THE
LAST
GENERATION

steffan postaer

INKWATER
PRESS

www.inkwaterpress.com

ISBN 1-59299-033-9

Publisher: Inkwater Press

Printed in the U.S.A.

For Camille
Born August 12, 1998

Never again will the sound of music be there
-No more pianos, saxophones and trumpets.
No industry of any kind will ever again exist there,
And there will be no more milling of the grain.
Dark, dark will be her nights;
Not even a lamp in a window will ever be seen again.
No more joyous wedding bells and happy voices
Of the bridegrooms and the brides

- The Fall of Babylon, Revelations, 18.22.23

It's better to burn out than to fade away…

-Neil Young

Contents

Acknowledgements

To Jeremy, Virginia, Masha and all the good people at
First Books and Franklin Street Books.
Nice folks in a tough business.

To my secretary Doe, who helped edit, format
and critique this work.

To Marian, the brilliant designer who created its cover.

To my wife, Susan, for all the reasons why.

And to every one who reads this book…

Thank you very, very much.

Three prologues, the first of which is...

Labor

It is calm, the tropical night providing no discernible weather except heat. Festooned in their most elaborate ceremonial guise, the tribal elders surround a tent. The leader chants softly, his ancient brow covered in a heavy sweat. They have been like this for nearly 24 hours, trance-like, full of jungle teas. They are hoping as much as waiting. The small tribe's last capable female is in that tent.

The other women keep their distance. They are frightened, having all lost babies to the same quiet evil. They clutch their empty bellies in shame. Still, these women do not envy the one inside. They want her to succeed, desperately so, for she is their sister and, more importantly, their existence.

Just before dawn she erupts from the tent, emitting a strange wail. Hunched over, the woman runs toward the jungle and disappears into it. The tribesmen do nothing to stop her. They know where she is going.

Just like so many of the tribe's sisters and daughters before her. To the river.

Pain

Chaos.

A woman is strapped and screaming. Doctors are pushing and running alongside the gurney. Trailing them a throng, some press, others police. The mayor is there. They are all struggling to keep up, to put on their surgical masks. One man trips and falls. He yells for them to wait, but none do.

Inside the operating room, various medical personnel are attempting to hold everyone back. The lead surgeon pushes the woman's legs apart. There is blood. Her shriek dissolves into a long moan. She chokes, starts spitting up. A nurse wipes the patient's mouth and places a rubber device between her teeth.

"No," she yells, spitting it out with surprising force. It flies across the room, hitting a reporter in the face. Against the woman's wishes, a strong anesthetic is applied. She's out and the doctor goes back to work. The priest's prayer is muffled by a mask, still the only sound in the room. Finally, the surgeon rises up from between her legs and lowers his mask. "The miracle will have to come from someplace else," he says, looking at no one.

Later, after most of the spectators have gone, the man who fell earlier approaches his wife. He sits down by her side, saying nothing. His teary eyes mirror hers.

The lone nurse looks away. She decides to leave. Seven months is a record for this hospital for an "Event Pregnancy," but it satisfies no one.

And it's not much of a story either. After some perfunctory interviews, the press depart as well. They wanted a baby as much as the parents.

Analysis

Given the situation, I'm thinking how incredibly arrogant it is for me to even be here," says Eleanor, fiddling with the contents of her purse, a force of habit. As Eleanor speaks, she shakes her can of Altoids, sometimes the entire session. It soothes her like a rattle could a baby.

"What situation is that?" asks the psychiatrist.

"You know. EFS. The world coming to an end. It's in all the papers," replies Eleanor sarcastically.

"The world isn't ending, Eleanor," says the doctor. "You are unable to have a baby. It's not the same thing. You know that." His eyes close as if his point were beyond reproach.

As if.

"Last I checked, nobody was having babies," she says. "I would call that a situation." Eleanor's shrink continues to insinuate that she blames herself for current events. And maybe she does.

"You take it right on the chin, Eleanor. You think the world's problems are endemic of your own, that your inability to bear fruit is why the entire orchard is barren." The psychiatrist never opens his eyes. "Don't you see what you are doing to yourself?"

Apparently not. Eleanor remains quiet, half expecting him to yell DO YOU? DO YOU? DO YOU? But he doesn't. Just when she thinks she's being interrogated, she realizes it isn't so. Such is the nature of therapy. The lines of trust are forever being pulled in and let out. Tested.

"Why do you think you are arrogant for coming here?" questions her doctor, breaking the short silence.

At first, Eleanor doesn't hear him, engrossed with the contents of her purse, rooting around between the lipsticks and coins and vials of pills. Even therapy intimidates her.

"I suppose..." Eleanor stops, looks up at her doctor, and is suddenly annoyed. "Does it really even matter? I mean, haven't we already had this conversation a million goddamn times?"

"You know repetition is part of the process," lectures the doctor. "However, I'm not so sure you've used the word 'arrogant' before. Not in the context of coming here. Why arrogant?" The psychiatrist rolls a pencil back and forth in his hands almost like he's trying to start a fire. And maybe he is.

"Arrogant," retorts Eleanor. "The act of being so full of oneself that you actually spend four hours a week whining about trifles while civilization is...is—" Eleanor takes another tack.

"Does it really matter whether I make peace with my mother?" she asks. "Does it matter that my ex was having an affair while I was having a breakdown? Does it really matter that I carry the gene for Lupus?"

Crying now, she fumbles for a tissue.

He hands her one of his own.

"Does it really matter, Doctor? I mean really?"

The psychiatrist makes his way around the cluttered desk and sits down next to his patient. He listens to her cry for a while. Then he gives her a hug.

"Yes, Eleanor. It does."

An explanation of...

Embryo
Fatality Syndrome

EFS usually occurred at the end of the first trimester or beginning of the second. Rarely much after. It was generally not painful, except in later occurrences when the hurt could be significant.

Developing embryos eroded into a viscous state of gelatinous globs without any semblance of form. Lifeless spit. Jell-O.

Said less graphically, the embryo dissolved. And it was this symptom which made EFS so different from all other kinds of miscarriage, and also what made the syndrome so very hard to understand. Without legitimate fetal tissue, there was little to study. The cell matter dissipated inside the mother, which she then purged via menstruation. Save for the most rudimentary structure cells, the reddish-gray material was void living matter. No free radicals or foreign bodies could be detected in the residue. Again, like Jell-O.

Of course, unprecedented efforts had been made in search of a cure but all proved futile. As stated, EFS happened quite rapidly, perhaps in seconds. Up until its occurrence, the unborn child was healthy. Then, in an instant, gone. Doctors were baffled. The fact that they knew so little about EFS was maddening, but the strange realization that they might not ever know was terrifying.

No one was giving up. Still, the symposiums and think tanks, so rigorously attended at first, were beginning to show signs of petering out. Lacking new information, there was nothing to discuss. No real point. As one beleaguered physician said, "There were a million other ways to ruin a week and only so many more weeks left to ruin."

Doctors needed a culprit. Something evil to slay. A virus. A contagion. As of yet, they had no takers. Not a goddamn clue.

"Like trying to save snowflakes as they fall," is how a renowned biologist from Pakistan put it. "Watching. That's all we do," said another, as one developing human being after another... died.

Obviously, in vitro fertilization had been attempted. Year after year, it remained the most common medical procedure. But the same thing happened to new human life, whether it started outside a womb or in: Embryo Fatality Syndrome. An egg could be fertilized without difficulty. They'd been doing that forever. Bringing it to term just didn't happen. Cells divided in the usual manner, forming a discernible embryo with a minuscule heart intact and palpitating. Then gill slits. The slight bending of a tailbone. The blunt protrusions that three hundred million times before had become arm and leg.

But no more than that.

Death came swiftly, the epidermal membranes collapsing into the liquid around it. The effect was not unlike that of a paper towel absorbing water, then breaking down. As documented so thoroughly, the embryo dissolved, becoming vague, disappearing, all in a matter of seconds. The life inside these women had been a mirage. There, then wavy, then gone. Not real anymore.

EFS had been filmed and analyzed in microscopic detail, every cell observed, from start to bloody finish. There was nothing gleaned except for the obvious—obliteration quiet and quick.

EFS happened in the host wombs of chimpanzees. Gorillas. Orangutans. Even cows.

Below the sea. High above the atmosphere.

In different temperature extremes, under varying pressures.

Even in cyberspace.

Their embryos went in a heartbeat, existing humanity had become like the rented palm plants ubiquitous to office buildings: unable to reproduce, biding time, in a corner by the elevator.

Waiting to die.

MAX POPULATION: < 6,127,111,000

CURRENT: > 3,027,356,000

It begins...

On Location

Y ou can't take it with you and you can take that to the bank. That is, if you can find one that's open." Jack was trying for sarcasm but the words came out wearily. That and all the "that's."

He bit his lip, starting over. "The rainy days are here, my friends. And without any eggs, I ask you, why feather your nest? I'm 32 years old, making me one of the young ones. The so-called Last Generation. After me are fewer and fewer. Before, hardly any." Regretting all the clichés, he stopped speaking, rose from his stool and sauntered around to the other side of the bar.

The bartender, Dan, watched but did nothing as Jack tapped himself another beer.

"Remember all those apocalypse movies from the last century?" More animated now, he motioned his sister to follow him with the camera. "Androids and guns. Weird monkey viruses. Charlton Heston falling down before the Statue of Liberty screaming, 'We finally went and did it! We finally went and did it!'"

"Goosebumps," he said, taking a swig. "Oh, make no mistake, the end is coming all right. Only not the way everyone thought it would. No asteroids hurtling toward us. No alien invasion. Nothing, frankly, for Bruce Willis to do. Because it's coming slowly, crawling just... like...a... baby."

"Okay, cut," barked Muriel, putting down the camera. She wiped her brow, able to push a few long strands of red hair out from one of her deep green eyes. Thank God her brother hadn't gotten up on a soapbox. *More so, anyway.*

Jack set down his beer. "How are we on film?" he asked. "Should we try another take?"

"We're fine," she answered. "Only, next time watch the hands. Be less expressive with your gestures. You were spilling your drink."

"Excuse me," he replied sarcastically. "I can't help it if mankind's demise has a melodramatic component." Jack shook his beer, letting the suds fly about the room. "Cheers to Armageddon! Cheers to the end of the world!"

Grimacing, Dan peered from over his crossword puzzle. He could see where this was going. "I need a six-letter word for shut the fuck up."

Silence. Then–

"Stifle," yelled brother and sister, happily returning the serve, back on the same team again.

"The last child born in America is currently nine years old. His name is Harvey Whelm." Jack pointed to a photograph tacked on the wall. "He's a cute kid. All-American, all right. Almost made-up looking. And what if he is? After all, the world only knows little Harvey from magazines and television." Jack hoisted the various periodicals to the camera and there he was. Paddling a canoe with a trio of fake friends. Sitting on the president's lap. "They could have called the movie Harvey, but the name was already taken."

"Hold on," said Muriel, reloading. It was her idea mentioning the old Jimmy Stewart picture. With all their clout it wouldn't be too hard finding a clip at the Film Center. She sighed. The segment would work better as voice-over, but they were shooting him live just to be safe. On her cue, he continued.

"The actual title of the film: *The Last Child*. And despite being played by a woman in her late twenties – *very late twenties* –

Harvey is a damn fine specimen of a boy. He plays horse with his daddy in the driveway. Helps his mother in the kitchen, though only when prodded. Even wants to be a big-league ballplayer when he grows up."

Jack stopped speaking, tapped his nose.

Picking up the signal, Muriel moved in for a close-up.

"It's not likely," he continued, "because what's left of America's pastime is, well, past its time. All the great players and most of the good ones got out of the game a long time ago. Those who had money took their fortunes and split." Jack looked away from the camera, turning his gaze toward the window. Leaves were blowing. It was getting dark. "Major League Baseball is now this palsied tournament between four terrible teams. And the only people watching are very old, even older than the players who are also very old. Needless to say, there are fewer of them every season. Fewer of everybody." Outside, the leaves and debris spun harder, creating one of those hapless, little tornadoes that meant nothing and did nothing.

Jack considered his meandering dialogue about Harvey Whelm, baseball, and the rest. Instead of elaborating, he began to sing. Yes, sing.

"Take me out to the ballgame! Take me out to the crowd! Buy me some peanuts and Cracker Jacks. I don't care if I ever come back..." The whole song.

"Cut." Muriel hated when he ad-libbed but she refrained from giving him a hard time about it now. It would make an effective segue. Good enough. Besides, the movie about Harvey was as he described it. Likewise, the game of baseball. She gave her brother a kiss.

"Well?" he asked, eyes twinkling.

"Fabulous. Now, if you'll excuse me, I have to pee." Turning away, she handed him the camera. Sometimes it wasn't sad what they were doing. Sometimes. Rushing to the ladies room, she covered her eyes. Muriel hated crying in front of her brother. Not sure why. Hell, she wasn't even sure why she was crying at all.

"So, what did you think?" Jack asked, aiming the camera at Dan.

The bartender gazed through the lens, thought about telling the young man enough for today. Call it a wrap, as they say. Lame or not, he still enjoyed the game of baseball. Wasn't sure he appreciated Jack dogging it that way. His night crowd, sorry group that they were, would be filing in pretty soon and he'd just as soon sell them their highballs without the entire spectacle. But he liked looking at the redhead and, of course, reconsidered.

"You were fine, kid. A regular Barrymore."

Jack laughed. "You probably don't think I know who that is, do you?" He did not expect a reply and none was forthcoming.

The bartender pulled the tarp off his lone pool table, wrapping and shoving it behind the radiator. The bar's habitués were comprised of a half-dozen guys, all older. They didn't seem to mind the two siblings and their camera. Dan figured to let the young professor make his movie or documentary or whatever the hell it was. He'd paid his fifty bucks for the beer and location. Didn't bug anyone. And it wasn't like the female was hurting business either.

"Fall in, Sis?" Jack hollered to the back. Receiving no answer, he laughed. As usual, Jack was unaware of his sister's fluctuating mood.

Equally oblivious, Dan couldn't even remember if the bathroom was clean. No matter, he reasoned. She wouldn't complain. Women didn't sweat the little things anymore.

He thought about his wife. Connie left him, having joined a cult when the babies stopped coming. The Congress, it was called. She said that because they were the last, they were the most important. And that God himself would be calling them together for some big to-do. That he was going to make things right again. Who fucking knew? What did that even mean, make things right again? Losing his entire family didn't seem very right.

"Can I use this?" Jack gingerly held Oscar by the gut.

"May I ask what for?" Dan's legendary patience was ebbing.

"Because he's so dead," is how Jack answered the question.

"I know. I made him that way."

"No kidding? Wow." Jack considered the stuffed bobcat. He tapped one of its plastic, unblinking eyes. "I won't hurt it. I promise."

"Of course you won't."

Jack took this for a "yes" and began placing the creature in various spots around the bar, staging his next shot. "You are going to be a star, my friend," he said to the dead cat.

The bartender didn't surprise easily, by this or much of anything else. Oscar was part of the bar and he couldn't believe they'd wanted that. He folded his newspaper, placing it beneath the counter. Dan's Place was a dump. A certifiable one. And he sure as hell wasn't keeping it up. Why should he? That had been Connie's job. And besides, barring some miracle, he was going to be the saloon's last owner anyway. Even so, the place was quintessential. Wasn't that what the kids had called it? They said it was a tattered remnant of the American experience. When he'd asked them why they wanted to make a movie about such a crappy topic, Jack merely asked him why he kept on selling beer. He took their fifty bucks. Dan didn't think it would be much of a movie, but then, he didn't know what to think. As a rule, young people pissed him off. But with fewer of them coming in, he stopped being so critical. Soon they'd all be old, just like him. Just like everybody. For all he cared, these two could stay in this bar their whole damn lives.

He knew he was.

Sex & Television

Raphael kept pushing his Camel into the ashtray but it wouldn't go out. He left it there, watching the ember fade.

"Did you like it?" the woman lying next to him asked. She was not sure... about a lot of things. She thought sex should be fun and wondered why it wasn't now.

"I liked it," the man said. He coughed.

"Then how come you're not saying anything?"

"I don't know."

She thought about this. "Want to go again? I mean not right now," she giggled, feeling foolish.

"Why you so into it, anyway?" he asked, mildly annoyed, still on his back. A strange bug ran along the ceiling above him. With myriad thin, fine legs it looked almost like a feather.

"I don't know," replied the woman. She could see his teeth in the dark, whiter than the pillow.

"What did you say your name was?" The creature was directly above him.

"Nora."

"Nova?"

"Nora."

And just like that, Nora started crying, two big tears scurrying down her cheeks like bolting silverfish.

"Ah, Jesus," intoned Raphael. He rolled over and found the clicker. On television, a familiar black reporter was wrapping up his story.

"So, with government putting all its time and money into medical research, the day-to-day business of governing has all but abated. No more budgets. No more crime bills. No more infrastructure to plan. 'New construction is hardly a necessity at this point,' the president had said earlier today."

The newsman was sexy but not the story. Besides, Nora's heard it all before and was sick of it. She plucked the remote from Raphael's hands, changing the channel.

A very large number scrolled across the bottom of a white screen accompanied by bad music. *Very bad music.* The kind you heard in department stores. The figure got smaller by the second, but it was still pretty big.

Millions or billions? Nora wasn't sure. She always did suck at math. Muting the volume, she wondered and hoped if the man who picked her up last night was going to say or do anything. Something. Please. Doubtful, she surfed the few remaining channels in relative quiet. Her crying faded. She then drifted off, dreaming of babies.

The Free Thinkers Society had a popular show on PBS called *Cooler Heads.* They only talked about one thing. Debated it. Fought about it. Cried about it. And the whole world listened. *Cooler Heads* was translated in virtually every language known to man. It was just talking heads uttering big words. By late twentieth century standards, the show would've bombed. But this was a different time, albeit only a few years hence, and *Cooler Heads* had the daily ratings of a major sporting event with the numbers getting larger as the population grew smaller. Even in futility, the human race was still the only game worth watching.

When Nora awakened, Raphael was sitting on the floor in front of the television, its volume set low so as not to wake her. He was buck-naked, smoking a cigarette, and listening to an obese southern lady. Saying nothing, Nora watched him watching. She thought it was sweet he'd turned the volume down. Sweet the way he stared at the TV screen, head bobbing like a newborn, taking it all in.

"People have always known they were going to die. Ain't nothing new there... it's what separates us from all other God's creatures. Makes us special," bellowed the large woman.

A balding, white smart-ass cut her off: "Our opposable thumb and brains are what make us special, Mrs. Wilson," he lectured, wiggling his thumbs in front of his face.

Nora would slap him if she could.

"Not the same. Those are just tools," countered Mrs. Wilson. "Civilization depends on our known mortality. It is why we have religion. It is why we have children."

"*Had*," retorted the smartass, still playing with his thumbs.

Incredulous, the woman barked: "Are you saying religion has gone the way of our children?"

"I'm saying it will," he replied curtly, undeterred.

Nora threw a pillow at the screen, hitting her new boyfriend instead. "You shouldn't be watching this."

"You shouldn't be throwing things."

In his all-too-rare smile, Nora saw opportunity. "Come back to bed," she said, patting the down comforter.

Raphael lifted his eyebrows. "Why should I?"

"I've got opposable thumbs and I know how to use them." And with that she employed one, zapping *Cooler Heads* right out of the bedroom.

* * * * * *

"By the end of our lifetime the world will be comprised of perhaps a few thousand individuals, most of them at least ninety years old, many older."

Nora was looking at some dated fashion magazines. Sometimes she got off on *FutureScape* but not now. Looking at gnarly old men and women did nothing for her. She had wanted to be a model and now her youth, like everybody else's, was behind her. Their world was ending and in one lifetime would be over. Deal with it. Don't wallow in it. That was her credo.

For the many curious others, however, there was *FutureScape*. A companion piece to *Cooler Heads*, *FutureScape* endeavored to pre-view the future, dramatizing the questions, rather than merely ask-ing them. What was to become of all the emptying cities and towns? Would the remaining people group together in pockets or divide and separate into the vast opening landscape? No one really knew. In meticulously-produced segments, *FutureScape* hazarded to guess, taking creative pot shots, playing out scenarios. Many well-known actors had roles in the productions, seemingly out of obligation. Cer-tainly not for money.

This episode depicted an Amish village of sorts. Men on horses. Women in gardens. Folks doing chores. Only here, Utopia wasn't in the fickle climate and nondescript geography of Indiana. No, in a diminishing population, those who remained had options. So natu-rally they'd opted for a secluded mountainside in Bel Air. The morn-ing swim was good for an aging body, to say nothing of Southern California's pleasant climate, a sultry-voiced narrator pointed out.

"Maybe the movie stars were gone, but not their lifestyles," she winked.

Yet even though these aged, new age pioneers lived in the world's most dramatic houses, they lacked power to run the dream kitchens inside. Instead, the resourceful inhabitants cooked homegrown veg-etables on a grill next to the pool, such strange surrealistic cave-men. But like the lady said, these days you didn't need power to live in Bel Air.

Accordingly, the Last Generation also dined on deer and other wild creatures. As EFS was exclusive to humans, game was increas-ingly abundant. Save for a few benign predators, the animal king-dom went unscathed, free to behave, populate, and ultimately re-take the land mankind had so unceremoniously usurped.

There was a God, Raphael thought... and he had a sense of humor.

Raphael stared at the various computer-generated animals running rampantly through the gardens of Bel Air. He smiled, imagining coyotes roaming down Hollywood Boulevard, sniffing the golden stars lodged in concrete. Mountain lions sunned themselves in the middle of a freeway. He looked at Nora. Beautiful, but, like him, a dying breed. Game over. The End. But not so for lions and tigers and bears. Oh my. They were coming back... down from of the mountains, up from extinction. The idea made Raphael feel good, like method really was in the madness. Like his death and the death of humanity had meaning. There was a silver lining after all. It wasn't the end of the world. It was only the end of people.

The episode concluded with the tribe of elders forming a circle, chanting to themselves and to the pristine blue skies of a people-free Southern California. They weren't scared of dying. Hell, why should they be? They were in Heaven.

"You think we'll be like that, Ralphy?" Nora was behind him now, hands on his shoulders, staring over his back at the television.

"I don't know. We're on the young side now. I suppose if we make it that long, anything is possible."

FutureScape had a way of making the end of the world look inviting. Raphael knew better. From what he'd seen on the news some places weren't transitioning so easily. Los Angeles was one of those places. Folks from the barrio, South Central, everywhere really, were hip to all those mansions up in the hills. They began moving in, taking their chances whether occupants were there, let alone cared. The film industry was an old crowd to begin with. Sans natural heirs, their swell estates sat idle, modern ruins, castles with pools instead of moats. There was no shortage of unnatural heirs. See a name in the obituary and, just like that, a family was loading up a truck and heading north and west, a migration not unlike that of Monarch butterflies. Or, if you will, the "Beverly Hillbillies." So massive was the incursion, the Times had to stop running obituaries. And, even so, the people kept on coming, knocking on doors until finding an open one.

They were met with some resistance. Violence visited these neighborhoods like never before. Even though the concept of real estate would soon not matter, quite a few remaining well-heeled families were beside themselves. Wanting no part of the vulgar interlopers, they fought hard to keep them away. But despite the news coverage and random gunplay, the immigration continued. The laws of supply and demand no longer applied. Even the police, both public and private, at first up in arms, had begun losing interest.

FutureScape had one thing right: in the scheme of things it just didn't matter who resided in all those big, lavish houses. In a mere generation, all humans would be gone. It would be the den of mountain lions. Raphael envisioned a female cat sunning herself on an extinct movie producer's diving board… licking its paws… purring. Surreal. The Cheshire Cat.

He grinned.

Made love to her.

Nora moaned, buckling and winding her legs around his. This was sex. She held him inside her long after he came. Still believing in miracles, she wanted his seed. Though that's what he thought. Hoped so anyway.

But Raphael was not thinking of babies. His passion had no ulterior motive. It just was. In addition, he felt less ambivalent, not as hostile or distant. He just kept seeing that lioness. On a diving board. Purring.

"Well…" This time he asked. "Did you like it?"

"Hmmm," she replied.

"Good."

Like always, Austin, Texas stayed hot at night though mercifully dry. The two lovers left the window open, lying atop the sheets, relishing the wind as it played across their skin.

Each mumbled thanks before falling asleep. For what, though, each other? Perhaps in a time void of miracles a little one was here.

God Only Knows

I don't know what to tell you. The arrogance of man, it's pathetic." Jack was fuming. He didn't know whether he was yelling at his sister or the camera. He'd gone off like a discarded landmine.

Muriel filmed him anyway.

"I mean, we think we're created in God's image, right? Therefore we can do whatever we want. Right? RIGHT?" He admonished the stuffed bobcat, his finger weaving in front of its tattered dead face. "But I'm here to tell you, it's not right!"

Her brother was drunk. No bout a doubt it. But she continued to shoot. Hell, she was drunk too. And besides, she agreed with him. We were born is all, not created. Wasn't that what she'd always told him? Damn right it was. Only now he spouted off like it was his rhetoric. Typical Jack. She zoomed in on her brother as he stepped on a chair and then onto the table.

"Top of the world, Ma! Top of the world!" Jack wavered, trying to balance himself. He held up the bottle of Johnnie Walker like a torch, imitating the Statue of Liberty. He began singing the National Anthem, blah-blah-blahing where he didn't know the words.

Still rolling, Muriel looked behind her at the door, hoping not to see Dan. It was getting about that time. And she could think of a dozen reasons why this would piss him off.

Abruptly, Jack stopped and went slack. Contemplating the bottle of Red Label with one eye, his sister with the other, he bent down, placing the scotch back on the table.

She reloaded, not sure what her brother would do next but knowing he wasn't done.

"Thing is, we are not created in God's image," he said, having regained his footing. "God is the image. And we created it. We created God in our image."

Muriel had never believed in God, really, but her brother's comment still made her cringe, even now, even though she agreed with him. Whether she were an atheist or agnostic, Muriel still had a conditioned response to blasphemy. Whirring, the camera absorbed Jack's words, committing them to celluloid.

"We happily peopled this Earth, never thinking twice. I mean, why should we? We were *miracles*, each and every one of us. We wanted our place in the sun. Our acre. It was our God-given right, right?"

She moved the tripod below him, shooting up at her brother. The klieg was still a sufficient source of light, but only if he stayed out of shadow.

Jack continued, "I mean all this talk about multiplying and reproducing ourselves. My stars, such vanity. Like we were so good for the world that the world naturally needed one or two more of us. Are you married?" he asked at the camera. "When are you two gonna have kids? How come then? Let's go people. Get out there and be fruitful. Multiply, dammit! Don't you know that every sperm matters? That every sperm counts?" It was an obscure, vulgar song from the Monty Python oeuvre, and he sang it not prettily.

It also happened to be when the bar's owner came in from the back.

"Hey. Hey! Get down from there. Pronto!" Dan heaved the three cases of beer he was lugging onto the nearest table and approached

Jack. Yeah, he was pissed. "Damn it, Jack. What the hell is going on around here?"

Muriel turned the running camera on the old man. "We're filming, Daniel."

"You're drunk," he said to them, knowing drunk when he saw it. "And turn that damn thing off, will you?"

"A little drunk, sir," replied Jack, descending from the table. "Nothing to fear."

"I'll be the judge of that. And I thought I told you to turn that off."

She did, noticing, however, that without the camera's reassuring hum, she felt naked. Childish.

"We're sorry," said Muriel, meaning it. "We just got carried away. You know, what with the movie and all." She started playing with her hair like a little girl.

Jack began tidying up. He carried the whiskey bottle back to the bar and painstakingly arranged it along with its brethren: Black Label, Gold Label and the way-too-expensive-to-ever-be-opened Blue.

The somewhat mawkish display worked. Dan rolled his eyes upward, not so mad anymore.

"I'll make coffee. It looks like you kids could use some." Even though they weren't, he liked calling them kids. They certainly had acted like children. In a way, the whole scene struck him as nostalgic. He thought about the Frappel Twins in New York. He'd never seen the show, but heard it was grand. In it, the protagonists acted like children. He turned Old Oscar around so that he was facing the door.

Muriel pulled up a stool and watched Dan prepare the coffee. She still had a lingering buzz on, and her head felt like a balloon swaying on top of her neck. Still, she wasn't anywhere near as lit as her brother, who was now in the bathroom. She could see the yellow light escaping from under the bathroom door and heard him wretch.

"Do you mind if I ask you a question, Dan?" Like a lot of people, she became braver under the influence.

He didn't answer and Muriel presumed that meant 'sure, go ahead.'

"I was wondering if you had any sons or daughters?" She caught herself not using the word *children*, as if it were shameful to do so, as if the term had an unpleasant other meaning. Yet another oddity in post-EFS etiquette.

"Two daughters. Had 'em before it all started. Or should I say stopped? Sometimes I wish I hadn't." Dan turned around and looked at Muriel and saw his Mary and Kathleen in her face. "They're about your age, a little older. They were among the last." He told her their names, what color hair they had, eyes.

"Where are they now? Still in Wisconsin?" she asked, guessing no.

"Frankly, they're with their mother in a cult in Utah." Okay, he said it. "Hopefully not as crazy as she is," he added, laughing inappropriately. He tried to sound cavalier but, failing that, turned around, busying himself with something.

She sensed from his awkward tone that this wasn't the most popular topic around the saloon. But she could tell he was not indifferent to it, either. To the contrary, his quivering lower lip gave the old man away. Muriel didn't want to push, but she knew a little something about this cult and wanted to know more.

"The Congress?" she said tentatively, afraid of his reaction.

"Yeah, them." Dan had half a mind to take himself a shot of bourbon. Opting for the java instead, he poured them each a cup. "You know, they think it's special being the *last*."

"Maybe it is." Muriel thought there might be worse ways for members of the human race to spend their final years. After all, it was kind of like a family. And the great open spaces of Utah were probably a lot more remarkable than Madison was, at least in winter. Plus, from what she had seen and read, nobody got hurt there. But she could see from the look on Dan's face that this wasn't really true. He was in pain.

"They're getting ready for the big meeting. Supposed to happen soon."

"The big meeting?" Muriel leaned in closer.

Dan snarled. "God himself is supposed to attend."

"Oh, really? And which God would that be?" She wasn't being sarcastic, at least not entirely.

"You know, I'm not sure. Never asked. I guess every Congress needs a president." Dan chuckled at his little joke. He reached below the bar for some Bailey's. "What the hey, right?"

Muriel refused the liqueur. She wanted him to go on, wished she were filming. Either way, she hoped she could draw him further out of his shell.

"Do you talk to them?"

"Nope, it's not allowed. No phones." Then Dan realized he had no customers and noticed why. The front of the bar was still dark and locked up. He decided to finish his Bailey's and coffee before rectifying the matter.

"So how do you know if they're all right?" She lifted her empty coffee cup his way, hoping for more conversation as well.

"I don't… at least, not anymore," he said, filling her mug. "I used to get letters from Kathleen. That's how I knew anything at all. She was always less gonzo about the Congress than her mother and sister. But she must've got caught writing me… or something. I haven't heard from her in months. I'm sure she's fine, relatively speaking. She has her mother."

Dan stopped talking and looked toward the bathroom.

"What about your brother? Is he all right?"

"Relatively speaking," answered Muriel with a smirk. She knew he had to open the bar and got to the point. "Look, Dan, did your daughter write anything else about the Congress? You know, like about the big meeting? I'm just curious. It could help…" Muriel was going to say 'our film' but thought better of it.

Dan walked to the bar's entranceway and turned on the main lights. They flickered and popped, both inside and out. He unlocked the front door, opening and closing it out of habit. He came back to Muriel, this time on her side of the counter.

"In her final letter Kathleen said God was going to bring them the next child, maybe even to her." He shook his head, then looked up. "I think her sister would be the more appropriate candidate, don't you?"

Muriel stared at him.

Dan sighed. "I say that because my other daughter's name is Mary."

"God," was all Muriel could say. It was sinking in. His family had been sucked into an end-of-the-world cult, of which many existed. Obvious, understandable, and yet still sad. She shuddered. Who portended to be the father of this so-called next child? Wondered what kind of man had that kind of gall.

"Uh, do you got a mop or something–" It was Jack. He was standing, albeit wobbly, several feet away from them and staring down at his shoes. They were covered in vomit. "I stepped in something bad," he warbled.

We all have, Muriel thought, rummaging for a towel.

Congress

K athleen Hunt stepped out of the tub, careful not to slip on the tiled floor. She grabbed a towel and started drying herself off. Outside the slit window she could see the sun flirting with the mountains before it went down. It was cold and her flesh pimpled. She toweled herself and finished by dabbing it between her legs. She looked at the towel, and seeing only wet cotton, placed it there again, this time holding it longer.

"Oh God," she said to her reflection in the mirror. "Please let it be red."

It wasn't.

She did not want to be carrying his child, regardless of what it might mean for her status. But what could she do? The staff matrons knew she was late and they would report it. This time they'd insist on administering the test and if it was positive she could forget about leaving.

And if she lost the baby, like everyone else before her had, she could forget about living. Maybe they wouldn't kill her if she were truly repentant and if she were lucky. But things would be different, Kathleen knew that for sure. Matthew did not have much patience for the wives who failed him. And the more who did fail him, the more impatient he became. Look what happened to Mary.

Kathleen thought about her sister. She was out there somewhere, in the mountains, doing her penance, seeking absolution. EFS took her child, his gift to her, and now she had to pray–no, pay–for her sin. Probably she'd been given a loaf of bread and some matches and hopefully a coat.

The sun now rested on top of a spiked peak, the silhouetted point of the mountain just touching the big crimson ball and then piercing it. The sky bled across the horizon accepting its fate.

Kathleen turned away and slid to the floor. The room darkened, catching her in shadows. With the faceted edge of her mother's diamond engagement ring, she dug into the delicate inner wall of her vagina. She felt tremendous pain but stifled her gasps.

The presence of blood might fool them. For a while, anyway.

Yet even if her ruse worked, it only meant he'd be in her bedroom again. The situation was, as her dad used to say, lose-lose. Still, she had to buy time. It was her only move.

Her sister was suffering worse, she reasoned.

Unless, of course, she was dead.

The Show
with the Models

D o you think I would make a good mother?" She played with his earlobe. She could feel his still warm semen trickling down her thigh. Things were getting better between them. She sensed it.

"You'd make a great mother," said Raphael, believing it. He stared at her through the blackness. She looked like an olive, dark and firm. How a creature like that could not bear fruit was beyond him. Even her smell was ripe. Fucking world.

"I was just thinking," said Nora, still massaging his earlobe.

"Oh really?" he asked, sounding shocked, razzing her.

It was a bad move and she let him know it, popping him upside the head.

"Ouch!" But he wasn't hurt, far from it. "What? What were you thinking? Tell me."

"I was thinking how great it would've been, me and you... parents." And before he could respond, "Even though I know you don't think so."

Raphael turned away from her, pressing his face into the pillow, not out of anger but bewilderment. He'd never wanted to be a father and, now that he couldn't, he didn't know anymore. Besides, what difference did it make?

He envisioned sperm racing down her fallopian highway, maybe this time hitting pay dirt. But then what? A month goes by. Two. And just when she begins to show… Much later Nora got up to go to the bathroom. She was pretty sure he wasn't sleeping but remained quiet, leaving the light off. Even during the best of times, they tiptoed around each other. Everything was so fragile, she thought. Oh, well, at least he was still with her.

Nora stretched and positioned herself in front of the mirror. Except for hair that hadn't been to a salon in ages, she was still quite attractive. Maybe even a knockout. And way younger looking than she actually was.

Nora didn't have a headache, but she opened the medicine cabinet anyway. She saw it, lodged behind the Band-Aids, wrapped in tissue, sealed in a zip-locked baggy, just as it had been for a long, long time, way before him, way before EFS–her diaphragm, an obsolete artifact of the modern woman's medicine cabinet. As useless as an appendix, a womb.

"Your show's on," Raphael called out. "The one with the models."

"Coming," she mumbled, too quiet for him to hear.

Raphael was watching a hybrid fashion show called Later. Even though the program came on at midnight, Nora called it "later" for another reason. The models were later, as in much later, old. Forty-year-old women traipsed around like Lolitas, wearing outfits designed for Lolitas. Never known for its firm footing, the fashion industry had either lost touch all together or perhaps, in a desperate scheme to remain relevant, was trying to make obsolescence chic. Perhaps the mawkish display had a name: Oblivion chic.

Thin, young things didn't exist anymore. Even so, or precisely so, Nora found Later entertaining. There was something reassuring about knowing that every woman on the planet was in the same boat as she was. Flawless, unwrinkled faces no longer stared at you from magazine and billboard. The female form as icon was essentially dead. Shows like *Later* merely provided the final viewing.

Nora climbed into bed, first pulling the sheet up to her chin, then brazenly letting it fall. The television was muted. A Teutonic female strutted forward on a shiny glass runway. Lights flashed, revealing every mile, every imperfection.

To his credit, Raphael had fallen asleep.

She watched a few more of the "girls" and began fading herself. But before she did, Nora realized she no longer wanted to be one of them or even be like one of them. For that matter, she no longer wanted to be anyone else alive.

The epiphany, if that's what it was, made her chuckle. She reached down beneath the fallen covers trying to find the remote. Screw it, she thought, giving up. The TV won't bother me.

And so she went to sleep a bit easier than last night or the night before, unburdened now by the sin of envy.

The Last

Feeling yesterday's drunk, waiting for today's pills to kick in, Maura gathered her belongings from the motel room's floor and began piling them on the bed. She could hear Seth in the bathroom forcing up puke. Not pretty, she thought, pulling her panties out from under the sheets. Not pretty at all. He was too old for that shit. They both were.

"Sun's coming up, Seth," she hollered toward the bathroom, trying to disguise her contempt and failing. But what the hell? She had ten years on him and you didn't see her throwing up every hangover. Maybe he was dying; who the fuck knew? Either way, they had to get out of there. The bogus Visa card may have gotten them in last night, but it wasn't going to fool the day man. Not to mention they were at least a full day behind schedule. Minnesota was a big state and then they had all of Wisconsin to cross before reaching Green Bay.

A guy on the radio provided the temperature. Thirty-seven degrees, reaching a high of fifty. She pulled the plug rather than fumbling with a switch. She knew how cold it was. Almost Memorial Day and the lakes still had ice. It did nothing for her constitution, thinking about the numbers, not when you had a Harley outside.

She rapped on the bathroom door.

"Yeah, yeah, yeah," came the muddled reply.

The Black Beauties began kicking in. Clothes rolled, tied, and ready for the bike, Maura felt itchy and impatient.

"Jesus H. Christ," she exclaimed, tripping over Seth's unpacked duffel. "Do I have to do everything?" She walked around to his side of the bed and began gathering his things, such as they were. Levi's, tee shirt, sweatshirt, some nasty looking underwear and his beloved leather jacket. Seth's name was stitched in front over the right chest. And in much bigger letters, "The Last" was emblazoned on its back. She threw the jacket on the bed, next to hers. They were the last all right. The last people to get arrested in this room if they didn't get a move on.

"Any coke left?" Seth asked. Buck-naked, he trudged into the bedroom.

Whatever she saw in him she wasn't seeing it now. She could only imagine how foul the head must be. At least he wasn't fat as well as disgusting, excessive weight tending not to be a problem among drug addicts.

"Just some crystal," she said, in the end not being one to pass judgment. "It's on the dresser."

Seth nodded. Lumbering over to it, he bent over and inhaled. "Let's get the fuck out of here," he gasped upon rising from his snort.

"You might want to put some clothes on first," Maura replied, rolling her eyes. "It's nippy out there."

He shrugged but did as he was told. In five minutes they were stepping out into a frosty Minnesota morn. Overhead the sky remained black but the horizon line was visible and becoming more so, an edge beneath the forming dawn.

"Man, it's colder than Christmas," said Seth, speed-filled snot running down his nose. He packed the bike's studded leather saddlebags and got on the vintage Harley. Firing it up, the noise was startling, even to them. A cold morning had a way of emphasizing a hot engine. The sound rumbled across the parking lot, for sure waking some of the guests or, worse yet, the manager.

"Let's go," Maura yelled over the din, adding to it with the roar of her own cycle. "We ain't getting any younger."

True.

She figured they could make it to Eau Claire without stopping. She had a cousin there. Hopefully, he was still cooking his own meth, selling smoke, et cetera. A little help from the Doctor and they'd have enough for the cruise. And cruise they must, because this was a party Maura did not want to miss.

No doubt the world was getting smaller, but the rally kept getting bigger and bigger. Members rode in from most every state, including Alaska. Even other countries were represented. This year the estimated crowd was a hundred thousand plus. It would be the largest gathering since the Packers won their division in '97.

Maura shivered, teeth grinding, eyes stretched open against the wind. To take her mind off the cold, she went back to that game, remembered the ebullient crowd. Mostly drunks, faces painted green and yellow, a lot of men and maybe even some women shirtless despite a wind chill of minus a ton. The Pack would go on to win the Super Bowl, but that particular contest, the NFC Conference Championship, was the last football game she'd ever attended. The following year, when the babies stopped coming, football became less of a draw, even to the frozen faithful in Green Bay. It was a game that relied on the promise of future generations as much as it did past glories. And so it was the Packers won the very first Super Bowl and then one of the last. Football died soon after. But, and Maura wasn't the only person to say it, with bookends like that, at least the NFL managed to go out in style.

At ninety miles per, the wind felt like the endless slapping of an angry God. But at this point, high as she was, her skin could be peeling off her face and she wouldn't have noticed. Maura zoned on the road, feeling the engine rattling between her legs. She couldn't see Seth, but sensed him. She knew he was there. She could feel the crystal pulsing through his blood as well, making him right, making them go.

Movement was everything now, providing total absorption. In front, the sun was coming up, exploding high-octane colors into the sky. Maura felt something akin to happiness. Better than happy. Alive. The human race was ending, of that she was certain. But not today. Not this morning. Not right now.

Legs straddling the handlebars, Seth ripped past her howling at the new day. He must've been feeling it, too. Son-of-a-bitch was popping a wheelie.

But she wasn't worried. Not in the least.

After all, they were The Last Generation, Wisconsin chapter. Established one year before a new millennium, two years after the Pack won it all.

"Bound to Die. Sworn to Live."

A couple hogs snorting through America's dairy land.

The Last.

Man, it felt good.

Simple as That

You can't just go there and start filming," said Dan, shaking his head. "Those fuckers are crazy." Normally, he didn't use that kind of language in front of women, but this wasn't normally. He thought he'd seen everything from these two. "Among other things, you don't even know where they–where it is. And secondly, those fuckers are crazy." He was ranting.

"Well, I'm crazy too," Jack blurted out. "Aren't we, sis?"

Muriel looked at her brother and couldn't help but smile. An exasperated smile, but still. "Yeah, sure," she responded, despite reservation. Truth be known, she was feeling a might reckless herself. Maybe restless was the better word. Indeed, she was tired of Dan's dingy saloon. Cult or no cult, the expansive vistas of Utah were sounding pretty good.

"Look," said Jack, dialing it up a notch, "I don't know why you find the idea so unappealing. Your daughters might be in trouble. We could help." Jack convinced himself as he spoke, seeing the desert highway unfolding in his mind, warming to the romance of it. Like his sister, he craved the journey. He was rubbing his hands together.

"Oh, yeah. Right." The bartender had had about enough. He turned, reaching for a cigar box on the top shelf. He thrust the dusty carton onto the bar, opened it and pulled out a stack of Polaroids. They were pictures of his family. "Why don't I just give you these and when you arrive at the compound you can show them to the armed guards and ask if anybody's seen them and if so, can they come out and play?" Dan threw a handful of pictures at Jack, hitting both him and his sister. "You might not be on the guest list. Ever think of that?"

"We're sorry," responded Muriel, bending down to pick up the photographs. She gathered the man's daughters into her hands and placed them onto the bar. "We're sorry. We weren't thinking is all."

"Ah, bullshit," said Jack, breaking the solemnity. "If your girls are in trouble, and I think they are, then they're in trouble. Our presence won't change that. They'll either kick us out or let us in." Jack scooped up the photographs and placed them back in the box. "Worst case scenario, we'll be in trouble, too. I mean, what else is gonna happen?"

"They kill you and take your sister." Dan made the statement like he was replying to a knock-knock joke. He wasn't trying to be mean. Just providing the answer.

"I'm not afraid," Muriel shot back.

"And I don't intend to get killed," said Jack. "If we don't like what we see, we don't go in. Simple as that." He took a maraschino cherry from a container on the bar and popped it in his mouth.

"Simple as that. Simple as that." The bartender mimicked Jack's cavalier tone, adding a double shot of sarcasm. "Jesus." He bowed his head and then looked up, staring right at them, first the brother and then the sister. "You're not kids anymore, you know? This isn't just some road trip."

Muriel met his eyes and saw her father. Their daddy had been a dairy farmer, at one time possessing over four hundred head of cattle. When he died, the remaining cattle were sold off and the farm cut into three parcels, then four, later a half dozen, even more. At one time, the University planned on setting up an agriculture program in the primary milking barns, building a classroom there and everything. It never happened. Without babies you don't need milk. Or schools. Particularly schools pertaining to the manufacture of milk. After her father had to abandon farming, he bought the farm, so to speak, choosing to die quickly rather than just hanging around. Like everybody else in Platteville, he raised livestock, wanted grandchildren. Heirs. Some one to pass along the place to. A "couple-a-tree" as the saying goes.

He would have neither.

"You got a light?" Jack had been trying to pop a smoke into his mouth by slapping the back of his hand, a trick he'd seen in some movie. When he got it to work, he asked the question. He seemed disappointed nobody had seen him complete the trick.

For a supposed observer of the human condition, Jack could be so dense. He barely even paid attention to the old bartender. Muriel fished into her purse for a match and finding a book, threw it at him, hitting him between the eyes. Dope, she thought.

"What was that for?" mouthed Jack, the cigarette wagging from his lips.

Preempting this inane dialogue from going any further, Dan interjected: "You're gonna do it, aren't you?" He was looking at a baby picture of his oldest. It was faded but you could still make out the gaudy colors. Must have been Halloween, a costume party. She had on a tiara, and her outfit glittered like a sparkler. "I mean, no matter what happens here, no matter what I say." Dan put down the photo. He stared at the smoke coming off Jack's cigarette, watched the silver plume snake upwards, unfettered by wind or commotion. Where the hell were his customers, anyway? He sighed, resigning himself to the fact they were going.

A rattling fist at the door busted up their little ménage.

"What the? Ah, Jeez, I forgot the frickin' lock."

"Again?" Jack smiled. "You're getting old, chief."

Ignoring Jack, Dan shut the cigar box and made his way to the front. "So, I'm old," he shot back. "Forgetting isn't such a bad thing. Get me?"

Brother and sister contemplated the barkeep's deteriorating photographs, knowing all too well what he meant.

Plus 2 Make 5

ey, don't stop the party on our account." Maura strutted in
first, assessing the place and its three denizens. Sensing few
problems, her confidence, already bolstered by speed and a
lung full of fresh air, went that much higher. "PBR me, ASAP!" she
demanded, marching past Dan to the near corner, assuming a stool.
"Come on, Seth, they ain't gonna bite."

Even more impaired than his girlfriend, Seth traipsed in, passed
the owner, giggled, and sat. "PBR me, APBP," he said, stumbling over
the old advertising slogan and almost falling off the stool. "ASAP I
mean," he said, even louder, correcting himself as if it mattered.

"Look, I don't much care if you're stoned," began Dan, wearily.
"The Law doesn't much care anymore, either. But I don't want any
trouble." Dan made his way behind the bar and stood before the
now seated couple. "Got me?"

"Yeah, yeah, yeah… now how's about that beer?" Seth conjured
a look of profound boredom, implying here was yet another speed
bump in the way of their fun. "Got me?" he said, mockingly.

He reevaluated his position when Dan cocked the shotgun, placing it on the bar in front of him, in front of everybody.

"No trouble. Understood?"

In the movies, a moment like this was usually followed by all hell breaking loose. But this was real life and that was a real gun.

"Now then, draft or bottle?"

Uh-oh. Jack and Muriel exchanged shocked expressions. They'd never seen these two characters before and they knew Dan hadn't either. They also suspected they were high. What was Dan thinking?

"Draft's cool," said the female biker, surprised by the offer as well, though she tried not to show it.

"Two cold ones," said Dan, "coming up." He proceeded to draw them a couple of frosty mugs of Coca-Cola. Smiling, Dan placed the fizzing glasses in front of them. "Can I get you anything else?"

Jack gulped. The whole scene reminded him of a Sergio Leone movie. That or a Coke commercial. He loved when the two thugs submitted to Sheriff Dan, limply taking sips from their beverages. He loved it even more when they feigned satisfaction.

"Been riding long?" questioned Muriel, desperate to break the lingering silence, attacking the cowboy nonsense head on. It was almost rhetorical the way she posed the question, like she was talking to herself.

"Since dawn," answered Maura, settling down. She noticed Jack's smoldering cigarette and dug into her leather jacket for one of her own. "You got—"

"He does," said Muriel, anticipating the question, pointing to her brother.

Jack handed the tough-looking female a book of matches. "How about a draft over here?" he asked Dan. The Cokes looked delicious, strange considering he seldom drank soft drinks. In all the time he'd been there, he didn't even know Dan carried soft drinks. "ASAP," he added, trying to be funny.

Nobody laughed.

For whatever reason, Maura felt compelled to offer an explanation for their bravura appearance. "We were on our way to Green Bay but found ourselves sidetracked. So we decided to visit the capital instead."

Her audience remained puzzled.

A little paranoid, Maura continued babbling. "I would've gone to school here, you know, if not for the baby sickness and all. Still, I think Madison is a fine place. The lakes sure are pretty–"

Seth belched.

"And, well, here we are." She laughed unconvincingly, staring into the burning ash of her cigarette. She'd left out the unfortunate episode this morning with her cousin. They'd found him tied up and dead in the closet, his cabin trashed, his meth works in a shambles. Wrapped head to toe in gaffer tape, he resembled a silver mummy. Hell, he was a silver mummy. They left him there, of course. Had to. Calling the police would have only gotten them in trouble. Hondo was dead, long dead, and seeing as his death was dope-related the cops wouldn't have cared much anyway. Somebody was just doing them a favor. The rural stretch Hondo called home had pretty well gone pioneer. An eye for an eye, that sort of thing. The law was less and less a factor *in country*. Like the rest of civilization, it had retreated back to the towns and cities from whence it came. If a lake got fished hard enough, the remaining fish tended to find each other, gravitating to the middle, deep and center, just like people were doing now. Those that stuck to themselves had a harder time of it, like Hondo. Gripping her shaking fingers around the cigarette, Maura sucked hard, wanting to pull as much smoke into her center as possible.

"So, why were you two heading to Title Town?" Jack asked, not picking up any vibes, just asking. "Visit the Packer Hall of Fame?" He fished around in his glass for an ice cube, putting one in his mouth and crushing it. "I hear it's still open," he said, voice breaking from the broken cube.

"Something like that," answered Seth, determined to change the course of their conversation, preferably south of Green Bay if not the whole damn state. He hadn't appreciated finding a moldy stiff in Eau Claire. Kind of put the fear in him, suggesting it was time for a change in venue, a new direction. The hell with the big bash and to hell with doing any more speed. He wanted to go south where it was warm and drink margaritas. Maybe Key West or New Orleans.

He vocalized the sentiment. "Maura and I got to thinking how long this winter was and why not just be rid of it. So we took a right at 50 and haven't looked back."

Seth regretted mentioning their turn-off for worry of placing them near the murder. He still felt skittish.

"Those wouldn't be cigars?" he asked, turning his attention to the box on top of the bar. Without waiting for a response, he reached for the container.

"They wouldn't be," Dan cut him off, placing a big paw over the lid. He stared at Seth, now seeing fear behind the bombast. He'd have no trouble from these two, leastwise not from the fellow. "You want a cigar, I'll get you one."

He picked up his gun, walked back along the bar into the pantry, stopping at an engraved walnut humidor. A gift from his wife, he'd gotten it some twenty years ago. Lifting the lid, he remembered how much Connie had hated his cigars. And yet, she'd given him this. He grabbed a Churchill and then another. Why not? It wasn't that early anymore. And who or what was he saving them for?

"He's got pictures in the box," Muriel told the biker, sensing his curiosity and not seeing any harm in telling. "Of his family."

"Family?" whispered Maura. She'd thought these two might've been his kin. She could tell they were brother and sister and had just assumed he was their dad. Why else would they be in a place like this, let alone so early?

"Just looking for a cutter," hollered Dan from the other room.

"A wife and two daughters. They ran off to that cult in Utah."

Jack's look said it all. Why the hell did you tell them that? Apparently to no avail, for Muriel continued.

"We're thinking of going out there too. Not to join the cult. To make an intervention, I guess you'd call it."

He thought his sister was brighter than this, telling two strung out bikers their plans.

"The Congress?" whispered Maura. She'd heard a few things about them, most of it bad.

Muriel nodded.

Unless maybe she was recruiting, Jack thought, seeing as how the others' interest had been piqued. He knew the open road was getting dangerous, particularly out west. A couple toughs could shore up their little party, make for a better wagon train. Besides they would look great on film. *Very Easy Rider.*

"Weather's nice out west this time of year," she said, continuing her pitch until Dan came over with the cigars.

"They call these Macanudos." He handed one to the scraggly biker. "And they call me Dan." He snipped the tip off his cigar and gave Seth the cutter. "Now, what do they call you?"

"Excuse me, where are my manners?" responded Seth, half-jokingly, knowing full well they were pickled, like his brains. "I'm Seth and this here is Maura. And, um, Dan, if you're so inclined, I bet she'd like one of these fine cigars herself. Ain't that right, Mo?"

"If he's so inclined," she said, warming up to the whole set-up. Despite the business with her cousin, Maura had been upset about bagging the big rally, but she was feeling better about it now. She began mulling over the Utah trip and thought it could be interesting. Besides, maybe the brother and/or sister would be good for a roll. Lord knew Seth wasn't.

"I suppose you want a cigar, too," Dan said looking over at Jack.

"No, but I'll have another one of these," replied Jack, holding up an empty mug. He wasn't being cocky with the old man, merely familiar.

"Take one anyway." Dan threw him a stogie. "I'll get your soda."

Jack rolled the cigar between his fingertips. They'd spent a long time at Dan's place and had gotten kind of close. The film they were making had been as much a calling as a task. Not just something to do but something to do that was meaningful. Dan had become part of the process and in turn part of that meaning. They might not ever see him again, but then weren't those famous last words in post-EFS society? Nobody was going to see anybody again.

"Here you go, Fellini." Dan gave Jack a new drink to go along with the fresh cigar. Doing the same for Maura, he then lit everybody up.

They smoked for a while.

Still not yet 12 o'clock the morning light poured in, revealing the smoke, fashioning stripes into the bar's dank atmosphere. Replete with dark wood, bright rays of sunshine, and filtering smoke, the place resembled an antique painting. Beautiful as a Rembrandt. Heavenly even. And for a long while nobody spoke.

"Kathleen has red hair," said the father, opening up his cigar box, looking for the most current photo. "You can't miss her."

The Desert

Mary was cold but not excessively, the small cave affording her some protection. She was, however, exhausted, achy, and wanting nothing more than a soft bed. Hell, any bed. She thought of the lower bunk relegated to her as a child. As the younger sister she'd had no choice in the matter and therefore hated it. Well, she craved that bunk now.

Evening was coming, and she needed to prepare a fire. Unfortunately, wood was scarce and at these elevations what little could be scrounged tended to burn quickly. She'd found out yesterday, having gone through two piles in two hours. Still, a shoddy fire was better than no fire, especially against the unforgiving desert night. She rose to her feet, her bruised legs wobbling, tender from last night's fitful sleep on jagged rocks and freezing dirt.

Using her jacket as a halter, she carried branches and sticks, thereby eliminating the need for multiple trips. At least the physical labor was keeping her somewhat warm, if not alive. But the blue-pink twilight played tricks with her eyes, and she made several wrong turns stumbling to and from the campsite. Gone some thirty hours, she was already quite weak. The miscarriage, her second, had happened just three days before. This time he hadn't been as lenient with her. Now she had to take the so-called Good Walk. Purify her for the next time, if indeed there was a next time.

Mary laughed bitterly as she lit the fire. She knew Matthew was sleeping with as many of the camp's women as he could. He was probably on top of one now, filling her head with lies and her body with worse.

And yet she'd fallen for him. They all had. Even Kathleen, the brainy one, was under his spell. "The Congress chose HIM and he has chosen me. I will conceive for HIM, I know it. I will be the one."

Right.

Of course, her sister had said all this before Mary had gotten pregnant, lost the baby, and became pregnant again. She doubted Kathleen even knew about the second miscarriage, let alone her subsequent banishment—excuse me, Good Walk-into the desert.

A small flame discovered the kindling, spreading quickly. Mary sighed, bitterly recalling her indoctrination into Congress.

As was typical with arriving relatives, especially sisters, they were separated almost immediately after being welcomed and certainly before the rhetoric phase. Within days you received a summons. For that you might be given an evening gown, a pill to relax you. It depended on your looks, his temperament, the goddamn weather, whatever. One way or another, you went to his bedroom.

After which, they never saw each other again. Acclimating wasn't subtle. But then again, fostering community and encouraging group dynamics was hardly considered relevant to the cause. The Congress was about Matthew achieving objectives. About Matthew siring the first post-EFS child. About Matthew being loved 'en masse.' About Matthew as lover, father, brother, savior. About Matthew.

He had charisma, she'd give him that. By the time Matthew worked his voodoo on each of them, they were awestruck, each one assuming he wanted her and only her all for himself. And in many respects they were right. He had wanted them all, them all being the operative phrase. 'Himself' and 'had' were a concern as well. A very real one as it turned out.

The fire kicked up, illuminating the ancient sandstone around her. Under different circumstances Mary might have found it beautiful. Instead the flickering shapes frightened her, lapping and jumping at the blackness. She took out two of seven remaining slices of bread, methodically pushing them into her mouth. She chewed the dry pieces, not bothering to take any water. She just kept chewing until the bread was down and inside of her. She felt old, half dead. Appropriate, she supposed, for someone who'd been raped repeatedly, both physically and mentally. She threw more bone-dry sticks on the ebbing fire, watching as they all but exploded in the heat. At this rate, her fire wouldn't last twenty minutes.

The coyotes began their baleful one-note conversations. So many of them now their territory returning. Undoubtedly they were hungry, too. Mary shuddered, tucking herself against the rough cave wall.

Before falling asleep, she prayed.

For her sister. Hopefully she hadn't gone through the same.

For her mother. Though brainwashed, God forbid she was being raped.

And for her father. Oh God, take care of him, please.

As for her, Mary didn't forget to say a prayer, she just didn't bother. In the end, Mary didn't really care if she woke up at all.

People who experience the loss of someone or something invariably go through a grief cycle. There is no timetable and every person is different in how he or she handles it. Grief can last months, years or even longer. There are perhaps a dozen symptoms and stages of coping.

The first one is almost always...

Denial

Fiona increased the level of incline to seven, leaving her speed the same, six-and-a-half miles per hour, a fast clip considering the climb. Going into her seventh mile, she felt strong, like she could do ten easy. Without looking, Fiona reached down and turned up the volume on her headset.

At twenty-eight, Fiona knew she was one of the youngest. Which meant, if she played her cards right, she could easily be one of the oldest. Therefore, it was mandatory she take care of herself. Major care.

Barring some terrible act of God, Fiona Douglas was going to inherit the earth.

That terrified her. She kept having nightmares of being alone in, of all places, Paris. Not as in sans lover. Alone period. If her sister thought the streets were too crowded when she was there on her honeymoon, that's because she hadn't considered the alternative. An empty Rue St. Germaine sucked. Trust her, she'd seen it.

On the net, Fiona found other "under-thirties." Not many, but enough. They were having the same kinds of dreams, the same kinds of worries. She began hooking up with them. There were three in Sacramento alone. Actually four, but Michael had cancer and wouldn't be around very much longer. Sad about him, being one of the young-est humans on earth, yet one of the sickest.

Well, she wasn't going down without a fight. She had every in-tention of staying awake for the final act. They all did. The group was going to watch the last sunset together. It's all they ever talked about. She had to stick around. Destiny demanded it.

Fiona couldn't help but stare. Though everyone around her was older, most of them were in damn fine shape. Health clubs were booming, and hers was no exception. She had to wait for most every machine, even late at night. Even on Sunday, for Christ's sake.

Fiona watched an old lady flail away on the torso-twist like some gawky butterfly. Maybe if you used some actual weight, Grandma, she thought. The five-pound slab flew up and down the machine's axis, slamming into the top, then into the bottom. She hated it when people displayed bad technique.

Fiona strapped herself in, welcoming the tension as she pulled right, then left, then right. She could feel her abdomen burn, the apparatus teaching her stomach about strength and power. Her womb might not produce any children, but it would be surrounded by per-fection its entire, long, rock-hard life. Another twelve reps, she de-cided. Ten more pounds.

"Uh, miss… miss." He had to tap her on her shoulder. "Are you still using that?"

Strapped in the "abdominal," Fiona's thighs gripped the cush-ion, arms straddling the bar. Michael Stipe sang into her ears, into her. The song was "Night Swimming," one of his most moving and her favorite. Hypnotized by her reflection in the floor-to-ceiling mir-ror, she barely paused at the hand rapping on her shoulder.

"What?" she said to the man, pulling off her headphones. "What?" Though unaware of it, she was crying, tears intermingling with the sweat from her forehead.

Retreating, the man said, "I just wanted to know if you were done. Sorry." He wasn't up for any crying ladies today.

Just as well. Fiona had no intention of getting up. "I got another set to do," she said to her reflection more than him. "Maybe two."

"Whatever." And he was gone. Another person losing it, he thought, as he walked away.

Fiona remained in the exercise machine. She could hear the music, tinny and far away sounding, coming from her dropped head-phones. Looking down at them, she tried to make out the words but couldn't. Beads of sweat fell onto the gray carpet. Her wet arms and thighs were beginning to stick to the vinyl. People were grunting, weights clanked all around her.

When she looked up, her dead sister was in the mirror. She opened her mouth, started to say something, couldn't, and so she just sat there staring, slack-jawed.

One-and-a-half years ago, Serena killed herself. She took a few dozen tranquilizers and bye-bye.

But Fiona knew it was EFS that killed her older sister. It took her life just like it did all the babies. Serena had wanted to be a teacher and a mother. Unfortunately, those two jobs were the first to go.

By the second miscarriage, her husband had taken off, as did her grasp of reality. They found Serena in the attic, her Barbie dolls ar-ranged around her just so, like students. Her adoring children.

Disgusted, Fiona got up and out of the machine. How could she lose it so easily? She had to stay in control. She needed her wits, and needed them for a good eighty years. She had goals, damn it, goals. And here she was falling apart at the gym. That wouldn't do. That would not do.

She headed for the locker room to change into her swimsuit. One hundred laps in the pool ought to fix things.

He Ain't Heavy...

Ten years ago, a volley of bullets struck his brother during a skirmish between the Latin Kings and the Simon City Royals. Running down an alley, he must've fallen forward like a shot deer, all momentum and pain. Raphael saw it like that in his mind, anyway, more a freakish image than a haunting one. He could be staring at the ceiling or watching the cat jump off a dresser and, wham, there was Hector....

This time he'd been shaving, looking at himself the way one has to, when, face bloodied, his brother seemed to fall right out of the mirror.

"Damn," cursed Raphael, dropping his razor into the sink. With steam all around, the blood ran fast down his cheek.

"What's wrong?" called Nora from the other room.

Transfixed by the sight of his own blood and the sound of running water, Raphael didn't answer. Drawn in, he found himself twirling into the drain along with the hot, pinkish residue.

It was only his reflection.

"Raphael!" This time louder, over the din.

"I'm shaving," he answered back, preoccupied by the strange moment, not wanting any interruptions. "I'm all right," he added, just loud enough to carry.

Raphael missed his brother and, regardless of how unpleasant, accepted these briefest of memories without hesitation. He had no immediate family, and, like everybody else, he never would. He had only gaudy recollections, pieces of a nightmare.

He stared at himself in the mirror until it fogged over. At least, Raphael thought, young men were no longer being taken in and out by the gangs. Too bad the reason was because young men were no longer... period.

Putting a Band-Aid over his wound, Raphael went back in the bedroom to watch a rerun of *Cooler Heads* with Nora.

Cooler Heads Prevail

"We've been drunk for so long now it is merely the morning after," stated Michael Dobbs. He'd been a copywriter once, turning phrases for automobiles and chocolate bars before the industry dissolved into its own fatuity. People still sold goods to one another, but who had time to build brands or forge an image. "Our arrogance as a species knew no bounds," continued Michael, reveling in the opportunity to be heard. "I mean, all one has to do is read the Bible. 'Created in God's image.' Can you imagine the conceit it took to write that, to even think it? First we create a god to placate our rampant insecurity and then we say he created us in order to manifest his."

"I don't have to sit here and listen to this former huckster deconstruct Christianity–"

"Oh yes, you do," reported Michael, interrupting the theology professor with equal vigor. "You've been preaching for two thousand years. Give someone else a chance."

"*Cooler Heads* recognizes the professor has a point, but the floor still belongs to Mr. Dobbs." The moderator spoke without looking up. His job was to balance the program. Simple as that. "You will have ample time to rebut. Please wait your turn."

The professor settled back into his chair, folding his hands, dejected. Why were so many people attacking religion, especially now, when people needed it most? Weren't they afraid of the coming oblivion? Apparently not, he thought, glowering at Dobbs' shaven head. Atheist!

"The Judeo-Christian belief system is, by its very origin, a study in vanity. All religion is, I'm afraid." Michael spoke softly now, and carefully. He didn't want to come across as too arrogant. "God, and I mean every god from Allah to Zeus, is a creation of man, not the other way around. And now it's all coming to an end. Us. You. This. Only it's not coming as predicted in the testaments." He took a drink of water. Sure, he was being a prick, but he knew he was right. Knew it.

"Apocalypse?" he continued. "Hardly. Humanity is departing like air from a discarded holiday balloon. It's rather almost boring."

"Boring?"

"Yes, that's right, Professor. Boring. Our systematic annihilation is, by all standards, a big drag. Who'd have thunk it?"

"May I speak now?" asked the professor, ever polite.

"But of course," answered Michael, preempting the moderator. "Knock yourself out." Either way, he'd made his point.

"It is natural for people to be like that?" the professor asked. "Like him?"

The host looked confused and sighed.

The professor answered his own question. "Indeed, these are frightening times. But they are not boring ones. In words I'm sure Mr. Dobbs can appreciate, God brought us into this world and now he is taking us out. Unlike him, I am not cynical and sorrowful, I am ecstatic."

"I didn't say sorrowful, I said bored."

"I am certainly not bored, Mr. Dobbs."

"Well, some of us are," the moderator chimed in. He enjoyed interrupting, taking sides. After all, it was his show.

The theologian continued, "Like Adam and Eve, we are blessed to be cursed. They opened his great work and we get to be the final chapter. The glorious finalé." The professor stopped speaking, bowing his head.

Was he praying? The moderator allowed him a moment before moving on.

"Mr. Dobbs, rebuttal?"

It's not that Dobbs was unsympathetic to devout persons, not at all. But he knew EFS was no more religious in origin than the creation of man. If a supreme being existed, a god, then why would he, or she, have created such a half-baked 'pie' as Earth? He lit a cigarette (why not?), and spoke:

"C-plus," he said. "That's what we get. This is our grade. Or should I say, that is his grade?" Michael looked straight into the camera. "If, as the good professor maintains, there is a God, then his life's work is, I'm sorry to say, painfully mediocre. Think about it. Mankind is barely deserving of a passing grade. If it weren't for summer houses, Chinese food, and the passion of a good painting... I mean what kind of a supreme being comes up with puppy dogs and Adolph Hitler? A supreme weirdo, that's who."

The professor gagged.

But the host of *Cooler Heads* was smiling with abandon. Nothing made for better television than a good rant. Screw *FutureScape*. They played make-believe. This was happening.

"I mean, come on?" Michael posed the question again. It wasn't rhetorical. He seemed to be defying the professor to answer, or anybody really. "Puppies and Hitler," repeated Dobbs. "What is up with that?"

"Japanese beetles and roses," answered the theology professor after a pause. "Beauty and the Beast. There's poetry in these dichotomies. A method. God."

Beetles and roses. Dobbs smiled, remembering how much his old man had hated Japanese beetles for devastating his beloved Kennedy White roses. Every morning, he'd pull the beetles off his plants, stomping on them one by one. But the very next morning the purple-green creatures would be back, chewing away on his

Kennedy Whites, even more so than the day before. And again, he went out, continuing the cycle, like the seasons, like the postman, the sun coming up.

The moderator went to a commercial. It wasn't that he had sponsor obligations; he didn't, but quiet guests were of no interest to anyone.

The networks ran the same few commercials over and over. Redundancy was acceptable to clients and stations didn't have much of a choice. They only had four spots in the rotation and all except one were about other programs. The exception: Kleen Toothpaste. Apparently white teeth were still a priority. The last man on Earth would have good incisors. It wasn't even odd to say it.

"C+ at best," said Dobbs, after the break, having viewed the monitors. "Advertising toothpaste to a dying population–I mean, come on. What is up with that?"

Alone Again, Naturally

S o they left him.

Dan stayed back, preferring to think, however naïvely, that his family wasn't really in danger. Or maybe, and more likely, he just lacked confidence in the rescue squad.

Dan wasn't afraid to join them. At least not physically.

If he feared anything, it was that his wife and kids didn't want to be rescued. That they didn't want to come home or see him at all.

A moot point, considering the foursome probably wouldn't be completing the trip anyway. Something would come up. A fight. A distraction. Whatever. They weren't going to Utah, and, frankly, why should they? It wasn't even their kin who were out there.

A couple junkies and two disillusioned idealists. Oh please, Dan thought. He ran through his satellite looking for some type of sporting event. No luck though. Best he could do was a rerun of *Cooler Heads*. Yet another crackpot was going off on a rant. What this time? Religion? Baseball?

Muting the volume, Dan lowered himself onto a stool and began listening to the pervasive quiet. Just like old times, he thought, before they'd arrived. He wondered if he'd miss Jack's speeches. They had a way of getting real old, real quick.

No.

It was Dan who was getting real old, real quick.

A melee erupted on *Cooler Heads*. Several guests were fist fighting while the host appeared to watch, doing nothing.

Jack swore they would call if something happened. More promisingly, so did Muriel.

Damn, he was confused. Conflicted.

Turning off the television, he began cleaning up. Customers would be arriving soon.

On the Road

No matter how you looked at the map, Utah was a long way from Wisconsin. They decided Chicago would be an ideal first stop, it being just hours from Madison and on the way in general. Besides, all four had been to the Windy City before. They knew it and liked it. Selecting Chicago was a classic no-brainer.

A relatively short hop, but inarguably a boring one. No hills. No water. Just farms, fast food and a preponderance of pornography shops. Were farmers really that horny? Could a handful of locals really support such a business? Did they even want to? Muriel fired off her questions like a reporter. All Jack did was point out the full parking lots.

"Do you think we'll make it?" Muriel asked, trying not to sound nervous. It was difficult. After the rush of hitting the road wore off, a vibe of uneasiness seeped in, making her feel cagey and agitated. She worried. Were they really going to infiltrate a cult? Rescue brainwashed women? It sounded like the plot of a midnight movie.

"I don't see why not. These Civics go forever," replied her brother, not taking his eyes off the road. He was nervous about the enterprise as well, though not as much as his sister. The task of driving served as an adequate distraction.

"I didn't mean the car," she said. "I meant us."

"Look, Sis. The only thing we're going to do that isn't completely safe we haven't even done yet," Jack said, sounding more confident than he really was. "We can decide whether to cross that bridge when we get to it."

Bailing out was always an option. If some shit happened or was about to happen, they needed only to return. Unless standing on private property, they were only sightseers. And new sights might just do them some good. Do their film some good. Dan's Place had gotten all too familiar. Dan was too much like a dad. Members of the Last Generation knew better than laying down roots.

Regardless of the destination, moving on had been a good call.

Soon after crossing the Illinois border, however, Seth broke from what had been a very fast clip. He signaled, then pulled his motor-cycle off the interstate onto the shoulder. Maura did likewise.

"What the hell are they doing?" Jack took his foot off the gas.

Muriel shrugged, hadn't the faintest.

Jack didn't have a choice. "I guess I'm pulling over."

About a hundred yards separated them from the motorcyclists. Jack and Muriel walked the distance carefully. Cars whizzed by at what seemed like supersonic speeds and in surprising numbers. Windy and alien, a highway shoulder was an awful place to linger. Feeling disoriented, Muriel held on to her brother until they reached the others.

"Just look at it," Seth said as soon as the others were in earshot. Maura knelt behind her bike trying to light a cigarette away from the wind, indifferent to the circumstances, let alone what her boyfriend was saying.

"What?" asked Jack. "Look at what?" They were standing in the middle of fucking nowhere. Even worse, they were standing on an interstate in the middle of fucking nowhere.

"All of it." Seth waved his hand, gesturing toward the landscape.

Jack and Muriel focused on where he was pointing. All they saw was row upon row upon row of houses. Aluminum-sided, sparsely landscaped, predictable, as far as the eye could see. Houses. Small ones, and nothing any of them hadn't seen a million times before. Run-of-the-mill, if not below average, America, particularly the Midwest, was full of them, with names like Prairie Summit or Summit Prairie. The American dream starting for as little as ninety-nine, five.

"Um, it's a bunch of crappy houses, Seth," remarked Muriel, annoyed. Though not late for anything per-se, this pit stop, or whatever the hell it was, struck her as a complete, if not bizarre, waste of time. That and it was dangerous out here. Nobody obeyed the speed limit and the road was full of weirdoes. Muriel feared she was with two of them right now.

"And before this, it was farmland," opined Seth. "Remember? It wasn't all that long ago."

Not that a history lesson was appropriate right now, because it wasn't, but Seth had it right. Less than a century ago, settlers parceled the entire area, creating lucrative farms out of the verdant landscape. Countless acres of trees had been eliminated and an ocean of indigenous grasses turned over. Within a lifetime, an entire ecosystem was eradicated. The very notions of country changed from vast, lonesome prairies and grandiose hardwood forests to an endless grid of sweeping farms. Reckless, tall grasses had been replaced with regimens of soybeans. Buffalo replaced by cows. And the trees, it seemed, had all moved to Canada. America had gotten her first facelift.

The tract houses Seth now gaped at were merely part of its second.

Yet for Jack and Muriel that was America, farms and then subdivisions, from sea to shining sea. It was all they knew. Prairies were a chapter in a high-school textbook, somewhere they visited on summer vacation.

Granted, it was a lot harder to lovingly sing about low-cost housing developments. Nothing much rhymed with cul-de-sac. Or aluminum. Or pressure-treated lumber. Little pink houses for you and me.

Seth seemed ecstatic. "Can't you see? We don't have to buy the myth," he said. "Just look! It's over. It's all going back!" He began whooping like the third part Oswego Indian that he was. "No more of us means no more of them!"

Jack took another look at the rows of innocuous buildings, a closer look. And then he saw what Seth saw. It was in the faded paint, the scattered remnants of siding all bent and twisted, strewn about in cracked and sunken driveways. The once neat, little lawns were now dirty brown from lack of water and care.

It became obvious. Nobody was here. The developments were empty. Abandoned. Just endless rows of white boxes, lined up neatly like tombstones, lacking only for corpses.

Jack began walking back to the car to get his camera. Then he was running. The shot wasn't going anywhere, but he was excited. These were the kinds of pictures he was looking for and that his film needed.

Muriel shook her head, still not seeing it.

Maura smiled. If nothing else, it was nice to see Seth happy about something other than what he put up his nose.

The Pitch

He was good looking. Bald, but bald in a fine way, a way few men were. Yul Brynner. Michael Jordan. Those guys could do bald. And so could the tall, lanky man in khakis and a black tee occupying the screen on Nora's television. It was him. The leader of Congress. Matthew.

Raphael was helping their landlord put new fixtures in one of his other buildings in lieu of paying rent. Otherwise, for sure he would have made her change the channel. Nora knew Matthew gave a lot of guys the creeps, and Raphael was no exception.

She inched closer to the TV, turning up the volume. She was pretty sure it wasn't men Matthew was interested in.

"I want you to consider my promise when you consider your predicament." began Matthew. He spoke standing up, allowing you to see his whole person, all six feet four inches of him. He was leaning, just a bit, against a pink stone edifice, perhaps the side of a mountain, one couldn't tell. "You need me as much as I need you. Our fates are linked together. Intertwined by destiny. What you want, I need. What I need, you want. We, all of us, are the last of our kind for a reason."

Matthew started walking along the cool, pink wall. "Let me show you something. It will change your life as it did mine. Follow me."

This was a new installment in his series of 'paid-for programming' that Nora hadn't seen before. She decided to give him a cigarette's worth of her time. Maybe he wasn't all there, but he sure was easy on the eyes.

Matthew entered a cave and, as if by magic, lights went on as he proceeded. "Over here, on this ancient surface we see writings from another time, when the world was young." Matthew spoke evenly, running his fingers over the delicate hieroglyphics. "They tell the story of a strange and unthinkable sickness. What exactly? No one knew. Only that it was robbing women of their unborn babies, not unlike what is happening to all of you now. Indeed, to all of us."

His hand halted, resting on a series of peculiar illustrations. They depicted a multitude of pregnant women, each one virtually alike. Nora thought the drawings appeared Egyptian at first, but then noticed the figures were rounder and squatter. Each one had dark hair, brown skin and a protruding stomach. You could see the little person inside each female figure's exaggerated belly. One after the other and side by side they appeared. Down, down, down they went, into the depths and into the darkness: An endless procession of expectant women, all cradling their swollen bellies.

Instinctively, Nora caressed her own stomach. She imagined what it must have felt like to be with child. The protective instinct kicking in. The pride. The promise of a new life. She fantasized about its glory.

"And so, with this poor woman, it began." said Matthew, placing his finger upon one of the drawings. It was identical to all the others but for one eerie difference: Her belly was empty. No little person resided within the roundness. Nothing.

The camera moved in even closer. Other differences became obvious. Unlike her previous sisters, this one did not smile nor cradle her belly. On the contrary, the woman's arms flailed high above her head while her mouth stretched wide open into a freakish, large O.

As if in agony, Nora thought, like that tortured soul in Edvard Munch's Scream.

"And they continue," said Matthew, "until there are no more women at all. No more women at all."

At that moment, a light shone down the corridor revealing the other figures, too numerous to count. Upon first glance, the shift made it look like the women were all doing jumping jacks, so severe was the physicality of their screaming.

Nora lit another cigarette. Okay, she thought to herself, I'm intrigued. Now show me what this has to do with you. And do it before my boyfriend returns.

The illustrations in the cave had indeed gotten to her. The perpetual, silent screaming of all those anonymous women, how could they not? Was this freakish cave legitimate? Did Matthew posses some real knowledge of what EFS was, where it came from, and why? She took a deep drag.

Did he have a cure?

In extreme close-up now, Matthew's chiseled, serious face dominated the television screen.

"And then we have this. A final drawing before the blackness of the cave takes over." He pointed to a tall, thin figure of a man. A nude man. He was bent over backward, pelvis thrusting forward.

More than overtly suggestive, the man's penis was erect and also ejaculating.

There could be no mistake.

The camera lingered on the provocative illustration, as did Nora. She stared at the masculine rendering, the bold scratch in the wall delineating his cock, the little nicks flying from it, his semen.

Strange to be sure... but undeniably alluring.

Aroused, Nora began almost subconsciously to touch herself. Nothing heavy, a soft petting. Her moans were barely audible, mere purring.

"I am this man," exclaimed Matthew, arching his back. "And he is me." He extended his midsection forward.

Without clumsiness or question, Matthew's lean physique assumed the salacious shape of the cave drawing. The resemblance was scary.

Nora could feel it, yelping as Matthew thrust his abdomen forward. All of a sudden she wanted this man and with great urgency. Spreading her legs, she slipped a finger below and between, then another, her body allowing the penetration the way butter received a hot knife.

"Oh my God." And she sprawled upon the floor like warm liquid.

No prelude, the entire event a finale.

Still gasping, still stunned, Nora removed the hand from between her thighs. She beheld the appendage, its long fingers slick. Her hand palpitated as if containing a heart. And maybe it did. His.

Prone, Nora gazed up at the television.

And he was staring right at her, as if no time had passed, almost as if he'd been watching.

He smiled, tongue roaming from corner to corner.

"Let me give you life. The life that is promised." Matthew spoke quietly, beseechingly, imploringly.

Nora couldn't breathe.

Then he cried, "The life that is prophesied in this cave, in these drawings. Let me give you what you desire and deserve."

The air came in spasms. It was like she was having another orgasm. An aftershock.

With brutal, studied conviction Matthew continued. Rhetoric flew from the television and erupted. His mouth occupied the entire screen.

Adoringly, the camera relished Matthew's wet lips. "I did not discover this place. I was sent here."

Tighter. Worshipping his perfect teeth.

"I am the savior of the human race. I am the one who will give you a child. I am your last hope, your lover, your future."

Tongue like a snake, curling and pink.

"Come to me. Let me fill you with myself. Join me in Congress. Join me in Congress!"

Matthew hushed, and the screen became white. A phone number appeared, remaining for a period... a spell.

Plenty cf time for Nora to write it down.

When dealing with profound loss, the initial shock and disbelief are often followed by outward physical expressions of hostility, rage, and even explosive behavior.

This early stage or symptom of coping is...

Anger

Simon pulled back on the stick, causing his plane to crane upward. In seconds it was vertical. He then released two small switches. Simon couldn't see it, but he knew a plume of white smoke was tailing off behind him. Upside down now, the skyline of Chicago shot up and out below him.

Most of the buildings were empty, it being Sunday. But even tomorrow they would only be half-full, some less so.

Simon came out of the loop, finishing with a tail shimmy. The vintage F16 wiggled its titanium ass at John Hancock.

As a child, Simon once visited the top of Chicago's most famous building. "Some view," his father had said, holding him up that much higher. He could see the smokestacks of Gary.

He looked for them now, but without telltale smoke, they were difficult to find.

Simon remembered their odor and, when driving through to Michigan, his parents rolling up the windows, lighting cigarettes to cover the stench. But today Gary, Indiana, was a ghost town, one of America's first, with only hyper-blue space between him and its abandoned factories.

He signaled the tower. One more maneuver, a simple cross, and back to the base in Waukegan. Those were his instructions, the same as yesterday. And the 71st Annual Chicago Air and Water Show would be one for the books. The people below temporarily exalted, their mounting dread abated by sunshine, aerobatics, and copious amounts of beer.

Only, the simple cross maneuver wasn't on Simon's personal flight plan. And neither was the Great Lakes Naval Base. He ripped past Wrigley Field, soaring over the ivy like no Cub-hit baseball ever could. No, today would be different. Call it a homecoming of sorts. Simon was going back to high school.

Occupying an entire block, Lane Technical resembled a university more than a high school and a prison more than a university. A classic Chicago behemoth, it was maybe the second or third largest public school in America. Used to be, anyway. Enrollment was slipping as of late, down to an unhealthy zero. If Simon remembered correctly, green and gold were the school colors, the Warriors its team. A huge swimming pool was housed in the basement. Before the school went coed, students were made to swim naked. A hard detail to forget. For Simon, it was impossible.

Setting up had been easy. The military was so busy maintaining civic order and putting on dumb-ass air shows. Simon got the idea while taking inventory in an unguarded storage hangar in Minneapolis. But in a way, he'd been planning something like it for quite some time, from the moment Coach Phillips ejaculated into his bleeding ass.

And so Lane Technical became history a few years before the human race did. The first rocket hit the clock tower right in its face, obliterating the landmark for all time, the mortar and debris scattering for miles.

Over the Atlantic Ocean, Simon ran out of fuel and went down, happy.

Well, happier.

The Four Horsemen
and the Apocalypse

Before long, the John Hancock building loomed in front of them. A monolith, for some time it had been the world's tallest skyscraper. Even now it had presence, like a beacon guiding highway travelers into port. Regardless of the human condition, entering Chicago was still cause for excitement. They all felt it, like the way one is consumed by patriotism when fireworks exploded. Civilization beckoned. Mankind still had sway. The City of Big Shoulders could lift anybody's spirits.

As agreed, the small caravan exited the Kennedy Expressway at Addison Avenue and headed east toward the lakefront, more specifically to Wrigley Field. Belying his drug-addled persona, Seth was a huge baseball fan and wanted very much to see the famous old park before it or he was gone.

En route, they passed the massive wreckage of an old high school. Unlike much of the structure, the sign remained intact: Welcome to Lane Tech, Home of the Warriors.

The place looked like it had been bombed to pieces. Partial, crumbling walls teetered on the verge of collapse. Busted infrastructure dangled and jutted, rusting amid the elements. Oddly enough, no fencing existed around the perimeter, not even that yellow police tape.

From the street they could see all the way in and down what used to be a corridor. The endless row of dark green lockers provided a devastating commentary on the times, on the demise of an entire student body, of youth in general.

At a long light the caravan had to remain put at the intersection, parallel to the condemned building. None of the riders so much as exchanged glances. Jack would later regret not pulling over to shoot, but right now he wasn't capable of thinking pragmatically.

None of them were.

It wasn't the awful destruction that freaked everybody out. Seth and Maura had seen lots worse, their dead cousin for instance. It was the way the whole area went ignored. Like an open wound left to fester, or a leprosy bruise, or sarcoma blister. The broken school sat, an obvious symptom of something terminal.

Ironically, the Friendly Confines lay just ahead.

Good Morning

Mary Hunt awoke from a dreadful sleep. Being frightened and cold, she hadn't fallen into a deep sleep, remaining aware of the inhospitable desert surrounding her. Mary's mouth was parched, dry as the land, her tongue sticking to the roof of her jaw like a dead mollusk. Her head pounded. She was hungry, thirsty, and out of food and water.

Lovely.

The prognosis was not good. If today shaped up anything like the last two, she'd be missing the coldness of evening within an hour. Assuming a position against the sheltering rocks, she watched the sun climb and saw it turn from a cool pink to blazing orange.

Even sitting was hard. Her left ankle ached, probably bitten or stung by something in the night. She knew scorpions inhabited the area and that they liked to hide in footwear, sleeping bags, and the like. Her only question was, if in fact, she'd been poisoned, why was it taking so goddamn long?

The boulder supporting Mary's head heated rapidly. Already she could feel the vapors rising off it. Her vision blurred. Only by blinking could she keep things in focus. Across the horizon, mountains took form in an array of pinks and browns and yellows. Another time Mary would have thought them beautiful beyond belief, but now she could only read the writing on their walls.

You are going to die here, the stones told her. And soon.

Getting Ready for Bed

Aware her mother was alive, having glimpsed her yesterday, Kathleen had a bad feeling about her sister. Shivering, unable to stop the goose bumps forming up and down her skin, she pulled back the curtain, blocking out the crescent moon from its place in the darkening sky. She knew Mary was out there with the scorpions and snakes and coyotes, one of which she heard wailing right now.

"She's on the Good Walk, Kathy. But don't you worry, she'll be back. She has to come back." Those had been George's words of encouragement last night. They had worked laundry detail together. "That's *his* way," he'd said, folding socks.

Whatever the hell that meant. Like most of the men in Congress, George wasn't all there. Sweet, yes, but also very slow. Still, George wasn't a troublemaker and he did what he was told. Again, like most of the men in Congress.

More importantly, he kept his hands to himself. George didn't leer at Kathleen or any of the women the way some men did, especially men cooped up like him.

A nice guy? No doubt.

On the other hand, if there was one thing Matthew wouldn't tolerate it was competition. Matthew was the lone wolf here, the Alpha male. With few exceptions, breakers of this rule had been extricated from the compound never to be seen again. For those with a penis, the 'Good Walk' was a short one. But for the most part, these weren't the kind of men who'd be missed. And, honestly, who would even look? Thousands of people, good and bad, were disappearing every day. Hell, every minute. It had a numbing effect. Missing persons had become redundant, irrelevant, and even boring.

Kathleen sat motionless on the small wooden chair. She played with a shock of her long hair, twisting the reddish curl over and over between thumb and forefinger. The fake menstrual bit had worked, buying Kathleen a little time.

But for what purpose? Leaving was not on the itinerary. It was over a hundred miles to anywhere, and hard as hell for a lone woman to navigate. Easy as pie for Matthew's helicopter and Jeeps. Escape was possible, but not probable. Suicide could get you there a lot quicker.

Positive she was pregnant with his baby, she also found herself tired, nauseous, and depressed. She slept a lot. She tried to spend most of her work time in the gardens or doing crafts. Yesterday, she made a clay water vessel. This morning she cut flowers.

But after a few days of relative peace and quiet, for bleeders were left alone during their cycle, the visitations inevitably recommenced.

He showed up at your door early evening, an hour or so after dinner. Like right about now, Kathleen thought to herself. Sometimes he brought a little wine or a rose. If you were a new girl, he took special care.

Later in the 'relationship,' he often took his clothes off before saying hello. By this point he expected to be greeted with a willing hand and open mouth.

Kathleen remembered how eager she was that first time and shuddered, not lustfully but disgusted. She'd had wanted him so badly then. She not only believed in Matthew but was turned on by him as well. Madly, body and soul. After all, he offered the seed of hope, and these days that was quite an aphrodisiac.

In anticipation of Matthew's arrival, she lubricated herself with Vaseline. It was, for lack of a better word, easier.

It felt less like rape.

That's All Folks

A few days *after* and Nora still felt moved. She hadn't told Raphael. He would've only gotten mad, jealous, or who knows what? Bottom line was she'd gotten off with a guy on television.

But not just any guy.

Matthew.

Nora couldn't shake the experience. It haunted her, clinging to her like an odor, like perspiration. She felt woozy and had to sit, letting her "famous" blueberry pancakes bubble past done in the cast-iron pan.

It was Saturday morning, and she'd awakened with a craving. Whether it was for blueberry pancakes or something else, she couldn't be sure, but pancakes were what she was making. Sound asleep, Raphael snored like an old hound. Nora could hear him even in the kitchen. She broke from her reverie, flipping the hotcakes before they burned. Black around the edges, they were fine. The crispiness would give them character, a crunch like French pastry, right?

Whatever.

Nora turned off the gas, leaving them sit.

She didn't want fucking pancakes.

Nora wanted what? Him?

How about a life? A real life like her mother had had and her mother's mother. She did not want to be a part of this here and this now, this EFS, this so-called Last Generation. All of it.

This.

"Nora, are those pancakes I smell?" His voice boomed from the other room. "I'll take mine with butter. Don't forget the butter!"

"Yeah, all right. Coming," Nora answered, trying to clear her head. There was no point in dwelling on these things. She stacked the pancakes on one plate they could share and everything else breakfast required on another. She drew a huge breath, taking the air deep and exhaling it hard, hoping to purge more than just carbon dioxide.

"You remember cartoons?" asked Raphael when she entered the bedroom.

"What do you mean, remember?" Nora shot back. She set the plates down on a dresser, not really thinking about the conversation. Raphael often got lost in silly thoughts like that. It was one of the things she liked most about him.

"This is Saturday," he said. "Saturday morning. And look, no more cartoons. Nothing." Raphael folded his lip against his nose. He wasn't being maudlin, merely making an observation. On television a trio of well-dressed people were debating or arguing. Blah, blah, blahing. With the volume off you couldn't tell.

"Well," sounded Nora, taking his topic more seriously than perhaps it deserved, "no more kiddies means no more cartoons." She handed him a plate, not forgetting the butter. "No surprise there, right?" It was barely a question.

Raphael contemplated his lover's comment. Of course he knew the technical reason there weren't any more cartoons on television. Everybody did.

He had a vivid recollection of endless Saturday mornings a long time ago with colorful robots, space aliens, happy talking monsters, all blending into a happy, goofy collage that was a typical Saturday morning.

"All gone now." he whispered to Nora. "No more fun."

"Yeah, babe, all gone." Nora sat down next to him on the bed.

They both remained silent, holding plates but not yet eating, just staring at the people on television. After a while, a long while, Raphael picked up the remote and gave the TV characters their voices back. And just like that, the dialogue about the end of the world continued, with its same serious words, accusations, and predictions.

This time the fuss was over drastic action being taken by NASA. Another man and woman had been sent into orbit. The hope was that, free of earth's doomed gravity, they could conceive and bear a child. However, it wasn't the plan that was deemed controversial, but rather the couple chosen to enact it. Apparently they weren't married.

Raphael grabbed a buttery pancake, rolled it up like a tortilla and took a huge bite. Ordinarily he might have been interested in the topic.

Again, the sweet and comforting taste of breakfast took him right back to the Saturday mornings of his youth. Pancakes and bacon. Watching cartoons with his brother. His favorite had been the Roadrunner. But for some reason, he'd always rooted for Wiley Coyote, even though he knew full well that the hapless animal could never catch the smarter, speedier bird. That's probably why he rooted for the canine. He felt sorry for old Wiley. He felt the frustration every time the Roadrunner outwitted him, and his anger every time the Roadrunner said beep-beep. But just as the Roadrunner was never caught, Wiley never gave up. He could fall into a thousand-foot crevice, followed by being hit by a truckload of anvils, and, just like that, he'd pick himself right back up. Time after time after time. It was as if his resilience and determination had made him impervious. Immortal. That was definitely cool.

Shit, Raphael thought. Nobody on *Cooler Heads* was capable of doing that.

Raphael devoured his pancakes, stealing one from Nora's plate. On *Cooler Heads*, as it so happened, a doctor-scientist was describing in disturbing detail the way in which "ordinary" miscarriages differed from those associated with EFS.

"What happened to the couple doing it in space?" blurted Raphael, finding himself in front of two large, very graphic renderings of the internal female anatomy. They were both of the same reproductive organs but one looked different from the other. Darker, smaller, wrong. Undoubtedly the sick one.

Bleh.

Raphael turned away. How do you ruin a story about sex in space? He looked at Nora, gauging her reaction to the graphic material being televised.

Nora wasn't grossed out. To the contrary, she was watching the program with obvious interest, concentrating on it. Maybe this egghead from another land would know what to do. Maybe, maybe, maybe.

"You watching this?" he asked, knowing she was but wanting to change the subject and the channel. He gave her arm a tiny squeeze. "Are you?"

"Uh-huh," Nora mumbled, intent on her show.

Raphael didn't respond. He didn't need this crap. Not now, for God's sake. Not on Saturday morning. He wanted cartoons with his pancakes and bacon. Looney Toons. The Road Runner.

"Beep-beep," he chirped, trying to get her attention.

Plan B from Outer Space

They were instructed to keep their bodies together, him inside of her, for as long as possible.

It was unknown what lack of gravity did to the coital process. In less dramatic times, the question and subsequent answer would have been met with great amusement. Weightless sex was a fantasy nobody had ever experienced, unless of course NASA was lying. Nowadays, questions of that nature were kept in check in favor of more biological interrogatives.

If sex was the topic, science prevailed over kink. Would the male and female genitalia respond correctly in this new environment? And even if they did, would the sperm and egg? There was a real concern that sperm, once released into the female, would get turned around and travel backwards, getting lost en route to the egg. And, having found the egg, then what? Scientist's didn't know. For whatever reason there had never been an experiment conducted in space or, for that matter, in replicated space, involving actual procreation between humans. Insects, yes, and some small mammals, but never anything bigger than a rat.

If "natural" fertilization did not occur after two cycles, they were prepared to go in-vitro, but the feeling was to keep the process as natural as possible. And the entire event, procreation to birth, had to take place outside the Earth's atmosphere.

Four pregnant women had been sent into space and all experienced the same sorry results. Another two pregnant females were currently orbiting the Earth, but they'd been sent up pregnant. Hope and Future were the first couple to attempt conception in space, making them legitimate contenders. The Hope and the Future.

Astronaut 457, code-named Future, felt his member shrink and slip out of the vagina of Astronaut 472, code-named Hope. He let go of her body, floating up to the cushioned ceiling.

Below him, Hope closed her legs into a pretzel and began floating as well. As instructed, she went into a slow turning somersault, giving the sperm inside her every chance of success.

After watching his companion turn like a convenience store hot-dog, Future started crying, the tears orbiting around his face like tiny liquid moons. He didn't love Hope. She didn't love him. He knew they were trying to make a baby, not love. He knew what was at stake, but it was still sad. Damn sad. He flicked the tears away from his head. Hope just finished her fertilization exercises, and he didn't want her to see him crying. Among the many intangibles affecting their success was each one of them maintaining a healthy, positive attitude, particularly the female. All he had to do was maintain an erection. Somehow, it was felt Hope would need more.

Hope was sure. If tomorrow's test proved positive, they would no longer be, well, screwing one another. But, if you thought about it, and she did, nine months of no sex wasn't much better than a constant diet of *this sex*.

Wishful thinking, however, because EFS had yet to be avoided by anyone anywhere, this attempt being the latest in a series of ever-more desperate measures. Still, Hope was confident. Even though she knew the odds were against her, she remained confident. Hope was her name, right? You had to be, she told herself. It certainly came in handy when strapped down to a cushion having intercourse with a man met via the lottery. Besides, Future AKA William was a good man, attractive and smart. Nothing overtly displeasing about him. Well maybe his lips were too thin and his beard felt strange but other than that....

Emma AKA Hope also wasn't permitted to shower. Instead she had to settle for a disinfectant wipe. At least the terry pajamas were clean. In them now, she stared out the portal at her home planet. Blue and serene just like in a movie, it seemed to be floating away from her. Strangely enough, at that moment she felt her place in the grand scheme. She knew her role and accepted it.

We are all merely tenants, she thought, and our lease is up. The landlord doesn't want us to sign. We are not wanted anymore. End of story.

So be it.

Caressing her tummy, Emma apologized. She prayed for success but understood the likelihood of failure.

William tried reading but once again found it impossible to focus on the text. The book was a political thriller. Guess what? Politics was no longer thrilling.

Being the world's only father, now that was thrilling. He was pretty sure it would happen too. He believed, like them, that EFS was an earth-born contagion of some sort and, in lieu of ridding the planet of it, all one had to do was remove themselves from the planet. That's what he believed. Which was why, despite mixed emotions, he'd been eager to participate with the program in the first place. He was doing his duty, as was she. Together, they were saving the world. Spun like that and the sex took on rich new meaning. Maybe not romantic, spirited, or wild, but it sure as hell was deep.

On the other hand, what was that infamous quote? "If rape is inevitable, sit back and enjoy it."

No. There was no other hand.

When William made love to his partner, he'd done so with respect and purpose. The human race depended on them. William picked up his book, reading the embossed words off of its shiny back cover. He'd read the same self-serving paragraph a thousand times. It was as far as he'd ever gotten.

And again he put the book down.

God, he hated analyzing himself, over-thinking.

Last month they weren't even a couple and now they were fucking like lab rats while sometimes not even taking meals together. Weird, weird, weird. Why didn't they just send real lovers into space? Why them? He knew the answer. They were the most ideally suited specimens within the space program.

But still....

Future gazed out his portal at the unending blackness. He had no idea what time it was and that struck him as bizarre. He wondered what Emma was doing and, in turn, how odd it was that he didn't even know.

Odd world, he thought, looking at it.

The Friendly Confines

Wrigley Field didn't just look like a ballpark; other ballparks looked like it. Constructed early in the twentieth century, Wrigley was truly a fond farewell to the Victorian age. Festive and jubilant, it was the embodiment of all that was swell about baseball, leisure, even America. Think the Titanic but without water and, Cubs jokes aside, tragedy. That was the Friendly Confines. 'Welcome to Wrigley Field,' flashed the big red sign in front, its light bulbs working even now.

They stood before the old stadium, taking it in. Much to everybody's surprise, Seth rattled off the lineup from the infamous squad of '69. That year the Cubbies took a winning season into September and choked. He even knew the players' positions, batting averages, and so on.

Maura was impressed or shocked, probably both. "How the hell do you know Don Kessinger's batting average?" she asked. "How the hell do you even know Don Kessinger?"

"Just do," he answered, not looking at her. "Weak hitter. Good glove. Played shortstop. I think he died recently."

"Hey, so the guy likes baseball," interrupted Jack. "What's the big deal?" He didn't think Seth's knowledge of the team was anything profound. It was common knowledge that even though the Chicago Cubs always found a way to lose, an inordinate amount of people, and not just locals, were fans. The term 'die-hard' was invented here. The Cubs were America's lovable losers or something along those lines, even he knew as much. When Jack was a boy, he'd gone to a Cubs' game with his homeroom class. Fun he remembered, even though they lost by a ton.

Fun he remembered.

Recalling his recent diatribe on baseball, the one Muriel had filmed back at Dan's Place, Jack felt blue. And well he should. Above him a sign indicated seats were still available for Tuesday's match-up with the Astros. Alas, they were not. That contest had concluded nine years ago. Melancholy was appropriate. Baseball was a game no longer played, one of many games.

"What's eating you?" questioned Muriel, sensing her brother's flush of pain. Until that moment, she hadn't even been paying attention. Not to them anyway. She'd heard somewhere that Wrigleyville was also famous for being a gay neighborhood and she was scanning the area for signs. Other than an old man walking a poodle, she hadn't seen anything remotely queer. Alternative lifestyles intrigued her. Something about the whole scene made sense. Especially now. Why, she couldn't put her finger on. It just did.

"Jack's bummed out because they don't play the game anymore," replied Seth, seeing as Jack wasn't answering his sister. "He senses, as I do, the palpable loss of joy that comes with the loss of baseball. Nobody is having fun, anymore. We've decided not to play games anymore. It's like we've begun to mourn our own passing."

"Um, excuse me," interrupted Maura, wondering where this soliloquy was coming from. "Aren't people," she said, "more or less bumming out on account of the baby thing?" Nobody missed baseball and football, and the Green Bay Packers, more than her, "but even so," she added, "you've got to be young to play professional sports and in case you haven't noticed there ain't nobody young anymore."

Ain't nobody? Great. First Seth starts sounding like a Poindexter and now she's biker trash. They needed to get high. Or get out of there. Something.

Yet her point was well taken. The group quieted and stared at their feet.

"Let's have a cigarette," suggested Muriel. "And a seat." She pointed to a group of empty benches near the Addison bus stop. The bench they chose featured an advertisement for Regis Day Care Services. It was faded, though one could still make out the copy and phone number. Not bad considering it had to be twenty years old. The artwork, such as it was, featured a small Hispanic child holding on to the hand of his caregiver. The two looked at one another with the kind of big smiles one only saw in advertising.

"Do you see what I see?" asked Maura, reaching for her Marlboros. She didn't have to point. Right smack in the middle of the ad was a sticker for The Congress.

"How about we sit elsewhere?" offered Jack, not liking the feng shui. He motioned to the adjacent bench. On it was an ad for Rolling Thunder Amusement Park. It pictured a roller coaster with the head of a serpent in front and passenger cars for a body. Some thrilled kids had their hands up in the air screaming in delight.

"These benches are ancient," pointed out Seth, sitting upon the serpentine roller coaster. "But comfortable."

Maura smiled. There was the incoherent speed freak she knew and loved. Sitting down, she said to the others, "Take a load off." Maura could sense their anxiety. She kept on talking as a consequence. "We'll split in a minute. Just let me finish this smoke. Besides, we need some kind of a game plan, don't you think? I mean, for example, where the hell are we going to stay tonight?"

As instructed, Muriel took a seat on the bench. Just as well. Her right leg twitched. Bad sign. Something was troubling her. Here they were in the second biggest city in America, and what do they see? First, a blown-up high school. Then the fucking Coliseum. Was all of

Chicago ruins? And what about all these old ads? The benches weren't like that in Madison, were they?

Muriel couldn't remember. The sudden lack of recall made her uneasy and kind of panicky. She took a deep drag on her cigarette, which she'd almost forgotten was in her hands, and attempted to gather herself. Everybody was akimbo, she thought, if indeed that was the word she was looking for.

Akimbo.

It wasn't just her, however. Seth's monologue. Maura all defensive. She guessed the friendly confines weren't so friendly anymore. Muriel flashed on an old horror picture she'd seen in film school, not with Jack but on an actual date. It was shot at an abandoned circus, the film called The Carnival of Lost Souls. She couldn't recall the plot. A young woman had been drawn to an abandoned amusement park only to be tormented by ghosts and apparitions, people from before, the lost souls. It didn't make a lot of sense, but it was damn creepy. "This place gives me the willies," she said finally.

"I heard that," remarked Seth, feeling the same vibe as the rest of them.

And he thought he knew why. Only a hunch but, "a nice spring day. Classic ballpark. Yet something's wrong with this picture." He turned his gaze to the McDonald's restaurant across the street. Open but basically empty. A car or two were parked in the lot, probably employees. And that was it.

"Last I checked," continued Seth, enunciating his words, "there were still a fair number of people on this planet... "

"A few," said Jack.

"My question then is where the fuck are they?"

"These places don't work anymore," said Jack, catching Seth's drift.

"What do you mean, don't work? The McDonald's is open," countered Maura. "A lot of the places around here are."

"Maybe," replied Seth, undeterred. "But this place doesn't work as in work."

"I think he means conceptually," added Jack.

Here we go again, Maura thought. And me without my taperecorder.

Jack continued, oblivious. "We live in a world without children, right?"

Silence.

"Right?" he implored. When no one answered, he answered for them. "Right. No children. Okay, and where are we now? A baseball stadium. And not just any baseball stadium, mind you. The greatest one in the world. Now then, what's across the street?" This time he didn't wait for an answer. "Mickey D's. As in Ronald McDonald. Happy Meals."

"I remember Happy Meals," chimed Muriel, compelled to participate. "You would get a toy or some puzzles. Jesus, I loved Happy Meals."

"We all did," Seth said. "When we were kids." He flicked his cigarette as far as he could onto Clark Street, then looked up at the rest of them. "When we were kids."

As if on cue, a bus rolled over the smoldering butt. Like everything else, it was nearly empty.

"Don't you see?" Seth continued. "Without children, or even the idea of children—this whole place seems weird, ominous. It just doesn't work."

"Like an abandoned amusement park," retorted Muriel, recalling the eerie movie once again.

"Exactly," said Seth. "Or an empty..." Noticing Muriel had begun filming with their mini-camera, he smiled. "...Classroom," he said, completing his thought.

After experiencing loss, one is often unable to carry out previously held plans or wishes. As an alternative or 'solution,' that person may assume the characteristics and mannerisms of others.

This coping mechanism is known as...

Assumption

The bar was packed. Sometimes it seemed to Mick that everybody left in the world was gay or wanted to be. With children no longer part of the equation, in a way, everybody was. Without biological imperative, sex was just sex now. Go forth and be fruity. Mick blew a kiss to Neil, who made room for him at the bar. Neil had a thing for him, he knew, but tonight Mick wasn't interested, not that he'd ever been. He maneuvered his still nimble 43-year-old body around the perfumed admirer searching for a bartender.

"What am I, a parking attendant?"

"Sorry, Neil. Thirsty."

"Manners before alcohol, Mickey. Didn't your mother teach you anything?"

"And didn't yours teach you a little cologne went a long way?" Mick was officially having a bitchy conversation. He did try avoiding the queer clichés in his life, but guys like Neil made it difficult.

With tight jeans, ripped tee, that ridiculous policeman's hat, Neil was the embodiment of gay stereotype. Nelly Neil, they called him. His advanced age only made it scarier, the big, bushy mustache sealing the deal.

"Welcome to the end of the world. Can I buy you a drink?"

Mick turned to the voice, discovering an attractive woman wearing an even better looking suit. A crew cut and thick-rimmed glasses completed the look. Clark Kent as a woman. Or visa-versa.

Which was fine, provided she could fix a proper martini. He ordered it with a brand of gin she didn't have up front and had to go get. He watched her move, wondering if she was really gay.

"Pseudo," Neil chimed when she was just out of earshot. "I tell you, there's more and more of them. Their wombs go bad and they just—" He hunted for the words. "Come over."

"Pseudo-sexuality." Pseudo for short. Post EFS, it was all the rage. Artificial homosexuality. Reverse proclivity. More commonly seen in females, men went pseudo as well. In fact, the last guy Mick took home had been one. He'd confessed to Mick after struggling at the fine art of fellatio. The unarguable turn-on of doing a straight boy had come with a price. Oh, well, Mick thought. Bad head was better than no head.

He looked over Neil's shoulder. Maybe the pseudo was here. Mediocre cocksmanship aside, he was still gorgeous. Probably a real ladies' man once. He told Mick he'd recently left his wife and no family. That's how he put it, "wife and no family." He'd grown tired of her interminable melancholy. Like a lot of women, she'd wigged out over the syndrome. After miscarrying, she'd become terrified of sex all together and had blamed him for waiting so long to get married, as if that would have mattered. She quit her job, got fat, totally lost it.

Her loss, Mick's gain. Using his teeth, he pried the first of two feta cheese olives into his mouth. Clark Kent was mixing another batch of martinis. Someone had seen his and wanted one, too. Copy cats. He spun around, looking for Daniel.

EFS did weird things to breeders. Especially to the ladies. Sadly, many women were "blamed" for what happened to their unborn children. In many cases, they blamed themselves. The reasoning was specious but potent; while men produced viable sperm, women were producing nothing.

Mick set down his drink. He thought about the cruelty in that, the downright evil, remembering the AIDS virus and how everybody wanted a flight attendant for a scapegoat. Bad enough to be dying, but to feel guilty as well? Horrible.

"Now you stop that!"

Neil's indomitable laugh. A known pseudo was tickling his prodigious stomach, a former alderman no less.

Mick sighed, ordered another drink.

"Slow down, handsome," warned Neil. "The night is young. Even if nobody else is."

Mick ignored him and the bad joke.

Clark Kent handed him a martini, smiling.

Mick wasn't really buying into the concept of pseudo-sexuality. He did see the logic, however. These days being a sexy lesbian was easier than being a mother.

Pseu-Pseu-Pseudio

Maybe, Daniel thought, being straight had been merely a phase. Perhaps he was, as they used to say, curious. Either way, his wife certainly made the "transition decision" an easy one.

Blaming him, imagine.

EFS was happening to everyone. His tears had been real as hers, as real as anybody's. Shit, he'd wanted to be a father too. He had dreams of camping and Christmas mornings and helping with homework. She knew that. He knew she did.

And while his wife may have given up, he sure as hell hadn't. Part of civilization's finale, he was going out with a bang, figuratively and literally.

Daniel got out of the shower. Before drying, he checked himself out in the mirror. Smooth skin. Not too much body hair. Even less fat. He looked half his age and with the whole night still ahead of him.

That's when he realized what he liked most about the "boys." It was the forward thinking. They weren't trapped by endless family rituals and regimented expectations. Never had been.

Before EFS, that lack of obligation made them all pariahs.

Now it was freeing, unadorned, like being a kid.

Bottom line was homosexuals knew how to live in a world without children. It was all they knew. And now it was all anyone knew.

Being gay meant one lived in the present.

As in right fucking now.

Daniel stood, naked, dripping, and newly gay, and as it happened, thinking about something an anthropologist on *Cooler Heads* had said. A phenomenon, he'd called it. In absence of a biological imperative, a kind of hybrid evolution was taking place. Nature was reinterpreting itself. Mankind might be going extinct but not without having a good time. "Boys will be boys, right?"

Say what? From then on, Daniel had been glued to the set.

Another expert spoke on the subject from a gallery at the Seattle Aquarium. With some irony, Daniel recognized the venue from having visited it on his honeymoon. If memory served, that week he'd been straight. Very much so.

It was common, the marine biologist said, for certain live-bearing fish to change their sexual orientation if, in an isolated population, a shortage of one gender existed. The shift became necessary for survival. For example, a drought might diminish a mighty river into a series of puddles, trapping a group of females. Within days, the specialist said, male genitalia would begin to appear on one or more of the fish. In weeks, if the puddle held out, mating occurred. Fry were born and the species survived. Sexual metamorphosis could even be observed in aquarium populations, she said, or in your own home.

Pseudo-sexuality among humans was simply a variation, offered the previous scientist, tying it all up. The big difference among people, he said, was that survival no longer served as a relevant catalyst. Frankly, he continued, it wasn't relevant at all. People were changing their sexual orientation because they wanted to, because they could for pleasure. In the post EFS world, Darwinism had been replaced by Hedonism. Gay meant pleasure. "And these days," laughed the man, "that is enough."

Daniel put on his favorite black jeans, tucking a white Polo into them. He contemplated fixing a drink but decided against it. He was more comfortable now and wanted to prove it. Hopefully, to Mick.

In the foyer hung a photograph of Maggie. It was a black-and-white shot by one of their friends. She's holding a cat. She's smiling. He can just make out her diamond glistening from within the cat's fur.

"When the cat's away," he said, hitting the lights and opening the door, "the mice will play."

Make It A Double

Dan missed his kids. All four of them, he mused, accepting the realization with raised eyebrows. Kathleen, Mary, Jack, and Muriel. If it were Christmas, each one would have stockings hanging over the fireplace. *Hey, you get used to people.*

But it wasn't Christmas, and a part of him didn't think he'd be seeing any of them again. Dan didn't fear for their lives, leastwise not about the two bikers. He'd seen real trouble before, and they weren't it. If anything, they could be helpful when it came to fending off trouble. So should he be concerned? Not willing to go there yet, he did know this, when people left, *they left.*

"Right, Oscar?" Dan flicked his bar towel at the stuffed feline. "It's just you and me, baby."

"Hey, I'm here for you too, baby." Carl took a seat at his usual perch, furthest stool from the door.

"I know what you're here for," replied Dan, smirking. Carl may have been an alcoholic, but he was never a problem. He was the perfect customer.

"Maybe you do and maybe you don't," is how Carl returned the comment. He held his empty mug up for effect.

Dan brought the man another beer.

"A fresh glass? Someone hit the lottery?" Carl laughed at his own joke.

"What lottery?" Dan regarded his perfect customer. His familiar face. The Brewers' cap and taped-up glasses. And for perhaps the first time he thought about their relationship, if that's what it was. Truthfully, the repartee they shared was more like a game of checkers than a conversation, a move followed by a move followed by a move. But that didn't make it bad. After all, checkers was fun. Nobody got hurt. The arrangement, or lack of one, suited both men just fine. They'd already experienced their share of woe. You could see the pain in their eyes but it seldom came out of their mouths.

"What? Something on my face?" Carl wasn't used to being scrutinized, not since Betty died. And certainly not in this place, by this guy.

"Other than those ugly-ass glasses, no." Dan smiled, albeit weakly. "I was just remembering the first time you ever came in. Can you believe I actually remember a thing like that?"

"No, I can't," responded Carl, not sure he liked where this was going. Carl and Dan were the very definition of old dogs, and any deviation of protocol had to be considered a new trick. Still, he played along. "When was that, like ten, fifteen years ago?"

"Closer to twenty. Packer game was on. They were playing the Bears. How could I forget?"

"Easily." But he remembered.

"Betty was with you."

"Pissing and moaning, I bet." Carl laughed and it became a cough. He didn't smoke but he spent a lot of time in places where people did, such as here. "I think Bet was the only person in Wisconsin who hated football. You know, she once told me she appreciated EFS for getting rid of it."

Dan laughed, a rarity. He hadn't known Carl's wife very well. She didn't like bars and ballgames and, well, that was his life. Even Dan's wife found Betty stuck-up and overly critical. "Too precious," she'd called her. In retrospect, Dan kind of liked the broad's moxie, the EFS comment was a perfect example. What person, he thought, no, what woman would even consider putting a positive spin on something like EFS? Good old Bet, that's who.

"Hey Carl, can I ask you a personal question?"

"Could I stop you?"

"It's just—" Dan fumbled for the words. "Well, I know Betty was a bit of a pill. Always busting your chops—"

"I'm a drunk, Dan. A loser. She merely pointed it out. Maybe I should have taken heed, eh?" Carl swallowed the bottom of his glass. That he wanted another was a given. "Now what was your question?"

"Ah hell, Carl, you never were gonna be any more than the man she married. She knew that. You worked for a tire company. You drank too much. She still said 'I do' for better or for worse." Dan bought and brought his best customer another beer, setting it down in front of him. "My question is, what made her give up?"

"Give up? I never looked at it like that." Carl took a long hit on his new beer, wishing for some whiskey to go along with it.

"You know what I mean. Maybe she never won any popularity contests but she wasn't—" He couldn't finish. "What happened, Carl? Why'd they put her away? How'd she get like that?"

Committed for chronic personal neglect, it had gotten so bad she wasn't even bathing. One afternoon Carl came home from a 3-day trip and found Betty in bed, catatonic. The sheets were soiled.

"Didn't Connie tell you?" From the beginning, Carl had known Dan's wife never much cared for his. He could only assume she'd told him as well.

"Connie said a lot of shit. And, well, you know what happened to her." Dan turned around and then turned around again. He held a bottle, no, the bottle, of Johnnie Walker Blue in his hand, a couple of snifters in the other. "So, tell me, Carl. What happened to your wife?"

How long had Carl ogled that bottle? Forever. It was like the Holy Grail, precious yet unobtainable. For eons it sat up there while he sat down here. In nearly two decades he hadn't seen a single drop served to a single person.

And yet, here it was.

Carl licked his lips in anticipation, even though he knew he was about to say as sorry a thing as he ever would say.

He began. "Must have been 1998. I know it was right before the new millennium. Right before EFS. I owed a lot of money to a lot of people and I didn't think–" Carl stopped, took a deep gulp of air, wanting liquid. "How 'bout that whiskey, then?"

Dan poured forty dollars worth and pushed it forward. He saw a story coming at him like a city inspector behind in his quota.

Carl imbibed half the Blue in one toss, swishing it in his mouth first, then letting the fine distillation hurtle down his beckoning throat. After contemplating the rare, brief pleasure of that, he continued.

"Bet got pregnant." Carl finished his drink, shut his eyes and felt the warmth. It was like swallowing a new soul.

Dan poured himself one.

"And I, as you may have already surmised, was pretty adamant about us not having it. So, she didn't."

Dan winced. So that was it.

Carl looked right through the bartender, staring at a crappy painting of Africa, for some reason hung on the wall. Grimy as hell, he could still make out snow-capped mountains. Africa had hills? He'd always wondered about that but never asked.

A truck was backing up outside. They could tell from the beeping.

"As you know," resumed Carl, "the following year the babies stopped coming." His voice grew thin, barely a whisper. "At first, we pretended not to notice. But it was always there, lurking, taking up more and more of our space."

He took another sip. "I started really drinking then. My wife grew distant. Worse than distant, I suppose. Bottom line, Betty couldn't forget what she'd done. What I'd made her do. She never forgave me. Herself. Nobody."

Dan placed a hand on Carl's shoulder. The man felt tiny beneath his palm, vulnerable, like a small girl.

Carl cried, a soft whimpering. It was cold inside. Big, ungainly teardrops fell on the old wooden floor, as if from melting icicles.

That Toddlin' Town

Lodging became Maura's responsibility. There was a sizable chapter of The Last in Chicago. Most of them would be up north for the rally, but certainly not all. So, while the others worked on a pitcher of beer, she made some calls from a payphone.

They were in a bar called Nuts on Clark. Clark was the street. They were the crazies.

Maura got lucky. A woman in the Ukrainian Village said her old man left yesterday for the rally and, yeah, sure, they could come over. Just bring something to drink, she said. And, of all things, she demanded a bucket of chicken. Adamant, she mentioned the chicken twice. "Fried. Not that roasted shit. And only dark meat, you hear?"

"Sure," said Maura, hanging up. The woman on the phone sounded pathetic, and Maura thought she knew why. A craving for fried food usually indicated a serious hangover, or worse. Maybe she was coming down from something stronger, trying to kick a habit. Maura's choice would've been deep fried shrimp with red sauce. Or chocolate. After her last binge only Peanut Butter Cups satisfied. Whatever. She just hoped the chick was alone and that there were plenty of rooms to crash in.

Instead of asking the flake for directions, Maura looked up the address in the Yellow Pages. It only took a minute. Spend as much time on the road as she did, you got good at reading maps. It was a twenty-minute drive. Half an hour with traffic. She looked at her watch, a beat-up Timex she'd copped from her father. Still early afternoon. Plenty of time to drink before night fell.

And, frankly, who cared if it got dark?

In the booth, Seth was showing the siblings how to pop shots no-handed. Neck tilted backward, mouth around the shot glass, he resembled an ostrich. A dodo bird.

An improvement over the day before, Maura had to admit. She heard them laughing and couldn't help wondering how long the good times were going to last.

Apparently a while longer. From what she could see, they'd already polished off their first pitcher and were on to another.

Silly Rabbit

Of course she was pregnant. They'd been doing it like bunnies. Even post-EFS that part of the deal hadn't changed. Women got pregnant. Conceiving hadn't been the problem and never was. On the contrary, as a result of EFS, more women were getting pregnant than ever before. Everybody tried and for lots of different reasons. Starting a family was probably not one. It's like this: if some lady actually gave birth, she would instantly become the mother of all news stories. Next to her baby, she would be the most famous person on earth.

Nora knew what time of the month it was. Whether consciously or not, she'd wanted to get pregnant and did. What she did not know was how Raphael would feel about the matter. In the past, he'd only spoke of the futility of it. "Why subject ourselves to that kind of stress? You know what's going to happen. *You know.*"

She figured he'd be pissed.

And she was right.

"You're what? You're what!" By his own admission, Raphael wasn't predisposed to fits of joy. This didn't help.

And to think he'd come home feeling pretty good. He had a fine piece of tenderloin, intending to smoke it in the backyard.

Maybe drink a few Lone Stars with his woman, basically chill. That was the plan.

Was.

"Damn it, Nora!" He dropped the wrapped package of meat on the counter. The weight of it and the subsequent concussion caused a couple of glasses in the sink to fall over and break. Raphael gave two shits.

"How could you," he bellowed, and not in the form of a question.

"You did it, too," said Nora, albeit sheepishly. She looked at her feet, the floor, the cat dish. Cradling her stomach, she couldn't help but think how different things would have been under normal circumstances. Instinctively, she knew Raphael wanted a baby and that he would have wanted her to have it with him.

But she also knew the reality of the situation. Embryo Fatality Syndrome was not a matter of debate. Why Nora let herself get pregnant given THE REALITY OF THE SITUATION she could not answer, not really.

The silence became unbearable. Nervously, she began undoing the wrapper on the tenderloin.

"Leave it," he said.

"Please don't be mad at me."

"We were doing all right," said Raphael. "Under the circumstances, we were doing all right. And now what? Now how are we doing?"

There were a million ways she could have answered the question. Then again, there weren't any. She said nothing.

Raphael left the kitchen, the screen door slapping uncomfortably into its frame.

Nora watched him go, saw him get swallowed by the porch moths and the warm Texas night. Again, she picked up the roast, then, disgusted, set it back down in the sink. A tiny trickle of blood oozed forth from a wet flap in the wrapper quickly finding its way toward the drain.

Part of her believed the baby was not real. Part of her didn't. Nora knew the odds were brutal, but she also knew that if nobody tried anymore then it was over for sure, end of story.

She just couldn't let that happen. Call it maternal drive or call it stupid, but Nora was trying. She'd made a decision.

Perhaps, just maybe, she would be the one. It was not impossible. There was always that chance. EFS had come suddenly, without explanation. Who was to say it couldn't leave that way?

Overwhelmed, woozy, her legs buckled. Was it the bloody roast in the sink? Morning sickness? The argument? All of the above? Nora didn't know why she was falling only that she was, indeed, falling.

In that moment, she saw Matthew.

Arms outstretched, trying to catch her.

Save her.

And Nora fell, believing, heart and soul, she was going to be caught.

Tending the Flock

W here is she?"

"Which one, sir?"

"Mary."

"She is where you sent her, sir."

"Answer my questions succinctly. With a proper noun. Now, once more, where is she?"

"She's in the desert. On the walk. We can't be certain where exactly." A crony, Fred hated when it became so damn obvious. He also hated when Matthew feigned ignorance, as if to imply the seamy side of his affairs was not really happening. "We can look for her if that's what you want."

"I know full well what you can and cannot do, Frederick." Matthew said, chopping scallions for his omelet. He liked his onions sliced very, very thin, almost minced. Although Matthew had an ample staff, he preferred cooking for himself, richly enjoying the act of preparing food, maybe even more so than eating it. For some men, pursuing women was more satisfying than making love to them. Same thing here. Same thing.

"Hmmm," sighed Matthew, tasting an onion. "Perhaps you should retrieve Mary from the desert." He sampled a few more bits of browning scallion. "Yes," he warmed. "Upon further review, I have decided she has had enough," the Leader of the Congress said, stirring, then arranging his scallions into a neat little pile. "Assuming she is well rested, I shall see her tonight, suitably bathed of course. Make it happen, Frederick."

"Yes sir," nodded Fred. He wasn't so sure, though. Mary had been on The Good Walk for several days and the odds of her being "well rested" were getting shittier by the hour. He gave the woman about a sixty-forty shot of even being alive, let alone ready for trysting.

But denying Matthew's request would not bode well for his health, either. Frederick had no choice but to rustle up a team and find that chick, dead or alive. It's not like he hadn't done it before. He had. A hundred times. The desert was big but ladies were not. They seldom got far. Since the inception of Congress, they'd only lost three females to the Walk. And that was out of fifty-two. Of those, twenty-nine survived. The rest perished from hypothermia, food, and water deprivation or both. For Fred and his team, the goal was to try and find these girls before the canine packs did. Coyotes, wolves, and even wild dogs were out there, and in ever increasing numbers. Mountain lions, too.

"I'll get right on it," said Frederick, turning toward the exit. He figured he'd try the canyon first, checking out the usual caves. Hopefully Mary was hunkered in one of them, weak, hungry and cold, but not dead.

"Frederick, wait." Matthew did not even look up from his cutting board. He halved and quartered a red pepper, then began slivering it. "Pray tell, who's ready now?"

Fred sighed. *Ready* meant fertile.

"I don't know, sir," he lied. "I haven't checked the charts." There were two women he knew were 'ready' and, at least one who was probable, but Fred didn't feel like offering them up at this juncture. He was down on Matthew lately, and in no mood to help him get laid. Fred was beginning to question the whole situation, be it Congress, Matthew, or this business about a new child. Regardless, he'd kept his mouth shut this far and he would continue keeping it shut, for the time being, anyway. He reasoned saving Mary Connely from perishing in the desert would serve as more than adequate distraction. Besides, he liked Mary. He wished Matthew didn't. Frederick stood in the doorway waiting to be dismissed.

"I see," said Matthew, mulling it over. He contemplated a plump, vine-ripened tomato while considering his employee's less-than-desirable words. Detecting something false in Frederick's reply, he nevertheless elected not to pursue the matter. The sooner Fred got his posterior out in the field, the sooner he'd have his Mary back. Matthew turned on the burner, lowering a skillet onto the flames.

"Well, be off then and Godspeed. Be careful," he murmured, long after Fred had left the room.

Matthew continued to prepare breakfast, slicing a tomato in half, separating the mushy, seeded portion away from the better, firmer flesh. With the very tip of his knife, he clipped the fruit's skin, creating a flap. This enabled him to remove its skin with one pull. Doing the same to the other piece, he then sliced the tomato halves much like he had done the onion, but in this case careful not to harm the more fragile fruit. A tomato's firm consistency had to be maintained. It was critical. The integrity of his omelet was at stake. Integrity in all things was one of Matthew's credos. If one committed to an action, any action at all, it was incumbent upon that person to perform it correctly, without flaw. If he'd wanted salsa in his omelet then he would have made salsa.

In specific order, Matthew began sautéing each of the ingredients. Onions first, then mushrooms, then tomatoes, and then he added beaten eggs with a pinch of vanilla and tablespoon of whipping cream.

While the omelet cooked, Matthew gazed upon the magnificent geography located just outside his window. This land had been created with integrity, imbued with it, so much so, he could feel it. Matthew wondered if Mary was feeling it, wondered if she'd learned from the grace of her surroundings about correctness and perfection. After all, she hadn't performed the most critical of functions, failing not only him, but also herself. Yet the Good Walk healed. The great Indian chiefs believed it and so did Matthew. A spirit inhabited these valleys and white-tipped mountains, a powerful, curative spirit. One that was capable of bestowing many blessings, of a kind, Matthew was convinced, that Mary needed desperately.

Matthew slid a spatula beneath the omelet and, in one quick move, flipped it over. Golden, delectable, perfect. The man planning to sire the next child stared at his creation and smiled. Ah, what you could make with an egg!

Hail Mary

Mary heard the helicopter landing, at first thinking it was a flood or a sandstorm, anything but a helicopter. Wind and soil blew on her and everywhere. In her mind she had been dead, finished, gone. And just when the coffin was dropping, she heard the wup-wup-wup of the helicopter blades.

"Hello, Mary." Frederick reached out a hand, grabbing her. Pulling.

Muscles screaming, bones cracking. From both of their perspectives, she felt like a ball of tinfoil being unfolded.

"Hey!" She knew Fred and didn't hate him, took his hand and let him lift her when the pain subsided. "A helicopter, wow. To whom do I owe the pleasure?"

"Let's just go." Fred said, helping buckle her into a seat. "I'm glad you're all right," he said, after they'd lifted off. "I really am."

"Of course you are. Got any water?" She may not have hated the man, but that didn't mean she trusted him either.

"I'm sorry. Help yourself." He handed her a bottle, his.

Mary drank most of it, leaving perhaps a finger. She held the bottle up, rattling it's remaining contents. "May I?"

"Please," Fred replied. "Be my guest."

She polished it off.

"Are you okay? You look all right, considering." He was correct about that. Considering she'd been out in the elements for going on three days, this woman looked great.

"Again, who authorized this? Surely not him."

"Who else?" Fred wanted to tell her anything but the truth. I defied the leader of Congress. I've stolen his helicopter. I'm taking you away. But he couldn't.

Besides, Mary knew the score.

She grimaced. Of course it was a relief being saved from certain death but what about tomorrow? What kind of life was that? Fred could offer little salvation there. She stared out the helicopter's portal, amazed at the distance she'd covered on foot.

"Matthew requested to see you this evening." Fred told her this outright because he had to, because she might want him to. He had to remind himself daily that these ladies, however pretty and smart, had given up everything in order to come out here and be with him. For all he knew, Mary wanted to see Matthew this evening.

"I'd rather not," she said. Mary wasn't worried about Fred's reaction, sensing like-minded antagonism in him as well. The other pilot eavesdropping concerned her far more. Despite aircraft noise, Lieutenant Smith managed to pick up an inordinate amount of damaging quotes while shepherding Good Walk participants back to the camp. Much of it was not of the "I'm saved, I'm blessed" variety. And like a good soldier, the lieutenant reported every bit of it to his beloved commander. Consequences invariably followed, occasionally dire. Thus, through bits of shared information, many women learned to fake their salvation in some form or another. Mary would, too. But not now. She just didn't have it in her.

"Not tonight," she said wearily. "I've been through–" She was going to say hell.

Frederick considered her plight. Really their plight. After all, they were all part of Matthew's covenant. But for obvious reasons, he felt much sorrier for the female subordinates, and for this one in particular. Since day one he'd found her attractive, and here she was confiding in him.

Recalling his earlier take on the women in Congress, he'd showed nothing but contempt, chastising them for failing as women and disappointing the leader. Only recently had he begun to re-evaluate things and started second-guessing the whole operation. At first maybe he was envious of Matthew's status, jealous of his obvious sexual charisma. Perhaps now he had another motive as well. An agenda.

Either way, it was critical he assume a top spot in the hierarchy of Congress. The more Matthew trusted you the higher you went. The higher you went the more liberties you got and the more liberties you could take. Infinitely easier said than done.

Frederick had become more introspective and more critical of his own behavior. He was also afraid of the truth, not only about his boss, about himself. He, like Matthew, had come to Congress not for enlightenment, but for the two oldest reasons on earth, sex and power.

He peered over the shoulder of Lt. Smith out the forward window and saw Morton's Peak to the right about two miles ahead. They'd be arriving in ten minutes. He leaned back toward Mary.

"You know," he said, choosing his words carefully. "You don't look so well. I don't think you're in any shape to have company tonight."

Was she hearing him right? Mary looked Fred right in the eyes, scanning him for what? Honesty? Compassion?

"If you pass out, I'll be obligated to take you to the infirmary." He reached into his coat, removing a small yellow envelope from the inner pocket. "Take three or four of these. They'll help. Trust me."

But could she? Trusting men was a class she'd have to take over.

"Brace yourself. We'll be landing any minute." He spoke loud enough for the lieutenant to hear but the look in his eyes was purely for her.

Oh, Christ. She poured five of the phenobarbitals in her hand and, without asking what they were, gobbled them down. Unfastening her seat belt, Mary fell forward as far and as hard as she could.

"Lieutenant!" Fred shouted. "She's fainted. How much further?"

Smith turned around, assessing the situation. He saw Mary on the floor and Fred taking her pulse.

"It's low," said Fred, urgently. "I don't know what happened to her. Jesus."

The lieutenant had no reason to question any of it. He'd thought the woman's overall condition was a little too good to be true. He remembered the last one they'd brought back. She hadn't even been in one piece.

"We'll be there in two or three minutes," said the pilot. "I'll radio for a stretcher."

Mary opened an eye, catching Fred's attention. She mouthed the words 'thank you,' along with a smile. Already the narcotic was working.

Either that or she just felt good for a change.

When bereaved people seek affection from others as a substitute for loss, this strategy is referred to as...

Replacement

The Frappel twins were teenagers despite what their parents claimed. A well-known lie, but there they were on television, in magazines, all over.

"The Amazing Frappel Twins!"

"Behold, the Last Twin Children in the World!"

And the people looked and beheld. They looked and beheld very much and paid dearly for it as a matter of fact. This is what they saw.

In the blue house, Jimmy had everything a boy his age could want: An elaborate model train, reptile menagerie, archery range, even a miniature racecar he could zip around in. Indeed, he was encouraged to play with everything, twice daily.

One-way glass separated him from the gaping crowds. Bullet proof, of course, not that anyone would ever harm little Jimmy. On the contrary, people adored little Jimmy. They loved him unconditionally. They loved him for his all-American haircut. They loved him for his colorful toys. But most of all, they loved him for his sister.

Ah, Janey. Sugar and spice and everything nice. She was everybody's darling. It was three o'clock and time for tea in the parlor. Her teddy bears made awfully gracious guests, didn't they, smiling adoringly at their little Janey. A quartet played Mozart, Brahms and other appropriate selections. An honest-to-goodness butler served frozen candy sandwiches.

And the audience ate it up.

"Look at Janey's hair!"

"Isn't she darling?"

"Such a little princess."

The lines to Janey's dollhouse went through the gift shop and around the block.

On their own, each of the children would have been immensely popular. Together they were transcendent. On days when they both attended "The Original One-Room School House," the surrounding amphitheater was packed. Monitors and speakers brought every choreographed nuance to even the highest elevations. Even so, front row seats were coveted beyond all reason. It was truly a last glimpse at childhood. When Jimmy pulled Janey's pigtails in one of many scripted displays, the place, as they say, went wild.

"Jimmy, stop it! I'm gonna tell!"

"Go ahead! See if I care!"

Hailed by critics as the "collective and idealized memory of childhood," the shows played to over seven thousand paying customers, six days a week, two shows on Friday.

Pure gold.

Hardly anyone believed the insidious rumor Jimmy's voice was changing. "Nonsense. He's got another year at least."

But alas, it already had, a long time ago. Which is why the producers began synching dialogue. Jimmy mouthed his lines, pulling his sister's hair just like he always did, just like any precocious twelve-year-old boy. The catcalls and taunts were then looped in.

And poor little Janey? Well, she was menstruating now, but that was easier to hide. Her bosom would be another matter, especially if it achieved her mother's prodigious proportions.

So finally, in anticipation of the twin's inevitable, yet unacceptable puberty, computer generated simulations of the two children had to be created. The technology was such that even the parents couldn't tell the real from the virtual. Indeed, after a recent show, when Mother Frappel attempted to pull a comb through her daughter's famous hair, the instrument just slipped right through the virtual child's holographic locks.

As a test it was a huge success, though the mother had to be revived by paramedics. Still, she did agree to let the producers go ahead with the charade. After all, it wasn't about the money.

The Frappel Twins were about humanity, the last vestiges of it, anyway. At least that's what everybody kept telling her, even her favorite columnist from his widely read column. "The human race needs the Frappel Twins," he argued. "We exist through them."

The show must go on.

Just as the real Jimmy and Janey had to grow up. Of course, they'd been given new identities. A full education. Counseling. Like always, the twins received everything they wanted.

Well, almost everything, for they had to be separated. Safety reasons were cited. Doctor's orders.

It was a difficult situation for the twins to accept, but their mother had agreed and therefore it was done.

Jim and Jane grew up apart and never saw each other again. When Jim died, Jane didn't know. Even under a pseudonym, his suicide was kept out of the papers.

Without the limitations that came with real children, the show became bigger than ever. Soon, new computer-generated kids were added. There was the Chinese pen pal. A Canadian cousin. Last year a new baby. If people knew all the characters were fakes, the people weren't talking. Like pro wrestling a century before, this thing was bigger than life.

"I'm gonna tell!"

"Go ahead, see if I care."

The children made up in the end. They always did. And everybody left happy.

Pure gold.

The Ukrainian Village

·

The Ukrainian Village did not have many Ukrainians anymore. In the middle of the last century they began exiting their community for safer, less complicated environs north and west of Chicago.

By the late twentieth century, Ukie Village had become a predominantly Latin neighborhood, mostly Mexican, but with Puerto Rican and Guatemalan residents as well. Their growing presence in the community had as much to do with the Ukrainians leaving as anything else. Old World Europeans weren't open-minded in the first place and the more colorful immigrants from South America frightened them with their louder, feistier culture.

Prior to the onset of Embryo Fatality Syndrome, the Village, or Pilsen, as it was sometimes called, had been undergoing yet another ethnic transformation. White people were moving in again, beginning with young, artsy bohemians in search of cheaper rent. Then, after they'd established a foothold, replete with hip galleries and coffee shops, a wary but entrepreneurial middle class began gobbling up the real estate. When the Hispanics arrived and settled, it was termed "ghettoization." If you were developing half-million-dollar townhouses, that was called gentrification.

Through it all, the old churches remained. Catholicism being the religion of choice for all of the above. Hanging out the window, Jack filmed one as they headed south on Ashland Avenue. It was a mammoth. Grimy from pollution and neglect, there was no denying its stately beauty, especially considering it had been built by the hardest working members of the working class. The church Jack's parents had gone to in Madison was like a ranch house in comparison.

His many tirades against organized religion were legendary, and by his own admission Jack was not a pious man. Still, he found theology a fascinating subject, particularly as it related to architecture and even more so as it related to current events. These days it was hard to dismiss the rhetoric of Apocalypse. Clearly mankind needed an assist and many were praying for God to provide it. Of course, just as many were beginning to wonder if God hadn't caused it. Regardless, Jack was pretty sure he could use the footage of a church somewhere in their movie.

"Here we are," said Muriel, pulling the old Honda into one of many open spots in front of the Manchester Arms apartment building, readily available parking a rare upside amidst a diminishing population.

Once again, Seth and Maura had led them to their destination without a hitch. Considering they were admitted drug addicts, the two bikers continued to surprise. First Seth with his knowledge in subjects as diverse as housing developments and baseball, and now Maura with her fine command of directions. Left to their own ministrations, Jack and Muriel would undoubtedly be in Indiana by now.

They all convened under the old building's red and white striped canopy. The Manchester Arms was one of several gorgeous, vintage buildings in the area that, like the church they'd passed earlier, had seen its share of better days. Torn in places, the canopy was dirty overall. Most of the façade's stonework needed serious repair. Great chunks of irreplaceable ornamental terra cotta were missing altogether, probably chipped off, pilfered, and sold a long time ago. Muriel seemed to recall a big market for that sort of thing with gardeners, decorators and random zealots of the Victorian era. Her grandmother had been all three, with rolling gardens full of gargoyles, obelisks, and other assorted architectural artifacts. Maybe she'd had a piece of this place.

"Hey, lay off the chicken," Maura snapped at her boyfriend. "That's our rent."

Seth put the drumstick back in the carton. "We've got 24 pieces," he whined, sounding like a small child.

"You can eat later." She checked her notes. "It's apartment 11B, third floor."

The doorbell didn't work, but the door's lock was broken as well. They made their way up a dingy, dimly lit stairway.

"I hope you know what we're doing," exclaimed Jack from rear of the procession. "This place is kind of creepy." He was being melodramatic. Though not the Ritz, they'd all seen worse.

"Like Dan's place was any better," said Muriel. Determined to keep a positive attitude, she didn't need her brother complaining right now. Besides, Seth and Maura cast a formidable first impression. She wasn't worried.

They had to knock three times before anyone answered. "Who's there?" replied the scratchy voice from behind the door.

"Hello, Eileen, this is Maura. I phoned earlier." She used the other woman's name on purpose, a small attempt to make her feel more comfortable. If Eileen was high, she was probably paranoid.

Nothing.

"With the chicken?" countered Maura, rolling her eyes.

"Open the door," groaned Seth. The box of chicken was burning his hands.

The sound of turning tumblers and rattling chains and finally the door opened.

"One of you know what time it is?" questioned the woman. "We don't have any clocks in here. Like Vegas, right?" Eileen wouldn't acknowledge the group, but she did move out of the way allowing them to come in.

Which they did, mumbling hellos. Muriel mentioned the time, eight-forty.

"Um, here's your chicken." Seth put the container on the first available surface, the closed top of an empty aquarium. He got the impression its contents had evaporated over time versus being drained. He could see dead plant remains and a broken statuette of a mermaid. "It's fried," he added.

After which they stood quietly, kind of sizing each other up. The apartment smelled of cigarettes and bug spray, among other things.

A slight person, Eileen probably had been all of her life, even before she started using, which clearly she was. There were bandages on the inner part of both her spindly arms. One showed blood, likely from today. Her hair was colored a false red almost orange and brown at the roots. If nothing else it provided merciful distraction from her skeletal face, if not the mangy, purple robe she was wearing. All in all, this was an unhealthy, unattractive woman. And unfriendly too. Her only greeting had been a question about the time, which she asked again.

"Eight-forty-five," answered Jack. "So, where–"

"You're guessing," Eileen countered. "It can't be that late." She flew out of the room and down the main hallway. "Coming, babies!" yelled the woman. She entered a bedroom and was gone.

"Okay... " Muriel let go her duffel bag on the carpet. "Now what?"

"Well," said Jack. "Vile as it may sound, we stay."

The others concurred, dropping their bags in a heap. Did they really have a choice? They were in a rough neighborhood in a strange city and it was getting late. Leaving had to be worse than staying.

Maura was about to say something when two gigantic rottweilers barreled in heading straight for them. Growling and barking, their huge claws made a metallic clatter as they smacked across the linoleum floor.

Needless to say, the foursome was terrified. They could neither run, scream, nor do anything in self-defense. The most infamous, nasty dogs on the planet were about to be having them for dinner.

That is, if the animals hadn't stormed right past them into the room occupied by Eileen. Immediately they heard chomping, slurping, and growling emanating from the space.

"What the hell was that?" asked Jack, dumbfounded.

"I can't speak for the rest of the world but that was almost the end of ours," responded Muriel, a hand over her heart.

"No fucking comment," was all that Seth could muster.

"I see you met Riley and Keiffer." No one noticed Eileen coming in but there she was. Opening the tub of chicken she began picking though it, looking for just the right piece. "Surprised they didn't go after this," she said. "Usually the dogs eat sooner. I guess I just forgot they were out there. You know if there's any wings in here?"

Maura shook her head no. As a matter of preference, she'd requested no wings on the order. Go figure.

"You feed them in there?" she asked, her eyes rolling toward the sound of carnage in the other room.

"It's okay. That's my bedroom."

"Of course," said Jack sarcastically.

His reaction prompted additional explanation. "Usually there's more animals around here, but they're all at the rally. Anyway, I like to keep 'em separate during feeding. Learned that one the hard way." Laughing, Eileen grabbed a drumstick and bit a huge hunk out of it. A greasy piece of skin dangled from her mouth.

"Speaking of bedrooms… " interjected Muriel.

Eileen looked at her funny. "Oh, yeah, right. Honey you can sleep wherever you want. You can have your own apartment for all I care. Keys to a bunch in the desk drawer. Plenty of room at the inn. Like I said, everybody's at the rally." Finishing off her drumstick in front of them, she picked up another. "You didn't bring any beer, did you?" She could tell they had not. "Don't worry, there's a twelve pack in the fridge." Eileen went to the kitchen to fetch one.

Seth shrugged and followed her. He could use a cold beer.

Wanting beds more than beer, everyone else went over to the desk to look for those keys.

Lone Star State

On his third Lone Star, Raphael thought maybe he'd have some Jack Daniels as well. He hated drinking alone, but then again he was fairly adept, it being pretty much the only way he ever drank before meeting Nora.

Before Nora.

He'd met her at this very bar. They played drinking games and ordered a pizza. Made a connection. Made love. They'd been together ever since.

So what had he been thinking? He didn't have to blow a gasket when she gave him the big news. So why did he?

Raphael figured it was on account of the bad news that inevitably came with the big news. Why go through a guaranteed miscarriage? Life was too short.

Life was too short.

He lit a cigarette from a pack left on the bar. Although it was not his brand, at least it was menthol. Raphael tapped his empty bottle on the wooden counter indicating he wanted another. He knew the guy, so it was okay. Mitch wouldn't take the gesture as an insult.

Before their fight, he and Nora had been in a good groove. Hadn't they? He thought about it for the umpteenth time. Yes, they were.

Not happy with a capital 'H' happy, but far from unhappy either. And that, my friends, was saying a lot.

Well, she changed all that by getting herself pregnant. His preferred plan would've been to just live the life they had. Why open a door that only led to misery?

"Haven't seen you around, Ralph," said Mitch, handing him another beer. He could tell the man was drunk but gave it to him anyway. Mitch made those kinds of decisions from his gut, no longer relying on protocol and laws. It'd been years since he carded anyone. Who was 21? Ralph wasn't a troublemaker and that was good enough for him.

Raphael smiled, staying quiet. He took a tiny sip from the bottle, then set it back down, twisting it so the label's familiar star shone upon him. He wondered how things were going at the Lone Star Brewery. He'd worked there many years ago, loading trucks. It was a tough job but you got free beer.

"You still with that fine lady?" This was Mitch's second and final shot at making conversation. Just trying to be sociable with an old customer, he wouldn't push it. But Mitch also remembered Nora, yes he did. Until hooking up with Ralph, she'd been somewhat of a regular. By no means a barfly, Nora was good at eight ball and easy on the eyes. Mitch had been truly sorry to see her go.

"I was with her." Raphael answered. "I really was." He hadn't reached the blotto stage yet, but was well on his way. He took another swig. He hadn't expected the bartender to ask about Nora, but why not? She was something they had in common. He liked Mitch, though he couldn't recall whether he had a wife or girlfriend or was pseudo or what.

"How's it with you, Mitchell?" he asked. "Got somebody special or are you just hanging?" Raphael realized it had been some time since he'd had a conversation with anybody other than Nora. He missed it all of a sudden and hoped Mitch would be game.

"There's Linda. And I still see Ruby, nothing major." Mitch thought about the two women he'd just mentioned. He cared for them equally, which was not much. With Linda and Ruby it was more about the sex. What else was there in terms of a relationship?

"Nora is what you'd call major," Raphael responded. He picked at the label on his beer, putting the little pieces into an ashtray. "Under normal circumstances we'd probably be married."

Under normal circumstances.

Mitch figured he was referring to EFS. Whenever anybody did they seldom did so overtly. He heard euphemisms like 'circumstances' and 'situation' all the time. It was like everybody on the planet was in denial, at least during small talk.

"So, then, you still seeing her?"

"Yes... No... Hell, I don't know." And Raphael didn't. That's why he'd been sitting in the damn bar. "We had a situation," he said, after a drink and a puff.

Situation. Well, that didn't take long.

Mitch wasn't sure, but he supposed the couple had had a fight, probably something to do with their relationship. In terms of boy-girl stuff, some things never changed. Even now girls wanted to settle down, boys didn't. Mitch would humor the guy as long as he didn't have to deal with anything too weird. Mitch liked his customers and their stories strictly by the book.

"Nora's pregnant," said Raphael, like some line from a movie. He fumbled for the pack of stale cigarettes.

Okay, now Mitch got the picture. This wasn't the first time one of his customers brought up the P-word or expressed the emotions that came with it. Just the other night a lady in the bar had said she was pregnant but kept on drinking. He didn't stop her. Normally, he might have. Mitch wished he could tell Raphael something that would make him feel better.

"She would make a great mother, Ralph... under normal circumstances."

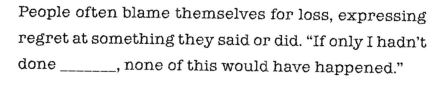

People often blame themselves for loss, expressing regret at something they said or did. "If only I hadn't done _____, none of this would have happened."

This unfortunate stage of self-blaming is known as...

Guilt

On this day the old woman got up from bed differently. On this day, instead of fixing a cup of tea and retrieving the morning news off her computer, Mrs. Lee visited the small garden and the hibiscus bush she'd planted there so many years ago.

On this day she knelt before the flowering plant uttering a solemn, quiet prayer.

Asking for forgiveness.

Asking for understanding.

She did not expect to receive either.

And so she remembered.

Vividly…

…On this day

It had been strangely sunny for that part of China, for that time of the year. Strangely sunny and warm.

Her husband, Lo How, said nothing as he prepared their morning meal. Nothing at all. He cut the duck from last night and added it to the bowl of sticky rice warming on the stove. Mrs. Lee sat rigidly at the table waiting, thankful, she supposed, for the silence in the kitchen and the rest of the house.

If she stopped from even thinking the little girl's name. If she were crying, it would have been unbearable.

Their other daughter, Lei-Lei, had been sent to her grandmother's house for this week and the next, however long it would take to retain some semblance of order. Some semblance of the way it had been before this strangely sunny and warm day.

Praying now, Mrs. Lee remembered not doing so then.

Lo How was her husband, and she would honor and respect his wishes, but on that morning it had been so very difficult. Her heart felt as if it were being sliced into pieces like the duck Lo How was preparing. She had no appetite and wondered how he possibly could.

Wondered how he possibly could.

Mrs. Lee did not look up as she ate. She heard her husband chewing. Did he force himself because of the energy it would provide? After all, they had a long drive and there would be no stopping. God forbid he was hungry.

When Mrs. Lee finished, she excused herself to prepare a bottle. She could hear the infant beginning to whimper and stir in the bedroom. The last thing she wanted was for the tiny creature to become upset.

She wanted her baby content for the rest of its life.

Mrs. Lee got up very slowly from praying. She stood before the hibiscus, attempting to find its best flower. She selected a blossom near the top, among the youngest.

A lengthy journey, especially for an old woman. She needed to get going now if she had any intentions of making it back before nightfall.

She drove in the slow lane, both hands gripping the wheel, her weak eyes fixed on the road in front of her. Mrs. Lee had made this trip every year since. She knew the way by heart.

Minutes after twelve she arrived at the park. Like every time before, it had been closed for the season, and she was able to park in the same spot she always did, the one closest to the path that led to the river.

She could hear the mighty river long before she could see it. The current was swift and white this time of the year, same as the first time they'd come. It was dangerous now and not suitable for fishing or swimming.

But Mrs. Lee did not come to this place for recreation. Not then. Not now. Not ever.

Before reaching the visitor's clearing, she detoured to the right. The going was harder, but she walked with determination. She came to a split pine tree, and it was here that she approached the river.

On this day as on that day.

She came to the edge, finding the same large flat rock from where they had both stood so many years ago. The water was kicking up a spray and her gown became wet. Never minding it, Mrs. Lee reached into her handbag, retrieving the hibiscus flower.

Mrs. Lee took the bloom to her bosom and held it there.

She shut her eyes.

And listened.

At first, the noise was deafening. The endless churning of the river seemed to swallow up all other sounds in its roar.

But gradually the din became its own form of solitude. Of course the water did not really stop or slow down, but once again Mrs. Lee found what she had come to the river to find.

A hint of a particular soul.

Releasing the flower from her grip, she watched the water take it away forever, just like her baby girl, so many years ago.

Rest Stop

Nora had been to Utah once, as a kid during her parent's 'See America' summer vacation. This was back when folks still took trips with their families. Back when folks still had families to take trips with.

Even though Utah was only two states from Texas, it was a long, complicated haul. But she had a map. She'd figured it out. Nora had thrown her favorite clothes and whatever else she could think of into a large duffel bag. She'd grabbed her supply of cash, about twelve hundred dollars, and, well, split. She didn't even leave a note. What was there to say?

Raphael had been gone only two hours.

By the time he returned she would be across the state line.

After driving many hours, Nora turned into a gas station. Because she'd left so early in the evening, it was still dark. She would have preferred not stopping until daylight but the car was running on fumes and the next filling station, an open one anyway, could easily be hundreds of miles away.

Pulling up at the station's one and only pump, Nora waited for service. And waited. She peered out the window, trying to ascertain if anybody was present. Edgy from lack of sleep, the desert night just made her more so. In addition to the pitch-blackness, her windows were filthy and she couldn't tell if anything was moving in or outside the ramshackle building comprising the station. A neon 'Open' sign flickered ominously.

"Screw it," she mumbled, getting out of the car.

Nora made her way over to the entrance, a simple wooden door without signs. Should she knock or just open it? She attempted looking through the windows but taped-up clippings, receipts and yellowing miscellany covered them.

Why must this be so damn difficult, she asked herself? Why must everything?

"Just pump your gas and go," a voice commanded from the darkness. "And you can't use the facilities unless you make a purchase."

Nora startled. Thank God the words belonged to a woman or she'd have pissed her pants, or worse. As it was, Nora wheeled around assuming the lone judo stance she'd learned as a teenager.

The woman was older than her voice implied, rail thin with white hair tied up into a pretzel. She held a pail in one hand and a flashlight in the other. Pointing the beam of light at Nora's face, she moved it up and down scanning her features.

"Sorry," whispered Nora. "You scared me big time." Realizing there wasn't a threat, she let her guard down.

Although it barely cast a beam, the old woman kept the light upon her. A truck rumbled by, silencing the crickets.

"Like I said, the toilet's off limits unless you make a purchase." Brandy had seen a little bit of everything out here and wasn't taking chances with this one, especially at 4 o'clock in the morning. Young ones. For all she knew, more were in the car. A bunch of sickos looking for an easy mark. But she had two shotguns inside, both loaded.

"I only want gas and, if you have it, something to eat." Nora needed a restroom as well but thought maybe it best just to hold it. She tried smiling. See, I'm a good person. You can be nice to me.

It worked. Brandy returned the smile.

"Pump switch is inside," she said. "Give me a few seconds, then press the handle. I got Twinkies, Little Debbie's, and burritos, chicken only." She set down the bucket and pulled out a wad of keys from inside her jacket. They were attached to her belt by a metal chain, the kind favored by bikers.

"Some Twinkies would be great," said Nora, heading to the pump. She would've preferred a chicken burrito, but Nora was fairly certain that what she'd seen in the pail had been chicken feed. She wasn't that hungry.

Brandy watched Nora from inside. It soon became obvious she was alone. No need for alarm. Or a shotgun. She grabbed a bag of Twinkies from a peg on the wall. One thing still bugged her: At this hour what was a woman doing all by herself on the highway? Shit, at any hour. Against her better judgment, she aimed to find out. Sure, prying could be dangerous out here, but it was always lonely.

Brandy took her chances, flat out asked.

"I'm going a ways up, to Driscol," replied Nora. The gas came out in just a trickle. She was reminded of her need for a bathroom.

"I know where Driscol is." Brandy put the Twinkies down on the pump cover and stared Nora right between the eyes. She could tell. "You know, you're not the first woman to pass through here going there."

All of a sudden Nora was flushed. Queasy from the smell of gas on top of everything else. "Do you mind finishing this up for me? I really do have to use your bathroom." She wasn't asking, more like telling.

"You'll need this." Brandy pulled a key off her ring.

Nora grabbed it on the run.

"Only door left of the building!" Brandy hollered. Sighing, she took the nozzle and continued pumping. She also took a peek into Nora's car. She saw a suitcase, a duffel bag, and a box of toiletries. And that was it. Brandy assumed the rest of her belongings were in the trunk. More likely, however, there wasn't anything else. The women going where she was headed tended to pack light.

At best, Matthew was little more than a desert Don Juan, a sleazy opportunist. At worst, he was a monster that fed on sad, confused women. Either way, too bad for this one, Brandy thought. She seemed awfully sweet.

He'd like her.

"No," Brandy spoke out. I can't let that happen.

Nora reminded Brandy of her own baby girl. Shelly had fallen for that devil's commercial as well. Out here a woman didn't have many options in life, making babies being by far the most popular. Shelly couldn't handle the thought of growing old without kin of her own. Unfortunately, she'd just had her third miscarriage. When Matthew offered her that ray of hope, she was nothing short of hypnotized. She became his.

Brandy hadn't seen her daughter in over two years. Neither had Lester, her former husband. They both got the same letter saying she was fine and not to worry. However, Lester had seen Matthew's commercial too. He saw the matter in more blunt terms. His wife had fallen for another man. He'd been dumped. Lester wasn't going to humiliate himself further by chasing after her.

Shelly's father could do even less on her behalf. He'd been dead going on four years.

Without any crime having been committed, the police had no right to investigate. They didn't particularly give a shit anyway. Utah maintained a well-known indifference to polygamy and that's how they summed up matters regarding Congress—a guy with a bunch of wives.

Shelly was 32 years old. She'd made a decision, albeit a foolish one. End of story.

What was taking that girl so long? Brandy went over to the door and leaned her ear against it. She heard a foul, retching sound. Now what? she thought.

Nora was sick, the result of being tired, hungry, and upset. The result of being pregnant. How had the old woman known where she was going? She'd not only known, but disapproved. It was in her eyes, and it had upset Nora. And now she was hurling a meal she couldn't even remember eating into a toilet as foul as they come.

"I'm sorry, Raphael," she bellowed, drooling, unable to stand. The nausea overpowered her.

"It's all right, child," Brandy said, now lording over her. "Just relax. You'll be okay." Nora had locked the door but she, of course, had other keys.

"I... I'm... " Nora threw up again, a foamy, whitish liquid.

"You're pregnant, aren't you?" Brandy wasn't really asking. She knew.

"I was gonna say I'm sorry."

Brandy ignored her. "And this Raphael, he's the father, ain't he?"

As if Nora didn't have enough problems, now she started crying.

"Let's clean you up and have some breakfast," said Brandy. "Eating sounds rotten now but it'll make you feel better."

Nora heaved again, but now at least it was dry. Maybe she was coming out of it. Even so, her head ached, likewise her stomach, bones, heart, everything. She was about as bewildered and turned around as she'd ever been in her entire life.

"I know how much you're hurting, girl," said Brandy, sympathetically.

"You do?"

"You have no idea."

"No, I guess I don't," she said. And slowly, with help from the old woman, Nora stood up.

Wake-up Call

Mary Connely awoke groggily, still tucked in under the sheets. Was her sister not up yet either? Such a lazy girl. Well, Mary was in no hurry. She decided to wait until she actually smelled bacon frying before getting out of bed. It was Saturday and it was cold, you needed a reason. Maybe later they'd go sledding or, better yet, maybe Shane would drop by and ask her to the movies or skating downtown. She'd received a pair of Crystal Flyers for Christmas and was dying to break them in. The door. Mary opened one eye to see who it was. Just Mom. She pretended sleeping while her mother quietly placed a breakfast tray on the dresser. The pungent aroma of coffee filled the room. Strange, Mary thought, Mom never came into our rooms with breakfast unless we were sick. And where was the bacon? And since when did we start drinking coffee?

"My God, Mother. What are you doing here?" Up now, the dream over. Her mother, whom she hadn't seen in months, was standing not five feet from her. "You know it's not allowed." She lowered her voice in mid-sentence, awake and cognizant of where she was, where they both were.

"And how are you, dear?" inquired Connie, ignoring her daughter's shocked reaction. She'd expected no less. She opened the window blinds. It was shaping up into quite a lovely day.

"I guess I'm all right," said Mary. "Considering." She resented having been pulled from her dream and didn't much care for reality either. Mary fell back onto the pillows, the phenobarbital still affecting her demeanor. What was her mother doing here? And why wasn't she worried about the ramifications? She shut her eyes, wishing her mom hadn't opened the blinds, maybe even hadn't come in.

"Honey, after what you've been through, I'd say you're doing fine." Connie bent over her daughter and wiped a bit of drool from the corner of her mouth. Then, surreptitiously, she dropped a miniscule piece of paper onto the bed.

"So," said Connie curtly, "did you learn something from your excursion? I trust you've been wizened by it?" With her eyes she indicated for Mary to read the note.

Excursion? Is that what she called it? Mary eyed the tiny letter. Something screwy was going on here.

"Tell your mother all about it."

"Okay… sure." She unfolded the paper.

We are probably being taped.
Play along. I'm on your side.

Mary took a deep breath and started putting two and two together. It appeared her mother was plotting something covert. Could she be having second thoughts about Congress and Matthew as well? Thank God.

"The Good Walk was, um, really great," said Mary, answering the question. "I'm sure I am a better woman now." She tried not sounding sarcastic. Mary knew the correct way to 'play along' was by acting thankful and contrite. Biting her lower lip, she wondered if she was capable. At this point, she wasn't sure about a lot of things. Really wanting a hug from her mother, Mary even had concerns over doing that.

A cuckoo clock sounded, of all things. Three idiotic tweets.

"I'm very proud of you, honey," stated Connie, sensing her daughter's anxiety, feeling it herself. Undoubtedly, some positive reinforcement would help. "You've been tested and you passed. Matthew will be very pleased to know that. We all are." Careful not to give anything away in her voice, Connie couldn't help winking. It was good seeing her first born. And, in a real way, she was very proud of her daughter. Surviving in the desert took courage and fortitude. Enduring Matthew must have as well.

Mary wished she could ask her mother any number of questions. How's Kathleen? Have you heard from Dad? Mostly what in the hell were they supposed to do now? But Mary knew she could not. Didn't dare.

Instead she said, "I'm ready to try again, Mother. That is if he'll have me." Mary sold the lines hard, perhaps too hard. The whole time she wondered where in the room the bugs were hidden.

She also wasn't sure where any of this was going. Nevertheless, Mary could tell her mother's demeanor had changed since they'd arrived. Just how much she would wait and see. The daughter smiled at her mother, even managing a wink herself.

"I'm here because of Matthew's kindness," replied Connie. "He cares for you. He believes in you, Mary." But while Connie spoke she shook her head, indicating that the bullshit meter was still running.

And so they communicated by reading between each other's lines, but it worked and both women felt more and more comfortable.

"Matthew feels you are the One. He sent me here to tell you that," added Connie. This time she was speaking the truth.

In fact, it was verbatim. Matthew had indeed sent her. He'd felt positive Connie could provide her daughter with the necessary measure of confidence and support, which, in turn, would facilitate a successful reuniting of the two of them. He was adamant about that happening and the sooner the better.

Connie suspected Matthew had an ulterior motive for involving her. He rarely violated his own rules, and separation of kin was one

of them. Yet, an uncustomarily large amount of dissention was per-
colating among the residents of Congress, an undercurrent of dis-
trust and regret, particularly from those who'd returned from the
Good Walk. It was becoming chronic and all too obvious. Perhaps
Matthew was merely being proactive. Mixing things up to keep the
girls focused.

Regardless, when he summoned Connie, she came promptly,
holding her tongue. Even though Connie was experiencing the same
remorse as some other members of Congress, she wanted to see her
babies even more. This was a rare opportunity. She would do as she
was told and, indeed, was doing so now.

"Is that coffee for me?" asked Mary, steering the conversation
back toward safe harbor.

"Absolutely," said her mother, playing along. "Cream and sweet-
ener, right?"

Mary nodded. So Mom was an ally. Great. But now what? It wasn't
like they could finish their coffee and leave. It was wonderful that
her mother was by her side. A dream come true. But at the same time
she knew Matthew was up to something. The leader rarely broke
protocol.

"Do you mind getting my makeup bag? I must look a mess."
Mary pointed to her belongings, having noticed them earlier on a
chair. She didn't give a damn about her face. She wanted a writing
instrument.

Connie obliged and handed her the shoulder bag.

What now? Mary scrawled on the back of an errant deposit slip.

Her mother read the note and said nothing. She picked up the
mascara and considered writing a reply. Connie opted not and put
the tools down. This whole interchange was getting silly and, frankly,
dangerous. Feeling paranoid, she eyed the windows and doors. They
were dropping notes like teenagers in study hall. Matthew would
catch them. They had to be more careful.

"I'll let you get your sleep, then," she said to her daughter. "I'm
sure you'll want to be rested and well for your next, um, opportu-

nity." Fidgeting, Connie got up from her place at Mary's side. "There's coffee and toast on the bureau if you get hungry," she said, heading toward the door.

"I love you, Mother," replied Mary, trying to remain in character. It was hard, considering her emotional levels were through the roof.

Connie halted and turned around. Suddenly it was another morning. Mary was in bed, sick with flu or chicken pox. She was surrounded by coloring books and dolls. She was a child again. "Feel better, sweetheart."

"I already do," Mary said, revealing much more with her eyes. "Give my love to Kathleen. That is, if you see her."

"I'll check in on you this afternoon," replied Connie, agitated. She wished Mary hadn't brought up her other daughter. They were pushing their luck already. "You just relax, okay?"

"Sure, Ma," Mary answered. "I know everything is going to work out this time. I feel so much better." A deep breath. More dialogue: "Tell Matthew I can't wait to see him."

Mary fell back down on her pillow. She had no idea how long this respite was going to last. A day? Two? If she took any longer healing Matthew might begin questioning her desire.

Connie grabbed the plate of toast, putting it on Mary's night table.

"It's right here if you're hungry." She blew her daughter a kiss, "See you later," and was gone. With an untidy whack, the door closed behind her.

For a long while Mary stared at the ceiling. She'd been through a lot, and she felt overwhelmed. She recalled taking pills in the helicopter but couldn't remember the man who had given them to her. What was his name?

He'd been nice, though. Someone good. He brought Mary back safely as well as providing her the means to avoid interrogation and, for the time being, intercourse with Matthew. In her memory he was like the man you kissed on New Year's Eve, maybe even slept with. The next day you forgot everything about him except for what happened. But he was a decent man, she felt certain.

Mary rolled her head, eyeing the pot of coffee her mother had left but deciding to pass. Still tired, the idea of sleep seemed a hell of a lot more attractive than lying in bed awake. She let herself drift, summoning remnants of the narcotic. Catching a wave of drowsiness, she then rode it into oblivion.

Friends

Seth woke up hungry and delighted to be only mildly hungover as opposed to ill, wired, and nauseous. Aroma wafted from the box of chicken stowed under his bed. He reached for it, careful not to wake Maura with his movements. He needn't have worried. Her breaths came deep and long with eyelids fluttering, all signs of REM sleep. He pulled apart a thigh, popping the oily pieces into his mouth. It seemed even tastier than the night before, more likely he was just hungrier. Maura mumbled something into her pillow. He turned and saw her butt shift under the covers. She stretched and the sheet pulled tighter over her body, outlining the curves. With teeth and tongue, Seth polished off the thigh. Having satisfied one hunger, another surfaced. He couldn't remember the last time they'd done it. Possibly that streak would end this morning. Maura rolled over, pulling the blanket up to her chin and began mouthing it. It was an unsettling image, and Seth's ardor passed as quickly as it had come.

Light filtered in from the lone window and Seth, having crashed hard last night, surveyed his accommodations for the very first time. Small, but with high ceilings, the room was about what he'd expected from an inner city Victorian. The walls were painted white and were dirty as hell, about what he'd expected from the inner city Victorian room of a biker. Fancy moldings were long gone, save a two-foot piece encrusted over the window frame. A ragged hole punched in the wall above him where there should have been a light fixture. All in all, it was the kind of place Seth had been living in for most of his adult life, worse than the hotel in St. Paul, but better than the trailer in Fargo.

Then, as if brought by a bullet, Seth's stomach began cramping so bad he thought he might be sick. The chicken was squawking inside him. He groaned, sweat beading up on his forehead. The pain was a hell of a lot stronger than ardor or hunger. Unfortunately, it was also familiar.

Withdrawal.

"What have you been doing with yourself, Seth?" asked the monkey, having jumped onto his back. "Long time, no see."

"Ehhh," groaned Seth. It was like the damn thing was banging pots and pans. "Go fucking away!"

As was typical in these matters, Seth forgot how delightful it had been waking up clear-headed. Equally typical, he began scouring the bedroom for drawers, boxes, and stashes of any kind. Like a car running on vapors, he had to find some juice or he would die. It was that simple.

First he checked the night table, it being where he would have kept his stash. The top drawer contained only a lone marble, some pennies and a dead cricket. What the fuck was that all about?

However, it was an altogether different story in the cupboard below. There he found a bong, (its bowl still filled with water), matches, small bag of pot, (mostly powder and seeds), even a couple of needles (where was the fucking dope?), and, oddly, a photo album.

But Seth didn't want pot, it would only increase his cravings, and so he pushed the paraphernalia aside, leaving only the notebook. He felt lucid again, the tide of withdrawal receding. Maura still slept. When she finally awoke would she have cravings too?

Oh, hell. Oh, well.

Already he felt another wave approaching. Seth opened the photo album. Expecting to see what? Motorbikes? Broads? A bunch of guys drinking beer?

On the first yellowed page was a grouping of canceled postage stamps honoring the singer, Elvis Presley. Arranged almost like a band, each little Elvis either sang, played guitar or both. That's what it looked like, a band of tiny Elvis's.

The next page contained a single color photograph of a young boy hugging the leg of a woman whom Seth assumed was his mother. She had short black hair, a decent figure, in general nice looking if fairly nondescript. The child, however, held on to her limb like he was clinging for life. He seemed about ready to laugh or cry. Impossible to tell which, his face that intense. There was pathos. There was ethos. Harsh fold marks crisscrossed over the snapshot forming a primitive crucifix. Seth didn't believe in God, not that God, anyway, but he couldn't help thinking of the Madonna and Child.

Seth choked up, a feeling in his gut even stronger than withdrawal. It was more profound and wrenching. Of course it was just a simple photograph of a boy with his mother. He surmised that the kid had become the man on whose bed he now lay. He figured his momma was dead.

Seth thought about his own mother. She was history too, having died when they were both young, without fanfare, without having lived much. Never a strong lady, the men in her life had mostly taken advantage of her. A fighter here. A drunk there. All of the above. Eventually she just gave up and slipped away.

Seth put the book back where he found it and lay down in bed. He stared at a hole in the ceiling and, just like that, started crying. Like a summer squall it came and went, leaving him empty, but cleaner feeling. Shake up the Etch-A-Sketch and the lines go away. Thinking was hard though. Likewise remembering. His childhood had been compromised by myriad circumstances. But he'd had one, hadn't he? There were pictures of him with his mother, weren't there? Somewhere? Sadly, he kept none.

A television went on in another room. Seth listened to the prattling voices, unsure who was making them and who was listening to them. Next to him Maura mumbled. The room was getting brighter. Seth wanted a cigarette, but oddly, the other craving had subsided. He ruminated on childhood again, his as well as others, and on the concept of childhood, period. For everybody it was just a memory now, an old photograph.

"Hey you," said Maura sleepily, tapping his naked shoulder.

Startled by her touch, Seth spun around.

"I look that bad, eh?" Maura pushed the hair out of her face. She saw the wetness around Seth's eyes but said nothing about it. His moods were his own.

"Hey yourself," said Seth, sitting up. He wiped his face with a shirtsleeve. "You wouldn't happen to have a cigarette, would you?" He wondered what Maura looked like as a girl. He saw Peppermint Patty.

"Yeah... somewhere. First things first." Checking that she had on pants, Maura got up and made her way to the bathroom. "Right back," she said, flinging open the door to the facilities.

And to Muriel.

"Good morning." Muriel sat on the toilet reading a biker magazine.

They both stared at one another, each acting like the proverbial deer in the headlights.

"Sorry," offered Maura, being the one guilty of intruding. "I didn't know the bathrooms were joined."

"Well, okay then, see you," countered Muriel embarrassed.

"Okay. See you." Maura grinned, closing the door.

Muriel brought her thighs together. What did she mean by that? See you. It sounded like a come-on. Weird.

* * * * * *

In the living room, Jack watched television with Eileen. He occupied the couch while she sat on a large, tattered loveseat. Riley and

Keiffer were on her lap, sort of. The dogs tussled with one another in a futile attempt for a better position.

On TV was an old sitcom featuring a group of young, impossibly beautiful friends who hung out in a coffee shop. In this scene, a rakish character named Joey was standing on a coffee table reciting lines from Shakespeare, or struggling to, anyway. He kept saying the wrong things. From big, purple overstuffed chairs two comely female characters, Monica and Phoebe, regarded him curiously. They were judging him for one reason or another.

If there was a plot, Jack didn't see it and he didn't particularly care. He was fixated by one of the girls. Clearly, Phoebe was pregnant. Her round belly was all Jack could look at. He'd never seen a woman that big before, that far along. He was agog.

"Jesus, she's huge," he said for about the third time.

"She's having triplets, that's why," replied Eileen, barely acknowledging him. "I've seen this one before." She attempted to reach over the dogs and tap her cigarette ash into the tray but could not. "Screw it." She flicked the dead ash behind her onto the rug.

"Triplets. And she's just hanging out with these guys? Helping out with some talent show?" Incredulous, Jack couldn't believe the program wasn't, in some deep, meaningful way, more about this amazing pregnant woman, and not the rube making an ass out of himself on the coffee table. Joey was now holding a skull over his head, reproaching it flamboyantly.

"Another time and place, Jack." Eileen said. "Get used to it."

Jack diverted himself from the television, contemplating his defacto hostess. She might've been pretty once. And loving. She certainly loved her dogs. But like all the other women Jack knew, Eileen was bereft of something. Empty.

"What?" she said, seeing that he was staring at her. The two rots looked up at him as well.

"Can I ask you a personal question?"

She hitched up her shoulders. "Shoot."

"Have you ever been... well, pregnant?"

"Yeah, I've been... *well pregnant.*"

"How along?" EFS had become a part of the zeitgeist. It was no longer considered a personal intrusion to ask questions like these or to assume the past tense when you did.

"First time three months. Second one went all the way to five." She laughed. "Oh, you should have seen this place, you know, when I reached five. Talk about special treatment. Even Mitch was nice to me." She pulled another Newport from her robe, then offered one to Jack.

Yes, he nodded.

She lit both cigarettes, tossing him one, not caring if it fell on the floor, couch or wherever.

"Um, was Mitch the father?" asked Jack, picking the burning fag off the carpet. Not his brand, the menthol jolted him. He suppressed a cough.

"Yeah, he was the daddy. Unlike some of the ladies around here, I don't sleep around," Eileen sneered. "Can't say that about old Mitch..."

Even though it seemed inappropriate, she laughed. Jack continued nodding. He had to picture himself as one of those bobble-headed ballplayer dolls before he could stop.

Eileen cared less. "All men are dogs, right, Keiffer?" She grabbed the animal's rippled neck and squeezed it lovingly.

Jack shifted in his seat. He never had a steady girlfriend. Did that make him a dog? Introspection made him feel crummy so he didn't say anything. Instead, he went back to watching TV. Another 'friend' was chasing, of all things, a small monkey around the coffee shop. The studio audience was going nuts. Alas, Jack struggled to find the humor. He worried about the pregnant woman. She was having triplets for God's sake! What if she got knocked over in the commotion? What if the monkey attacked her?

Another time and place, Eileen had said. Get used to it.

Still caught up in her own reverie, Eileen elaborated, "Yeah, boy, I'll tell you what..." She wiped an imaginary tear from her eye. "That fifth month was the best time of my life. Everybody was so sweet.

Bringing me presents. Asking how I was and all. I had wished it would never end." But it did end and her silence said as much. She blew a set of smoke rings. "I could stay pregnant forever."

She laughed and again it felt inappropriate to Jack. Even more so.

"When I lost her–it was a 'her'–I couldn't bear facing any of them. Especially Mitch. That prick. I went to my sister's in Oklahoma and, you know, I almost stayed there."

Essentially babbling now, the emotion took over. Eileen's expression was that of a wupped prizefighter. Her unattended ash clung a full inch on her cigarette. "So Mitch gets me the two dogs, right? They were the cutest little pups. Weren't you? Weren't you? Yeah…" She gave each one a kiss on the chops. "I tell you what, that was the first and last nice thing he's ever done for me."

Now it was Jack who laughed inappropriately. Must be contagious, he thought, stopping abruptly.

Eileen quieted down for a second. She spoke more slowly. "I knew the deal. First, other women. Second, his buddies. Third, his bike. Then me. In that order. Now you know why I didn't go to the rally." She licked her lips. "That and it's in fucking Green Bay."

Jack shook his head. Why didn't she laugh here, her first real joke? But then again, he hadn't either.

"The next episode is even funnier," she said, pointing her cigarette at the television. The ash fell to the floor, ignored. "Monica sleeps with Joey's roommate."

They watched the show for a while but the silence between them remained awkward. At least to Jack it did. He wished the others would wake up. He was getting hungry and restless. He was always restless.

"What's in the metal case?" Eileen asked.

With her cigarette she pointed, this time to Jack's camera equipment. It was packed, sitting in the hallway by the door. He'd put it there hours ago, hoping they'd be leaving hours ago.

"It's a movie camera," groaned Jack, realizing she'd want more information than that. "My sister and I. She's the one with the red, curly hair–"

"Muriel. I know who she is. I put her in Beth's room."

"Yeah, well, we're making a film. It's about what's going on. Um, you know."

Eileen's blank expression indicated that she didn't.

"The baby thing. How people are dealing with it and so on." Jack sighed. "Basically, it's my take on the end of the world."

"So it's a comedy?"

Then Jack grinned. First Eileen's a bag of hammers. Then she cracks like a whip.

"Can I be in it?" she asked. "Please? I've got something to say."

"I bet you do," Jack said. But then his smile faded. He kicked himself for not thinking of it earlier. She was perfect. He stood up.

"I have a handheld. It's easier than setting up the main."

If Eileen was disappointed by not seeing the big camera, she got over it fast. She claimed she only needed a minute or so to fix her face.

"Sure," said Jack. "Take your time." This wasn't that inane show with the models, because Eileen was no model. Jack regarded the television. A couple were kissing and the studio audience oohing. Click. Off went the love-in.

"Okay, I'm ready," she said. "Where do you want me, Mr. DeMille?"

Indeed. "There's fine," he said, positioning her by the window. And it was. An overcast sky diffused the light coming in through the murky glass panes back-lighting her nicely. "Okay... "

Jack began filming. "Now why don't you tell me who you are and then maybe talk about how it felt that time at five months. I liked that."

"May I say something before I forget?" inquired Eileen. "You can cut my introduction in later."

"Sure. No problem." Again he was impressed, both with her attitude and by her unforeseen knowledge of filmmaking. He turned on the Mini and gave Eileen the 'Go' signal.

"First of all," she began. "It's not the end of the world we're talking about. It's the end of us. Big difference, you know? The end of the world—that would be bad. This business here is Embryo Fatality System." She paused, thought hard about what she was going to say next. Really hard. This mattered.

Jack kept the camera rolling, wanting every provocative bit.

"For once everybody's equal," continued Eileen. "The rich don't have anything on the poor and the poor don't need anything from the rich. Black, White, Mexican, Chinese. It doesn't matter anymore. EFS is an equal opportunity destroyer. Sounds mean to say but that's the way it is. We're all in the same boat and the boat's going down."

She lit another Newport. Jack filmed that too.

"Now, I'm not trying to say people are no damn good and good riddance," she guffawed. "But people are no damn good and good riddance."

Jack went in tighter.

"One bad thing. When we're all gone, who's gonna take care of the dogs?" Eileen turned toward her pets; they had moved to a corner on the floor.

Following her eye line, Jack framed a shot of the two dogs and cut. He was pleased.

She smiled back at him.

He gave her a second before resuming. "Why don't you tell us a little bit about yourself?"

"My name is Eileen Gifford. Member in good standing, The Last Generation. Chicago Chapter."

In order to avoid the sensation of loss some people live in the past. Others choose to 'buy' time before accepting reality.

Either way, both are forms of 'dealing' with the situation or...

Bargaining

J ulie Dolan got into her 4-door Miranda, Buick and Honda's collaborative contribution to the world's shrinking array of transportation options. Even in a difficult market, it was a big seller and Julie Dolan loved hers. She headed for the Pasadena airport, just like always. Tomorrow was the weekly plans meeting in Denver, just like always.

Along with the human race, EFS was killing the insurance industry. Plans had to be made. You had to try, right? One such plan involved preserving and replacing embryos for expectant couples. They paid monthly premiums, which decreased every two weeks during a valid pregnancy. If and when EFS occurred to the couple, and it always did, a viable alternative embryo would be provided and the subsequent operation partially covered. The process of waiting and paying would begin again. It was weird, but it was insurance.

Julie found the whole thing desperate, even macabre. But these were desperate and macabre times. Still, she'd about had it. In her opinion, planning was folly. The so-called Fetal Replacement Program had yet to work, that is, produce a child, anywhere. Invariably, the same thing happened to the replacement embryo as to the original. Yet people wanted the program. They clamored for one. And so they provided it. Bottom line was nobody knew what to do and soon it wouldn't matter anyway.

Unlike a growing majority of people, her supervisor believed a solution or a cure was inevitable. "It's not if, but when," was her big line. But how, Julie Dolan wondered, do you "cure" a non-illness? Nobody was sick. What were the symptoms? People weren't being born is all. No more babies. Period. The trick instead was how do you sell insurance to somebody when extinction loomed for everybody? Vodka, fast cars, and movies–that you could sell. Insurance? For what?

Instead of exiting onto the freeway, Julie continued driving into town. In the late eighties, Old Pasadena had been revitalized. Bars packed them in. New ones sprung up overnight. Restaurants had long waits. Now these places only did business on weekends. It wasn't that Pasadena was falling apart, far from it, the town shone brightly in the California sun. There just weren't that many people around to enjoy it.

Julie passed the ice-cream shop she'd adored as a teenager and saw the Open sign. Painted, snow-covered mountains ranged across the window in contrast to the heat outside. She stopped short, parked, and left the rear of her car sticking out into Main, its front lodged in a red zone. Her plane left in roughly two hours.

She was the only customer. Behind the stainless counter, a man her age was reading a magazine. It still seemed weird not seeing a teenager doing the job. The man smiled at her, putting down his reading. Cope was currently one of America's most popular publications. Cope offered its readers mostly secular solutions to myriad psychological problems they were facing. Kind of a literary panacea, it was more enlightening than watching baseball and air shows, but with essentially the same purpose, alleviating fear.

"If you want to try a flavor, it's no problem," the man told her, holding one of those tiny wooden spoons.

Historically big on Rocky Road, Julie had grown out of it like everybody else. Rocky Road was like childhood, a thing of the past.

Why not, she thought.

"Two scoops. On a kiddy cone." She blurted out the order.

He filled the distinctive yellow cone with ice cream. "We don't call 'em kiddy cones, anymore. You want a napkin?"

Julie took the cone and a napkin and sat down. With child-like determination, she began eating. First the outer edges to prevent dripping and then the whole scoop, top first, working her way down to the cone. Delicious beyond expectation, she didn't look up once while imbibing the treat. Her tongue was numb from the cold.

"You got business in town?" asked the counter man, interrupting her reverie. "Sorry, I didn't mean to pry," he added quickly.

Now Julie looked up, realized her suit clashed with the surroundings. "I'm going to Denver. Plane leaves in one hour forty-eight minutes." She chuckled at her pointless obsession with the time and wondered why she even mentioned it.

"Wow. Wish I were in your shoes. I've always wanted to go to Colorado." He disappeared below the counter. Reemerged with a bag of walnuts. "Maybe soon I'll make it. You know, when more people are gone." He poured the nuts into their container. They made a hollow, clacking sound, strangely loud.

Julie considered the man. He seemed nice enough, if not a little odd in his chocolate smeared uniform. The all-American soda jerk. Behind him vintage fountain appliances gleamed, the sweet smells emanating from them almost tropical in their intensity.

"And I've always wanted a banana split," she said, cheerfully, resolutely.

"No kidding? Most ladies—"

"Tell you what," said Julie, cutting him off. "Make me a banana split and I'll give you Colorado."

"Excuse me?" He'd suspected she had issues from the get-go.

Julie stood. She wiped the ice cream from her mouth and walked over to the man. He backed away but she was undeterred. "Here's my ticket, first class. Car's out front. These are the keys." She reached back into her purse. "And this is one, two, three-hundred and some more dollars." She placed all the goodies on the counter in front of the flabbergasted man.

"You're crazy, right? I mean, not like you're-gonna-kill-me crazy but—" Then he looked at the money, the keys and into her eyes.

"And you've never been to Colorado," she laughed. "Hey, the ice cream will be here when you come back. If you come back."

He did have some money saved. He had it with him now, plus what she just gave him. He saw the snow-capped mountains before him, only a painting. He picked up a banana, peeled it back, and sliced it once the long way.

"Chocolate, strawberry, or vanilla?" he asked, shaking his head in disbelief. "You know, I've never ridden in first class, either."

"One of each," said Julie, feeling good all of a sudden, really good, like after a nap or when a fever finally broke. "Extra nuts," she told the man.

Last Call

J ust because Raphael left the bar didn't mean he stopped drinking. Six-pack in tow, he headed out on Highway 7 into the high country. He needed to think and to drink. The place where he would do both was seventy miles ahead. Based on the lack of traffic, he'd be there in less than an hour. Raphael owned the road. He punched the accelerator, hurtling forward into the dark, Texas night.

Though dry, the sharp curve in the riverbed seemed like an ideal spot for a campsite. The old cabin proved that for someone, some time ago, with a stand of desert juniper flanking one side, a steep, picturesque hill on the other. Naturally sheltered from the desert's arsenal, it didn't get the usual winds and high heat. Beautiful by day, at night it was even more so. Wrapped in down comforters, he and Nora would stare upwards at the infinite universe, forgetting how limited their lives had become. Typically a hardened, quiet man, on those occasions Raphael had been moved like never before.

He found the cabin unattended, door unlocked. Better yet, the wood that they'd gathered on their last visit was still present. Since it was such a gorgeous night, he brought a bunch of it outside. Not wanting to waste his flashlight batteries, Raphael got to work building a fire. Extremely dry, the kindling ignited easily and he heaped some of the bigger timbers onto the blaze. Within seconds he had the perfect campfire surrounding him in a cocoon of heat and light.

Raphael unrolled his sleeping bag, lying down upon it with his back to the ground. And there were the stars, even more abundant and glorious than he remembered. Fairly adept at astronomy, Nora had shown him many constellations. Then and now, like everybody else, he spotted the Big Dipper first.

Although the night sky could make a man feel inconsequential and small, it also had a placating effect. It's sheer magnitude and glittering architecture implied a sense of purpose and place in which Raphael belonged. In which Nora belonged. They had meaningful roles. They were part of the grand design.

And maybe, just maybe, thought Raphael, so was EFS. He had assumed the human race would continue just like the sun always rose in the morning. But there were no guarantees in the grand design. Stars exploded. Love could fade. Anything could happen. Everything could stop.

Raphael looked for the moon. Nora once told him it was a symbol of motherhood and fertility, that the moon was like a woman, full of hope and promise. Perhaps, he mused, on account of its round shape. Whatever, he missed seeing it in the sky. And he missed Nora by his side. So what if the pregnancy didn't last. She would. The question now was could they?

So many questions.

Raphael tracked a satellite as it glided across the starry ceiling. He wondered what it was doing up there, suspected it benign now, abandoned years ago. The governments of the world had more important things to concern themselves with than making maps or spying on one-another. On the other hand, maybe it was those two astronauts, the man and the woman. What were their names again? Hope and Future. Yes, that was it. Maybe the tiny moving dot was actually them. He said a prayer, wishing upon the moving object as if it were a star.

The emotions of the day and the beer of the evening had taken its toll. Raphael's eyelids grew heavy. He began to drift off, his thoughts trailing away like the multitude of benign satellites orbiting above, shooting stars, and random astronauts.

Chasing a moth, a bat flew down into the fading light of the fire. On the first pass, it missed the large insect. The second swoop he got it. And then the bat disappeared, the entire attack lasting only a moment. Raphael wasn't sure it even happened. What was that word Nora liked, the one she used all the time? Ephemeral.

Life was ephemeral and then you...

Sleep.

Turning Point

Having eaten, rested, and cleaned, Nora felt a lot better physically and was getting there mentally. What had she been thinking, chasing after some charlatan in the desert? She'd gotten pregnant and Raphael had gotten pissed. Nothing unexpected about that script. Nada. Of course he was pissed. Again, what had she been thinking? She handed Brandy the phone. Raphael wasn't picking up and neither was their voicemail.

"It's okay, honey," she said to Nora. "He'll come around. Important thing is you're going home, right?" Brandy hung the phone back up on the wall. Hearing no reply, she spun around. "Right?"

Nora nodded. She still felt foolish and chose to remain quiet. Sitting back, her eyes wandered across the walls of the gas station and back to the painting of Brandy's daughter. More than anything else, it was the picture of Shelly that had brought Nora to her senses. Not as a work of art–Christ, it was hideous–it was a reality check. Here was a woman so driven by her obsession to get pregnant that she'd given up her living, breathing family in order to chase after the false promise of a new one. Nora knew the details. Brandy hadn't left out anything. Shelly was gone now and even her mother had no idea how she was doing.

A car horn sounded from out front and Brandy excused herself. "I'll leave you ladies alone," she said, referring to Nora and either the painting or Nora's unborn child.

When she left, Nora got up and approached the painting. She could see Brandy in the woman's features, but she also saw herself in the young woman's eyes. Like Shelly, there was nothing she could do to protect the tiny life growing inside her. Unlike her, Nora would not succumb to desperation. Perhaps her baby was doomed but not so the rest of her loved ones. Raphael was real. And so was the quiet, simple life they'd been creating together back home. Home. She would return to it happily. Nora wondered if Brandy's daughter ever had that option. She doubted it.

"Well, I guess we better hit the road," she said aloud, perhaps unconsciously addressing the same phantom committee Brandy had. It was a good 700 miles back to Austin, maybe more, but Nora felt energized. Having pulled in for some gas, she was leaving with a second chance. Leaving for a new beginning. She liked the way that sounded. *Leaving for a new beginning.* It was like a song lyric. To say her spirit lifted would have been putting it mildly.

She figured she could make it to Albuquerque no problem. Even though tourism waned, on the way up she'd passed a motel still open for business. It had a pool and for some reason that also sounded terrific. Nora waved good-bye and good luck to the portrait of Shelly.

Heading back to her office, Brandy ran into Nora exiting it. They stopped, facing each other.

Pulling the hair away from her eyes, Nora smiled, her gratitude obvious. "Look, I still owe you for the—"

"Just give me a hug, sweetie. I'm sure that'll cover it." Brandy opened her arms to Nora. She wouldn't take cash or 'no' for an answer.

"Thank you so much," said Nora, embracing her. "For everything." She considered saying something to her about Shelly but decided against it. Brandy appeared to have accepted the loss of her daughter. Best just to leave it. For what it was worth, certain inevitabilities no longer frightened Nora as much either. Losing Raphael, however, was not one of them. She was anxious to get back to him, never more convinced that they were meant for each other.

Tying her hair back with a rubber band, Nora took one last look at Brandy, framing her within the coarse landscape of this remote desert. She blew the old lady a kiss and climbed into her car. Its windows dusty and dirty, she turned on the wipers. Swoosh, swoosh, the glass came clean.

Then Nora did something she hadn't done the entire trip, she flipped on the radio. Despite living in Texas, she secretly hated country music, but that didn't stop her from blasting it now.

Lonely at the Top

Miffed, Matthew threw his glasses to the floor. Rather than breaking, they slid down the hall. He would have preferred they shattered. Not only had Mary been unavailable to him this evening, as she was still recuperating, so was his other selection: Michelle Rafferty. A young thing from Detroit, Michelle was just 31 years old. And what's more, she was black, a rarity in Congress, rare in Utah period. Still being acclimated, Michelle was not available of her own accord. Unlike most of the women, she'd been coerced into joining, and by her parents, no less. He had half a mind to take the woman regardless of her inclination. Frustrated, he nevertheless couldn't bring himself to go *there*... not yet. The Next Child could hardly be the fruit of rape. Desire was mandatory. Whether it was Mary, Michelle, or any of the valid women, they needed to crave him. And they would, eventually. They always did.

Matthew scrolled his wall computer, looking for backup. There were the usual wanting whores, the older ones, mentally challenged, both. Not suitable for breeding, they did, however, serve an important purpose. It was imperative that Matthew's sperm be fresh and vital. More than 48 hours without an ejaculation was unacceptable. And since the humiliation of masturbating was out of the question, a group of females were always on call. And so, for maintenance, Matthew kept them around to keep his pipes clean, to keep the motor running. Yet tonight he wanted more than a tune-up.

He paused at the photograph of Shelly, a sweet potentate from just down the highway. The archive should've been removed from the file a long time ago. Even now, he couldn't bring himself to do it.

Instead Matthew zoomed in, relishing her again. Shelly possessed sensuous, lithe curves, but, in contrast to them, she had eyes like steel bearings and hair like black wire. She was the perfect combination of resilience and sexuality. Oh how he'd enjoyed taking communion with her. He'd been positive their coupling would result in pregnancy. And when it did, Matthew believed the blessing was finally upon him.

But of course it was not. The next child hadn't been Shelly's to give.

Matthew took the loss poorly, even personally. He'd gotten angry, more so than usual, than ever. Shelly was put on the Good Walk, but with less food than other girls and more distance to cover. After all, she'd raised his expectation then dashed it to pieces. She needed to learn from her mistake. Pay for her sin against him, against everybody. But mostly she had to pay for having hurt him so deeply.

Despite feeling rage, Matthew swelled beneath his robe.

Anger equals passion, does it not?

He unfastened the cinch, letting his member unfurl and grow.

Yes, yes, yes.

He commanded the images of Shelly back and forth across the monitor, scanning the full inventory of her. Seeing her once again, alive and in his bed, wanting it, wanting him.

Shelly did not survive her ordeal. How could she have, taken farther away and higher into the mountains than any before her? The freak snowstorm. Below zero temperatures. Two weeks later Frederick found only bones stripped clean by animals.

Matthew's erect penis pressed against the burnished steel cabinetry housing the monitor.

I will not touch myself. I will not touch myself.

And he did not, but his mind kept flashing on Shelly's perfect body. The warm opening of her. He moaned, steadying himself against the wall.

Frederick dutifully brought the remains back to the compound. Already pretty clean, Matthew ordered them boiled until free of all flesh, the flesh that had failed him. The bones were then crushed into a fine white powder, which he applied like salt on his morning omelet. Weak links to the soul, flesh and blood, but the skeleton was a person's architecture. An individual's character was maintained in her bones. That's what Matthew believed. He supped on the last distillation of Shelly as a kind of Eucharist. In this way, he absorbed and drew strength from her. In this way, she empowered him, gave him what her womb could not.

Cool steel brushed against his cock as Shelly's skin once had. He licked the video screen as it replayed the images. He pressed himself harder into the wall, into the steel, and into her.

Hello, It's Me

Dan was doing a crossword puzzle when the phone rang. The name of the President's cocker spaniel was the clue he'd been stuck on. It started with an 'S,' ended in 'y.' Dan didn't even know the President had a dog. A pink elephant maybe, he thought, picking up the receiver.

"Dan's Place."

"It's me."

Dan couldn't breathe, let alone speak. At that moment he was as incapable of it as Old Oscar. It had been over three years since he'd heard from his wife, since she'd taken the girls and left.

"I know you're still there," said Connie, finally. "I also understand how upset you must be... *at me*, I know." she whispered.

"I'm here," was all he could muster. Upset indeed–it was an understatement. But part of him rejoiced. *She was alive.*

"The girls are okay, Dan. I saw Mary yesterday. Kathleen, well, she'll be all right." A long pause. "Daniel, I made a mistake."

He heard his wife choke up. Dan wondered why she was trying not to cry. Seemed the least she could do. "Where are you?" he followed. "There... still?"

"Yes. He doesn't know I'm calling you. He doesn't allow—"

"He?" Dan knew but he wanted to hear her say it.

"You know... Matthew."

"Right. The guy who makes the Kool Aid." He paused. "Taste good, Connie?"

"Look, I don't have time to hash over what happened. I just want to get out of here. With Mary. With Kathleen. We want to come home." She stopped.

And Dan wanted them to come home, had wanted them to ever since they left. He just didn't know how to say it. His entire belief system had been undermined, wiped out, by their unceremonious departure. He'd lost the sun and the moon, everything in his orbit. Nobody had ever dealt him like that before.

Needless to say, Connie's call caught him off guard. Up until now, he'd had so little information, so few clues regarding their predicament. "Are you in danger?" he asked, starting with the obvious.

"No... maybe... probably. ...Christ." She sounded more exasperated than frightened.

All of a sudden, Dan realized the name of the President's dog: Sammy. Confused, a myriad conflicting emotions wrestled around inside. Part of him wanted to throw in the towel, give up. After all, Connie had been selfish. Profoundly selfish. She'd wanted her daughters to become mothers and that was that. Matthew would make it happen, she had said. The Congress was there for them, Connie had said. She was so damn sure. *We're going and you can't stop us!*

Hearing nothing from her husband, Connie resumed speaking. "I'll be fine... I have a certain amount of autonomy. Getting out of here is another story. Nobody ever has, you know? At least not to my knowledge."

"Look Connie," Dan said, gaining composure. "I think some, uh, friends of mine are on their way out there. I think they can help."

"He has armed guards, Dan. Military people. And they have weapons. If escaping is hard, then I'm sure breaking in is impossible."

Dan recalled a cult in Texas. They burned the whole place down and everybody in it. All because they didn't want anybody else getting inside.

"What friends?" asked Connie.

"I don't think they're planning to break in. Just coming for a visit." He hoped. Dan stared at all his liquor bottles, considered pouring himself a stiff one. He didn't even know what he was saying to her. Who knew what Jack and Muriel had in mind, let alone the other two? Dan didn't even know where they were. As of yet nobody had called. Jesus, this was not how he envisioned starting the day.

"Who exactly are they?" asked Connie again, agitated but curious. Help was help, right? If they made it to the compound, super. If not, that was their problem. Not cruel by nature, she'd learned.

"Some folks from the bar. A young couple. Two bikers from Minnesota. They're making a movie." Dan sounded like a dope and he knew it. Making a movie? That comment would only bear explaining. And he got the impression Connie hadn't the time.

"I don't think it's a good idea."

"They're okay people, Con," he said, sensing her discomfort. "I can vouch for two of 'em, anyway."

"Fine, whatever. I had my own plan but–Shit!"

The line was dead.

"Hello? Connie? Are you there?" But he knew she wasn't. He held the receiver to his ear, subjecting himself to the dial tone.

Now what?

If Connie was in trouble he had no way of finding out. It's not like Congress was listed in the directory. He'd tried.

Dan couldn't even contact the foursome. They might all have had cell phones, but he didn't know the numbers. How unbelievably half-assed was that?

Where were they? Chicago? Kansas City? Hell, he couldn't even find the goddamn atlas. Dan surveyed the long rear counter of the bar, searching. He'd used it a few weeks ago to settle a barroom debate. 'That's not the capital of such and such. Yes it is.' One of those.

He discovered the Atlas stacked between the Yellow Pages and, of all things, a Bible. He went to the back. Wyoming, Wisconsin, and voilá, Utah. Dan knew three things about Utah. It contained mountains, Mormons and, for the last few years, his entire family. He found the region where the Congress was located. The closest town was not very close at all, a place called Regerville. And Salt Lake City was twice again as far as it was.

Nowheresville.

Bewildered, Dan flipped the pages to his home state of Wisconsin, the Dairy State. Even on a map, he liked being somewhere familiar. He checked the bigger roads out of Madison. Going west there weren't many good choices. He knew they would eventually need to get on I-80, it being the main drag to the West Coast. But where would they pick it up? He traveled to the atlas' centerfold featuring the entire United States. Man-oh-man, Dan thought, eyeballing the two coasts. That's a lot of driving between here and there. Over two days now, they could be anywhere, even *there*, if they'd hauled ass. Interstate 80 cut the country in half horizontally much the way the Mississippi River did vertically. He followed the fat, black line as it meandered the Midwest and then he figured it out. Down and away, just outside of Chicago, that's where they'd gotten on. He was certain.

But guessing their coordinates changed nothing. He wasn't embarking after them. Like crosswords and solving puzzles, he just liked reading maps. Working out their itinerary gave him a modicum of satisfaction, but the atlas was as far as he was going. If his kin were meant to come home, then so be it. Adding him to the mix would only create traffic. Connie had said it best. Getting out would probably be easier than getting in.

He poured himself a finger of Blue Label.

His family was alive and, presumably, so were the people going off to find them.

"Here's to your health," said Dan, swallowing the libation.

He hoped Connie and the girls got out before needing the aid of such motley crusaders. He also prayed Jack et al knew better than to make like heroes. He honestly didn't know if they did.

He did know one thing, though. Whatever was going to happen, it would be happening soon.

Dan poured himself another round.

Mainly on the Plain

Iowa was flat.

Iowa was endless.

Iowa was grassy.

Iowa was flat, endless and grassy.

Many of the farmers' fields were no longer cultivated, the market for cash crops having diminished and, despite the competition from certain invasive brushes and weeds, the native prairie grasses were returning with an unexpected vigor. The result was as hypnotizing as it was breathtaking.

For Maura, mind numbing. Driving over them, she counted the white lines in the middle of the road. Every time she would reach a hundred, she started over. Over and over again. Still, it kept Maura's mind off the amber waves of grain closing in on either side of her. Maura liked the open road; she was a biker after all, but she preferred the more diverse terrain of Colorado or Minnesota. A lake would be nice right about now. Or a hill.

Seth, on the other hand, was in heaven. He derived comfort from the tall, undulating grasses. The prairie touched a chord in him, one he seldom felt. Maybe it was the Native American who appreciated this place. He imagined the massive herds of buffalo he knew had once roamed here. Great beasts, he hoped they would be coming back like the grasses they once feasted on.

On his right he noticed an old combine being swallowed by the verdant growth. Ancient, rusty and decrepit, the apparatus reminded Seth of the many assembled dinosaur bones he'd seen in museums. As their caravan passed by, a flock of crows erupted from the empty hulk. We're going extinct and so are our machines. Simple as that, Seth thought. The fossil record was already being shaped. He zoomed by it gladly.

"So this is what happens to a farm when it's not being farmed," observed Jack. "I like it."

Muriel nodded in agreement. "You think the same thing will happen to our farm in Wisconsin?" Neither one of them had been home in ages, having spent much of their adult lives in Madison. She was surprised by her own ignorance, and disappointed as well.

"I always just assumed somebody was taking care of the place," responded Jack, not sounding very confident. "I could be wrong." He felt the same vibe as his sister, shame and disappointment, mitigated, however, by circumstance.

"I know it sounds sad, but I kind of hope you are wrong," said Muriel, wistfully. "This is all so beautiful." The sun eased lower, its light now shimmering upon the endless, swaying green and yellow stalks. A glorious hue, and one that she only remembered seeing during harvest. Yet here it was, early. Like magic. So this is the land when it's not addicted to a particular growing season, Muriel thought.

"It's like a cathedral," she said.

"Except man didn't build this one," replied Jack.

"No," Muriel responded, whispering now. "Man's undoing did."

Jack leaned over the backseat and grabbed his camera. Directors called this part of the afternoon the 'golden hour' because it often led to the best film of the day. He rolled down his window and started shooting.

The small motorcade made its way between an audience of tall grasses, heading west through the Hawkeye State, and toward the setting sun.

Exit to Eden

E den, 11 miles.

   She'd been driving for six hours before seeing that sign. Austin was yet another hundred miles away, and she didn't feel like stopping. Especially considering Raphael hadn't picked up the phone or even responded to her messages. She'd left a dozen from the motel. Nora was eager to see him and patch things up. She was eager to get back.

   But then she saw the sign. That sign. Their sign.

   A sign?

   Eden, Texas was a special place. Their special place. She remembered the bonfires, showing him the constellations, making love. Even though there was a cabin, they'd usually slept outside, under the moon and stars.

   Raphael always did the driving, but Nora would find it.

   At the next exit, she did.

   A visit might be good for the soul, she reasoned. If only to say a prayer.

   It couldn't hurt.

After loss, people can feel abandoned and let down. They look for someone to blame, such as parents, colleagues, and even God, often having hostile reactions to them.

Whether directed at others or focused on the deceased, these two stages of the grief cycle are known as...

Hostility (a)

Y ou know it's a farce."

"What I know appears not to be relevant anymore."
Mervin was downloading his numerous files when Edward
walked in.

"So, you're actually going to go see her?" Edward needn't have
asked. He knew his boss and mentor and best friend was as good as
gone. Mervin's computer made a heartbreaking sound every time he
deleted a file. Bye-bye. Bye-bye. Bye-bye.

Mervin didn't reply, just kept doing what he was doing.

"Come on, Merv." Edward hated losing his cool, but it was hard
not to. He calmed down... some. "You're a scientist. A doctor. She
was probably raped by an orderly and too scared—"

"Probably. What does that mean, *probably*?" Mervin barely looked
up from his computer.

"It means odds are she had intercourse." Edward stared at his
colleague. The bald head. The distinctive oval glasses. He wondered
how such a brilliant man could be so irrational. Surely, he didn't
really believe?

"Would you say it's 80-20?" responded Mervin. "Eighty she did,
twenty she didn't?" He still hadn't looked up. Just kept tapping

and clicking. He had an old computer and downloading required many steps.

"I suppose if you're going to assign a number–"

"Well, Edward, suppose there's a 20% chance that something unconventional did in fact happen to this Sally Winfield. Something remarkable." Now he looked up.

"You mean, like a miracle?" Edward rolled his eyes. "Mervin, you've never even been to a church."

Mervin didn't bristle. He'd already wrestled with that one. Even though he was a scientist, and an atheist to boot, this transcended all that. He would try to explain.

"Science has gotten us nowhere," he said. "All our knowledge and yet here we are. Edward, the future is being taken away. For centuries we had all the answers. Well, I'm afraid EFS comes without a scientific explanation. My theory is the solution doesn't either." Mervin turned away from his computer and toward his colleague. "Perhaps it's time for a miracle."

Edward knew of the Winfield woman. He had seen a piece about her on television. Other than a few more years of education, she hardly differed from the countless fanatics who'd claimed the same thing. Immaculate Conception? The real miracle was that Mervin was buying it.

"I agree," said Edward. "Now is the time for miracles. Scientific ones." He sat down on the bench beside his mentor. "This Winfield lady isn't the answer. Instead of falling into a depression or going pseudo, she's elected to play the Madonna role. The Divine Carrier Syndrome. You are aware of the phenomenon?"

"As you know, I wrote a paper on it." Mervin understood his colleague's frustration, but would not tolerate condescension. He went back to his keyboard and paused. He sighed and turned around.

"Look, I realize Mrs. Winfield is probably not going to give birth," said Mervin. "I really do. But she is pregnant and she is credible. I do not feel this is a case of Divine Carrier. There are corroborating witnesses and her character is impeccable." Mervin cracked the

knuckles on his right hand. "She's no wacko, Edward. I believe her."
Then his left. "There is a reason to believe here. There really is."

Edward backed off. Resigned to the fact that a distinguished colleague was losing it, he watched the former Nobel Prize winner save
and delete and download his entire career. It reminded him of a kid
playing a video game, frittering away quarters.

At his own desk now, Edward accessed a coded file he'd been keeping on Mervin. It contained dated observations of peculiar behavior,
random notes from his weekly lectures at the university and other
damning bits all pointing to the mental collapse of Dr. Mervin Henry.

DCS, or Divine Carrier Syndrome was easily diagnosed. Other
than being pregnant, victims of the syndrome were often smart, in-
tuitive, and secular. Indeed, it was those very traits that enabled persons like Ms. Winfield to create and perpetuate the myth. Mervin
knew that.

A healthy Mervin did.

Edward began typing the final paragraphs in what he assumed
was the epilogue to a brilliant career. If Mervin did an about face on
DCS, it would undoubtedly raise some eyebrows. If he got on that
plane to see Winfield, it would end his credibility. The great Doctor
Henry looking for our savior in the womb of a divorced orthopedic
surgeon. Edward shuddered at the thought.

They had been so good together, like Edison & Watson. Now they
were more like Dr. Frankenstein and Igor. The flames of ridicule would
destroy them both.

Edward stopped typing. He looked at the collection of pictures
tacked on the wall over his computer. His dog, a woman he no longer
dated, and then there was the one taken of them many years ago at
a conference in the Bahamas. They donned identical Hawaiian shirts
and were drinking these things called Zombie Smashes. Overly pale
and inebriated, they were smashed zombies.

Back then, Embryo Fatality Syndrome was merely the problem
that they would be solving. It wasn't a question of if, only when.
After all, Mervin and Edward were the scientists who'd conquered

the AIDS virus. Even the vaccination was named after them: ME-1, short for Mervin and Edward.

The antidote for EFS would be called ME-2. At least, that's what Edward always told people. "Get it," he would say at this party or that meeting. "Me too!" But the cure never came. A few months turned into a few years and the dynamic duo of the medical community became also-rans like all the rest. In a decade they'd be has-beens. In two, dead. Sure, there would always be plenty of grants. They were still the world's most bankable hope. But the buzz was gone and, along with it, the magazine articles, talk show appearances, and awe-filled interns. The interns, Edward thought, had been the hardest to give up. He stared at the photograph of a zaftig brunette, fading on the wall.

The EFS Dialogue Conference no longer took place in Antigua or Harbor Island. Last year's was in Chicago. Next up, Cleveland. The most recent gathering was at a local university and had only drawn stringers from the press. Without 'news,' it wasn't a story. As such, it merited little more than fifty words and a file pic.

Edward fired up his first cigarette in twelve years. Why quit? Hope and Future were only the names of a couple goddamn astronauts. Down here it was Desperation & Futility.

Look at Mervin. He babbled at the podium now, rummaging through his crumpled notes like a mad scientist. He stopped wearing bow ties and started sporting undershirts to work, to class. He'd lost touch. Edward likened it to the deterioration of an Alzheimer's patient. Mervin's interest in theology became an obsession with religion. It seemed he had given up on science altogether, crossing over to the fictive world of channeling, reincarnation, and, now, Immaculate Conception.

"Fuck it," Edward exclaimed and proceeded to send Mervin's file to all 927 people in his mailbox. "Fuck Mervin. Fuck EFS. And fuck me." And with that, Igor took out Dr. Frankenstein.

He yanked the photos off his wall and, one by one, lit them on fire.

All except his dog. He put Grover in his pocket. In the end, a dog really was his best friend.

In the end.

Hostility (b)

Dwight was sick of hiding. No, not sick. Bored. He didn't even think they were looking for him anymore.

Didn't they know how dangerous he was? How bad? Because he was, he was! Eleven cut people, men and women, all killed. Their hands and feet disappeared without a trace. So, Dwight thought, why aren't they trying to catch me? What's a fellow have to do?

"Bastards!" He threw a thawing foot at his window, unconcerned if it flew outside. Let it hit a bobby for all he cared.

It didn't. The gawky appendage fell way short, landing on a small table. A perfect strike, it knocked over all the pictures of his family as well as those of his victims. The dead man's foot landed upright and sat there like an absurd piece of art. The killer contemplated the foot-art for a bit, then shut his eyes and fell asleep, the ale finally catching up with him.

When Dwight awoke it was dark outside. The processed Guinness poured from his uncircumcised member in a steady torrent, filling a bowl already stuffed with decaying feet and hands. Likewise, he ignored the corpse half submerged in his bathtub. Two days old, it was only just beginning to rot. He hadn't even gutted it yet. Maybe he wouldn't. Why should he? Not like there was any more room in the icebox.

Back in the parlor, Dwight popped on the telly. He started surfing. He went past the usual crap like *FutureScape* and *Cooler Heads*. Oh, how he loathed all that yackety-yak and make-believe. Where was the good, old-fashioned news, damn it? More importantly, where were the stories about him? Embryo Fatality Syndrome may have kept people from coming into the world, but, shit, he was taking them out. Didn't that count for anything?

Dwight stopped at something on the local channel. In a church, it looked like. Bunch of women proceeding up the center aisle, all holding their bellies. Each time one got to the priest, she exposed it to him. Then he dabbed them there with holy water. Blessed them, it looked like. Dwight got off his can for a closer examination. Bingo.

"Them bitches are pregnant!" With child every damn one of 'em! They're being blessed against the EFS. Of course! Of course.

Dwight fell back onto his couch, transfixed. Some of the ladies were pretty. Some of them were pretty old. Many wept. Yet, there was something else. They all seemed so important looking on the television like that. *So very important.*

Dwight realized these were the kind of people he needed to see. After all, a few more years and there wouldn't be a capable female left in the world. The pregnant ones were special then. Rare and special.

Their deaths would be regarded that way as well.

He ran to the bathroom and stared at his corpse. No wonder they don't care. The damn thing was ancient, dead even before he'd killed it. Same thing with the bloke who once had been attached to the foot. The whole lot was just hookers, bums, and miscreants. Old and decrepit, they offered nothing to a dying world. They only offended it. The people he'd been killing were unpleasant reminders of what lay in store for everyone. Bloody hell, Dwight thought, peering at the waterlogged stiff. No wonder people could give a shit. He'd been doing them all a favor.

Dwight fetched his knife. He had to clear out the tub and make room. He knew for a fact Larry's wife, Nell, was almost two months pregnant. He'd seen them at the pub just the other day and had wished them luck. She'd accepted his good wishes, carrying the hope that somehow she'd be the one.

He pulled a gleaming blade out from the dishwasher. She'd be the one all right.

Planted Seed

K athleen Connely did a superb job of remaining off radar and, as a result, Matthew hadn't seen fit to pay her a 'visit.' No way of telling how much longer that would last. Not a soul knew she was pregnant, but many were aware of her cycle and that, in fact, she was ready to get pregnant. And what they knew, he knew. Twelve days had passed since faking her period. By any measure, time was fleeting. People kept track of these things. He kept track.

Undisturbed by anyone thus far, Kathleen was in relatively good spirits. She worked in the far gardens, keeping out of sight, out of mind, and the strategy had worked. Except for deerflies and a pair of nosy rabbits, she'd been left alone.

Kathleen loved gardening, having developed a deep appreciation for it as a kid on the family farm in Wisconsin. So competent in the ways of agriculture, at the tender age of eleven, her daddy had entrusted her with a quarter acre of land to do with as she pleased. On it, she'd grown radishes, strawberries, tomatoes, and even some of the more difficult crops like asparagus and endive.

Today, Kathleen sowed tomatoes. A special hybrid from central Mexico, they were tolerant of the hot days and frigid nights common to the region. In forty-five days everybody's salads would be full of them. Three at a time, she pulled the plastic receptacles from the flat. Then she tipped and prodded the small plants out of their tiny containers and into the dirt. Having already dug a slight trench, it was only a matter of popping them in and covering the roots up with dirt.

Kathleen laid another trio into the furrow, pushing in the loose soil around them. The watering would come last, after she was done. Reaching for another set of plants, she felt nauseous.

The baby.

She smiled. Yes, he was the father, but it was hers too, after all. Like most women, Kathleen wished she could have the baby, a baby, a child to nurture and to watch grow. Among other things, she would impart to her child an absolute love of the land. They'd spend hours in the garden, hands to the dirt, laughing and chortling, arguing about which plants they should grow.

She sighed, wiped her brow, and grabbed the final two sprigs from the flat she'd been planting.

And then she dropped them.

Grimy and wet, a small envelope, like the kind one receives with a bouquet of flowers, rested on the flat. On it, in lovely script, her name was written in full.

Kathleen Connely

She recognized the handwriting almost as quickly as she had her own name. She'd seen it on Christmas presents, report cards and notes to the principal.

Mom.

Kathleen knew her mother was alive from observation and gossip, but she hadn't communicated with her in ages. Until now.

She grabbed the tiny envelope, shoving it deep into her back pocket. Open it later, she thought. Open it later.

Kathleen sowed the remaining two tomato plants. Grabbing the empty flat, she then got up and headed for the planting shack. There she'd find running water to wash her hands and, more importantly, privacy.

Checking that no one had followed her, she closed the lone door. A dingy window provided the single room with its only light. With some trepidation, she opened the envelope.

47th post from MW corner.
Fruit to kitchen S4. Bin 4.
Special Pie!

Okay, so her mother's secret note was a grocery list. Fascinating. Certain she missed something, Kathleen reread it several more times.

Nope. A grocery list.

Special pie? For who, why, and so what?

47th post. What the hell did that mean? It had to be something nobody else but she could know. She read the lines yet again, committing them to memory, then ripped the note into miniscule pieces, scattering them like seeds. Burning it would have been easier, but matches weren't allowed in Congress.

In case any one was watching, Kathleen turned on the irrigation system, setting it for a moderate trickle. To busy her hands she grabbed an empty fruit basket. Taking a deep breath, she left.

In the southwest corner of the compound, it was a straight shot to her mother's coordinates. But as far as Kathleen knew, and she knew more than most, there weren't any fruits being grown in that area. The orchard was by the main entrance. She headed to the northwest corner anyway.

A vague path existed between the last crop row and the tall barbwire enclosure. Kathleen walked down it with purpose. The fence was being erected right about the time she'd arrived. Kathleen recalled seeing the work detail coming back from sinking posts.

Posts. The 47th post. Whatever fruits she was supposed to gather must be growing by that part of the fence. Unfortunately, there was a hell of a lot more than forty-seven. Kathleen picked up her pace. She had to see the actual corner before beginning her count. Regardless, she couldn't imagine finding any kind of fruit growing there. That part of the garden was used for corn and other vegetables.

Kathleen was correct. There were no fruits growing off the 47th post. *On* the 47th post, that, however, was another story. Wrapping its way up the pole was a bramble of gooseberry, the tiny reddish fruit ripe for the picking.

Acidic, gooseberries were not among Kathleen's favorite fruits, especially given her father's allergy to them. The little devils nearly killed him once, his heart racing so bad the paramedics had to calm him with sedatives. The allergy was rare, said the doctor, but also quite deadly. Dad had stuck with pumpkin pie from that day forward.

Kathleen plucked one of the berries and held it for a while, rolling the tiny red ball in her fingers. The stain looked a lot like blood, like if she'd crushed a mosquito.

What if someone else had the same unfortunate allergy as her daddy, someone she might soon be having dinner with?

Him.

Operation Gooseberry

He would be seeing one of her daughters tonight, but Connie wasn't sure which. So she'd set up her plan to work either way. She fluffed the pillows on his bed in the blue room, one of five private chambers on the compound.

To say she was uptight right now required mastery in understatement. Connie had pushed the start button and now her whole family was at risk, more so than ever. But she had no choice. Her husband said others were coming. She knew it was time to act.

Connie prayed Eve bought the story and was doing her part to complete it. In the kitchen staff, Eve was in charge of deserts. A baker by trade, Eve adored cooking for Matthew despite being ignored by him and would be devastated if she found out her pastry had harmed him. That said, she'd been told Matthew requested a special pie made with gooseberries in addition to strawberries. Connie implied the new ingredient was part of Matthew's divine plan, intended for fertility purposes. She'd find the berries in today's harvest, bin #4.

All things considered, Connie wasn't worried about Eve. She would do as she was told. An order from Matthew's personal secretary carried a lot of weight in Eve's messed-up little world. She'd make the pie.

And since the pie wasn't poisonous in general it posed no threat to anyone but him.

Connie surveyed the bedroom. Recently, she'd reprimanded the cleaning staff for shoddiness, not good considering how anal Matthew was, and tonight was no time to take chances. It looked in order, however, and she moved on to the bathroom.

She put a point on his toilet roll, which she knew he'd appreciate. Nothing's too fine for his Lordship's ass. She checked the mirror for spots and smears. Anything that impeded his ability to see himself would also bring trouble.

In doing so, Connie couldn't help but notice her own reflection. Since being appointed his secretary, she hadn't been outside. It showed. Her face was pale, if not sallow. And she'd put on weight. By far, garden detail had been her preferred duty. Still, the new job was a promotion and one she couldn't turn down, not only because it was Matthew's will but also on account of the rare opportunities it afforded her. This put her in his inner sanctum. He trusted her. In time she would know things. Important things.

Like his fear of water. Hence the desert location and conspicuous lack of bathtubs.

Like his fatal allergy to gooseberries.

She left the garden job willingly, but not before planting the shrub.

Regarding herself in the mirror made Connie uneasy. She no longer saw a wife and mother. Looking away, Mrs. Connely massaged her empty ring finger, something she did during stressful times.

Why on earth had she ever come here, leaving her husband and taking her kids? Bereft of answers and bewildered, she could only sigh.

Mindful of the time, Connie pressed on. Later today a bus was coming from Canada and they were short on bunks. The carpenters needed to get going on the addition, which she was supervising. No, Connie couldn't answer her own questions. But that wasn't important now. Coming to Congress was no longer the issue.

Getting out was.

Speak of the Devil

So, how are the Connely women?" asked Matthew of his personal secretary, their mother. Sharpening his Swedish carving knives, he held up one of the blades to the window, examining its new edge in the light. He shot her a glance, a dagger itself.

Dagger eyes.

Connie remembered that that's what Dan had called her sharp, pointed stares at him. "Stop hurling those 'dagger eyes' at me," he'd bark. It was a look usually reserved for married couples, not whatever this arrangement was.

"My daughters are fine... *considering.*" She replied, neutering as much of her attitude as possible. It was difficult. "But, then, you already knew that."

Moxie. That's what Matthew liked about the elder Connely. She was a loyal servant to him, but without a slave's mentality. Matthew appreciated that combination in a woman, that is, as long as her commitment was beyond question. A breach in loyalty would not be tolerated. No, no, no.

"Tell me anyway," said Matthew, putting the knife back into its wooden case in the drawer. He only now tired of the little dance they were having.

"Mary is still in the infirmary. I, uh, haven't seen Kathleen," Connie replied. She demurred. Matthew could turn in a moment. "I hear she's currently working in the gardens," she added, fishing for information, at the same time spot-checking a line of crystal drinking vessels. Connie volunteered little but when asked a question she answered it truthfully. Her best strategy was to avoid being questioned.

But he wasn't finished.

"Ah, the gardens," Matthew responded. "Didn't you once care for them as well?" He faced her, forcing Connie to look up at him, prompting an answer.

"Yes, sir. Until you requested me to do otherwise." Where was he going with this? He couldn't possibly know of her recent activities. She'd be dead by now if he did.

"Hmmm… " Matthew poured himself a glass of water from one of the eight pitchers situated throughout his quarters. There always had to be a fresh ice water in each bedroom, bathroom and the kitchen. Another one of his special requests.

"I trust you're content with my efforts so far?" Connie asked, raising her eyes to meet his. She challenged him here, knowing full well that he was. She could tell as much by the way he often confided in her, revealing things, and showing inklings of vulnerability. Connie supposed Matthew appreciated having a woman for a confidante and one whom he wasn't taking to bed. She also assumed that he was not particularly comfortable with male companionship in general.

"So far," he answered. "And I am also pleased with the efforts your lovely daughters have put out with regard to the cause. They've both performed admirably under their varying circumstances. You must be very proud."

"Thank you, I am… proud." His choice of words, "put out" and "performed," rankled Connie, but she bit her tongue. What choice did she have? Sweetly smiling, the resolve to see him vanquished grew stronger with every such humiliation.

"Thank you," replied Matthew warmly, oblivious to any animosity. The light faded, prompting him to check his watch. "I think it's time for my nap. So, if you'll excuse me, Daddy needs his energy." He topped off his glass of water, turned to leave.

Matthew did not see the betrayal unfolding.

Certainly not from the likes of Mrs. Connely. After all, she'd come to Congress voluntarily, enthusiastically. And she'd brought her two daughters. Hardly the actions of an antagonist.

"Oh, Connie, I almost forgot," he said, reappearing in the doorway. "This evening's meal, I'd like it served in the yellow room." He thought for a second. "Set the standard table. A bottle of champagne."

Connie reached in her pocket for the small pad she always carried. Matthew likely had a very specific menu in mind.

He did.

"And if one of your daughters could join me."

It was not phrased as a question. Blankly, she stared at her pad.

"You decide which one," he added with a smile. "I trust your judgment completely."

She nodded slowly, trying not to show emotion, and put the pen and pad back into her apron pocket. He hadn't said what he wanted for an entrée, or had he?

Hopefully, Connie prayed, he'd save room for dessert.

Reunion

Raphael got up early, and went for a hike, and was now some distance from camp. Taking a sip from his canteen, he sat down among a group of large rocks surrounding the area. It was almost high noon but significant cloud cover kept the temperature from soaring. All in all, it had remained quite pleasant. The unbearable heat and humidity that often crushed this part of Texas hadn't.

That and a great night of sleep had done wonders for Raphael. Nothing like the proverbial wide-open spaces to get a man right. If he had a hangover, it was gone. With every breath he purified himself, absorbing the landscape, inhaling the atmosphere. A clan of vultures wheeled atop forming thermals in the bleached sky. Even though searching for carrion, they seemed…what was the word Raphael was looking for? Righteous.

Save for a ruined fence separating an abandoned cattle ranch from the indifferent desert, the land was void of people. As it must have been a long time ago, Raphael mused, and would soon be again. He didn't have to see it on *FutureScape*. In fifty or sixty years the world was going to look like this.

He laughed. Planet Earth didn't give two shits about the passing of humanity, no more than vultures did about a wounded squirrel. Even less, Raphael thought, laughing harder. At least the birds got a meal out of it.

Hardly an appetizing thought, none the less, Raphael was reminded of his own growing hunger. Before setting out, he'd eaten an apple and some cookies. All he had with him was a stick of gum. He took another sip from his canteen. There was cereal and dried meats back at the camp. Maybe, if he were lucky, he'd get a squirrel of his own. He patted his right ankle, feeling for the pistol he carried there. Raphael was far from worried. He was elated.

On his way back he even whistled. "Hi-ho! Hi-ho! It's back to camp I go…"

Until he saw the vehicle heading toward camp. Or rather, he saw the effect of a vehicle: something shiny and moving, a trail of dust in its wake. The debris seemed to linger in midair, like airplane smoke, or the tail of a comet.

Raphael squinted at the moving object, wishing it were a mirage, knowing that it wasn't. Could it be the law or maybe the owner of the land he'd been camping on. All the times he and Nora had visited it never occurred to them to seek permission. For one thing, whom would they ask? Until now, he'd never even seen another person.

High clouds passed in front of the sun, lessening the glare from the approaching vehicle. Raphael was able to pick up its shape and color. He gulped when he saw the apparatus on top of the car's roof, thinking police lights.

He picked up his pace. Better face the music, he figured. And anyway, how bad could it be? Besides trespassing, he hadn't broken any laws. What other choice did he have? He could ill afford having his car towed. And no matter how beautiful and spiritual, this was still in the middle of nowhere, and hardly a place he wanted to be stranded in.

Then he noticed they were ski racks, not police lights.

And unless the sheriff's patrol drove around in beat-up, old Hondas it wasn't the law either.

It couldn't be... no way...

Raphael rubbed his eyes. *Maybe it was a mirage.* He began running to camp as fast as he could.

And she to him.

"Slow down!" he yelled, waving his arms, remembering Nora was pregnant.

Not a chance. Nora sped up, as surprised at finding him as he was she. Hopefully, he'd be just as happy about it too.

He was.

For a full minute, they hugged, saying nothing. The miraculous fate reuniting them trumped all memory of their breakup. There were no hard feelings.

"Do you suppose the well still works?" she purred, speaking into Raphael's ear. "Because I could use a bath." She cried tears of joy, had visions of a bonfire, tequila, and that extra wide sleeping bag.

"Don't know," smiled Raphael. "But I'm feeling a little dirty myself."

Maxwell

Heading up the caravan, it was now Jack and Muriel's choice where and when to exit the highway. They'd been hoping to make it through Nebraska on this leg, but serious-looking storm clouds were forming, and they had to be mindful of their motorcycle-riding compatriots. This was tornado season and they were in tornado country. Anyway, to a pair of bikers even a slight rain made traveling miserable.

Muriel scrutinized towns coming up on the map.

"Maxwell," she said. "It's not too far."

It was also the name of a pony they'd kept as kids. Jack smiled when he heard her say it. If he ever had a son, Max was among his top three name choices. He'd forgotten the other two because the subject rarely came up.

"Perfect," he replied. "I think it's starting to rain."

Having booked a couple cheap rooms on the outskirts of town, the group piled into Muriel's car and headed toward the square. There, they encountered a prototypical main street replete with restaurant, bars, and even a movie theater. But unlike a lot of towns its size, Maxwell bustled. People waited at the traffic light less out of habit than because of actual traffic.

"That diner looks pretty sweet," Maura said, pointing. "Across from the movie house."

"I was leaning toward the bar, myself," Jack chimed in, Seth concurring.

"Plenty of time for that later," countered Muriel. "It's not like we're trying to catch a movie." She laughed at her own remark, as did the rest of them. They just assumed the theater was closed. Most these days were. Since she was driving, Muriel made the call. Or rather, her stomach did. The diner prevailed.

The boys were ecstatic to find that the diner sold beer and they ordered a couple pitchers along with their burgers. Muriel opted for a milk shake, but, succumbing to peer-pressure, she switched over to brew when they'd requested a third. The rain came, but not very strong, followed by dusk. The street lamps flickered on and coziness prevailed. In no hurry, the foursome lingered over plates, delighted to be able to smoke cigarettes and hang out.

"Is this place perfect, or what?" Seth commented, feeling the vibe.

"The whole damn town is perfect," added Muriel, and she grew self-conscious about having used the word 'damn.'

"Maybe we should pick up the real-estate section," joked Maura. "Finish out our lives right here." On the other hand, maybe she wasn't joking. People changed locales all the time now. Why lay down roots?

"*After*," said Jack. Someone had to remind the rest of the group just what it was they were doing.

"I meant *after*," she answered, not sure if she did. Maura understood the trip they were taking had a serious side... a potentially dangerous, serious side. But she also knew that they didn't have to do anything. The bartender in Madison aside, no one's kin from this entourage were in peril. Maybe nobody was even in peril at all. Regardless, she was glad the group wasn't obsessed with Congress, one way or the other. They'd get there. Or they wouldn't.

"And just when you think the town can't get any more trippy." It was Seth. He motioned to the theater across the street. "Ta dah!"

The marquee lights were on, every bulb lit. And, what was even more unbelievable, a sizable crowd was milling around out front, waiting in line. Movies Tonight! The sign flashed. Movies Tonight!

"Okay," said Muriel. "When we exited the highway we were in the state of Nebraska... what state are we in now?" She was surprised, as they all were, that so much was going on.

With few exceptions, small towns were dead or soon to be. Even pre-EFS, obsolescence was rampant. Only nobody seemed to have informed the good people of Maxwell. Quite a contingent had gathered beneath the gaudy marquee.

"More like Mayberry than Maxwell," Jack said. The others looked at him dumbly. "You know that little town on TV?" Nope. Still not getting through. The golden age of television hadn't made an impression on any of his cohorts. "Anyway," he said, adjusting the topic. "I, for one, would like to see whatever the hell is playing at that particular movie theater." Jack poured the rest of the beer into their mugs, topping his off last.

Seth signaled the waitress for their check. She was a wholesome woman and one who had probably grown up around the corner. She, like everything else in Maxwell, exuded small town, USA.

"Say, Ellen," he said, reading the name off of her nametag. "Seen any good movies lately?"

Ellen grinned. "You all aren't from around here?" she asked, sizing them up. "I don't mean to be nosy or weird or anything. Just curious is all."

"No problem," said Muriel. She warmed to the waitress. "Although Wisconsin really isn't much dif—"

"Keep the change," Seth cut in. He handed Ellen three tens, then winked at her. Something about small town chicks.

Maura rolled her eyes. She'd have been irked by the display, if it hadn't been so painfully rendered.

"Meatloaf up!" hollered the cook from behind the counter.

"Well, 'fraid that's me," said Ellen, hurrying. "By the way, the pictures start at eight. If you want a seat you better go now. It's a real popular show."

"Loaf up!" The holler came louder this time.

"Sorry, folks. Gotta go. And I just love that jacket," said Ellen, smiling at Seth before twirling away. "It's so boss."

"I can't believe she just said 'boss,'" said Maura.

"I can't believe she's gotta go," Seth deadpanned, smitten.

* * * * * *

At nearly one hundred years of age, the Maxwell House Theater, yes, of the coffee, was in excellent shape. Classic movie posters from the Golden Age on up adorned its red and gold-walled interior. A smoldering Clark Gable embraced Vivian Leigh on one side. The no less charismatic shark from Jaws leered at passers-by on the other. "What're you looking at?" questioned Maura, sliding by the toothsome monster.

The walls lacked current propaganda, so the group had no idea what they were seeing. And now, already in the theater, it seemed awkward asking. In lieu of a teller who could have told them, admission to the show was solicited via a Plexiglas container just inside the doors. A sign above it asked patrons to 'give what you feel.' The waitress from the diner was right. The place was damn near full, and for a second it looked like the foursome might have to split up. But then Muriel spotted two pairs of seats, one in front of the other, and they took those.

Like on dates, Jack sat next to Maura and Muriel next to Seth. The two couples fidgeted in their seats, sexual tension having so far been nonexistent during their journey. However, any such pretense dispelled when Jack and Maura pretended to make out. Muriel slapped her brother on the head. Maura turned around, laughing. "Serves you right," she said to Seth, mocking him. *Seen any good movies lately.*

At Seth's expense they all laughed, Seth too. Maybe it was the old theater or beer, but in some aspects it did feel like a double date. For one thing, they were all having fun.

The lights dimmed and they, like everyone else, hushed up in preparation for the show to begin.

A title card appeared on the screen:

The Weavers at the State Fair
Tecumseh, Nebraska
July, 1996

The film began with an extreme close-up of a pig's face. The animal was rummaging through a pile of hay blowing the dead grass with its snout. A young boy groomed the swine. They were in a stall and the child attempted to wash the pig's back but couldn't quite reach it. Mom laughed off-camera, then apologized. A man's voice cut in introducing his son, Will, and his prize-winning pig, Beluga. There was a large yellow ribbon with loud, cheering sounds, some of them coming from the previous couple. Then the camera cut back to the kid again, posing with his pig. After a few seconds of blue screen, a blurry shot of a merry-go-round revolved, going in and out of focus. The same guy said he was sorry but it was getting kind of dark and he still wanted to grab a shot of little Jennie and to please bear with him for a second. He found the girl, chasing her as best he could with his camera.

"Oh my God," Muriel whispered to Seth. "Those are just videos of somebody's kids. They're showing home movies." She turned to her left, eyeing the old woman two seats over. Dressed nattily, hair up in a bun, she was eating sunflower seeds out of a plastic bag, smiling at the primitive images flashing before her. Hearing the people in front of her laughing, Muriel looked up. The little boy was jamming a hot dog into his mouth as part of a contest. For a surreal second, Muriel wondered if the hot dog had somehow come from the kid's prized pig. She turned toward Jack to see if the whole thing was freaking him out too.

At first she couldn't tell. Something obscured his face. A small cylinder. She heard a subtle whir emanating from the general vicinity.

Good Lord, he's filming.

Art imitating life? Was that the phrase she was looking for?

On screen, another child stuffed hot dogs into his mouth while two girls squealed with delight. Muriel watched the people watching the movie, observing them laughing. She looked back at Jack filming.

No. Now life was art.

Life had become art for the Last Generation. Yesterdays' lives were now coming attractions.

Connie's Choice

Kathleen. Connie had to. If for no other reason, it gave her the chance to visit with her other daughter. And how could she choose otherwise? Mary was still recovering from her ordeal in the desert and the miscarriage before that. She was, thankfully, okay. But intercourse… with him… now? If indeed Connie had any say in the matter, she just couldn't let Mary be subjected to that. No way. Not again.

Connie lay in bed for what would have been her afternoon nap. But too many logs were on the fire. Her mind blazed. She wondered about the pie. If she saw Kathleen, she could at least confirm the gooseberries had been harvested and delivered. Having the dessert be part of his meal would be easy by comparison. After all, she was his personal secretary and, on top of that, he'd authorized her to tend to things this evening.

But how?

Connie sat up, frustrated and not sure how to proceed. Could she merely walk across the compound to the dorms? Had Matthew even meant what he said when he'd asked her to choose? If so, had it been communicated to the rest of the staff and to the guards in particular? And what was she supposed to do if and when she found her daughter? Tell Kathleen to put on a party dress and head on over to the yellow room? Hell if Connie knew. She hungered for a cigarette. She wished she could talk to Dan.

A knocking at her door. Three solid raps.

"Who is it?" She had no clue.

"Fred Morgan. I'm in charge of–"

"Oh, yes, I know who you are," she said, cutting him off. *One of Matthew's goons.* "Just a moment please."

Whatever was going to happen had just started. Connie got up, straightening out her robe and opened the door.

"Hello Frederick, what can I do for you?" she asked. For various reasons she'd ridden in the helicopter with him before, but not recently, not since her new appointment. She certainly wasn't planning on flying anywhere now.

He surprised her. "I'm here on behalf of your daughter. I've been instructed to take you to her." He mustered a thin smile though dropped it when she didn't reciprocate.

"Which one?" Connie asked.

"You tell me."

She answered straight away. "Kathleen." Done. "Look, we're not flying... are we?"

"Oh, no, Mrs. Connely," he chuckled at the misunderstanding. "You know, I do have other duties here besides piloting."

"I see... well then, let's get on with them, shall we? I haven't seen my eldest child in ages." It was getting late. She grabbed her topcoat and proceeded out the door ahead of him. At least this one had manners, Connie thought, as they exited the building.

"So," Connie asked, as they crossed the pavilion, heading to which dorm she still did not know, "might you be the pilot who recovered Mary, my other daughter, from her... walk?"

"I might." Fred replied, wondering if she was going to ask. Nothing against Kathleen, but he was glad she hadn't selected Mary. He considered telling Connie about the business with the tranquilizers but resisted. Based on her current behavior, he couldn't deduce whether Connie was happy or sad about tonight's arrangement. In addition to being the girl's mother, she was, after all, *his* personal secretary. And despite the noticeable dip in morale, his own notwithstanding, the vast majority of people in Congress were still very devoted to Matthew. Who's to say Mrs. Connely wasn't one of them?

"I owe you my gratitude then. The ladies don't always do so well on those walks." Connie knew of what she spoke. One of her more unpleasant new tasks involved dealing with the aftermath of so many missing women. Records had to be kept. Others destroyed. One never knew when a disgruntled lover or distraught parent might show up. You needed your stories straight. Ignorance of events, good, bad, or otherwise, was not tolerated in Congress.

They went by the part of the garden where Kathleen had been working. Connie looked down the long fence in vain, attempting to find her berry plant. Why, she had no idea. Connie searched anyway, straining her eyes against the diminishing twilight.

"We're almost there," said Frederick, noticing Connie's restlessness. "She's in building eight. It's, as you know, one of the nicer ones."

Where Matthew kept his favorites.

"Look, Mrs. Connely," he said with a degree of hesitation. "You should know that I'm not *all right* with some of the things that go on around here."

This was a rare piece of blasphemy coming from him, a lieutenant, no less, and she froze. She put a hand to her heart, feeling it flutter.

Fred stopped walking as well. Speaking truthfully relieved him. The boss may have been a monster, but he'd bet she wasn't. Not Mary's mother. He continued. "I've done everything I can to keep him away from both of your daughters. I don't know if it's any consolation, but it was my idea to let you see them. I just thought it might be easier on the girls."

So, even in the highest court the King's subjects were disillusioned. Still, if Frederick was having second thoughts, why in the

hell didn't he just leave? He had access to a helicopter. Of course,
Connie didn't know how serious his misgivings were. She decided
not to ask him. She herself could not remember at what point she'd
lost faith in Matthew and the Congress. It didn't happen overnight.
Before planting the berries she now hoped would kill Matthew, she'd
also planted plenty of produce that had sustained him. Maybe
Frederick was just beginning to examine his own conscience, just
beginning to see. She looked over his shoulder at the dormitory buildings silhouetted by the setting sun. First things first, she thought.
We're almost there.

"I'll be able to see her then?"

"Absolutely," he answered, resuming their pace. Connie Connely
was roughly a football field away from seeing her kin. He presumed
that that was foremost on the woman's mind. Yet, he also had an
idea she probably wondered why, if he wasn't 'all right' with things,
did he continue to be a part of them? It was a damn fine question.
Maybe asking it was a necessary part of the answer. "You have about
an hour before Kathleen needs to be anywhere," said Frederick.

Connie was well aware of Matthew's dinnertime, six PM sharp.
Like a schoolboy. Like an athlete.

"Until then, I'll leave you alone," he said, at the doorway. "I'll
have a cart sent for the two of you at a quarter of. Please be there, on
time, that is." He stammered at his own slip. Be there? Where else
would they be? "She's in room twelve." He tried smiling and took
Connie's hand and shook it.

"Thank you, Frederick. For everything." Connie said, doling out
an extra squeeze. "I'll see you later."

"I hope so," replied Frederick. And he did.

* * * * * *

Dumbfounded. Kathleen was dumbfounded. The last person she
expected to see at her door was her mother, especially considering
yesterday's coded note in the garden. She didn't know what to say.

Connie led by giving her daughter a long, deserved hug. There were a million things she would have rather told her daughter, but instead she said, "You're to have dinner with Matthew tonight... I'm afraid."

Over the warm evening wind, women's voices carried. A group was in vespers, singing hymns.

You're afraid. Kathleen expected the message, just not the messenger. First she was confused, then, all of a sudden, a little peeved. "Do you mind telling me what the hell is going on, Mother?"

"Yes, yes, of course." Connie replied, flustered as well. "God, I wish I had a cigarette. May we sit down?"

"Yes, let's," said Kathleen backing into her residence, a modest studio patterned in the adobe style.

Her mother grabbed her, "No, here," she whispered. "He could be listening."

Kathleen didn't argue. They both sat on the porch stairs.

"First of all, the note and the berries, did you figure that out?" Connie kept an eye on the darkening horizon, a militant gaze for any unusual activity. If anything, the choir had gotten louder. It sounded as if they were singing *Amazing Grace.*

"I think so. It's done."

"Then you know he has an allergy to them." Connie paused. "Like your father. Matthew is in better shape but the reaction should be just as severe."

"And let me guess," Kathleen said, putting the pieces together. "He's having the pie with his dinner tonight. And, as you are so inappropriately trying to say, he's having his dinner with me."

Connie took a deep breath, then let it out. "That wasn't the plan, but that's what's happening. Honey, I never intended for you to be the girl. But he forced me to choose."

"Choose?"

"Between you and your sister. And so I had to pick you. Mary is still recovering from the Good Walk. She's weak–" Connie started crying. The whole mess had been her fault. What in God's name had she subjected her beloved daughters to? Why was she still? "I'm so sorry." It wasn't much of an answer.

Kathleen didn't say anything. There was plenty for both of them to cry about. Plenty. The whole thing had twisted *beyond the beyondo*, as her dad would've put it. It felt odd thinking of him as she was looking at her mother. It felt odd, period. Kathleen put an arm around Connie's shoulder, and they sat on the stoop like that for a while.

"How is the little meatball?" Kathleen inquired, referring to Mary by her childhood nickname. She now knew at least part of the answer and it was not good. If her sister had been on the Good Walk, that meant she'd been pregnant, miscarried, and punished. Kathleen closed her eyes. *Pregnant.* Yet another thing her mother didn't know.

Connie looked up. She'd been playing with her ring finger again. "Mary will be all right this time," she said. "I think one of the men here is looking out for her." She meant Frederick.

"*Here?*" Kathleen said, standing. "You've got to be kidding." She went into the apartment to fetch a tissue for her mother. She cringed when she saw the Vaseline jar beside her bed.

Graciously, Connie took the napkin and wiped her eyes. She gazed upon her daughter. A long time had gone by.

"I must admit, you're looking well," she said, more cheerfully. "Must be the gardening. You know, when I had that detail it did wonders for–"

"I'm pregnant, Mom."

Now it was Connie's turn to be dumbfounded. The hits just keep on coming, she thought, not knowing what else to think. Or say. Her daughter's announcement would be considered bittersweet even outside of Congress. And when you considered all the mitigating circumstances–well she couldn't.

"It's his," Kathleen told her mother unnecessarily. "Think I should tell him the good news over dinner?" This time she was being sarcastic. She got up and went back inside to her closet to start getting ready. What else could she do? Yes, telling Matthew would get her out of tonight's date. But it would also serve as an admission of per-jury. Her latest 'period' had been documented.

"Nonsense," Connie replied. She followed her daughter in the room, whispering. "You don't have to go through with this. I'll report to Matthew that you're pregnant and he'll–"

"Take Mary instead," said Kathleen, stomping on her mother's thought, killing it forever. "Mom, it doesn't really matter. I was going to have to sleep with him again soon anyway. Look at it this way, at least I won't *get pregnant*." She threw a couple outfits on the bed. "Which one?"

Connie shook her head in disgust. That question again. Helping her daughter pick an outfit to wear on a date with the father of her baby should have been a wonderful moment between them, not a horrifying travesty.

Ignoring the dresses, Connie looked at her watch. "The cars are coming for us at a quarter to six."

"Don't worry. I'll be fine." She gave her mom a final hug. "You better go." When Connie left, she decided on the black outfit.

More funereal, she thought.

The Snake

Before the rattlesnake found them...
They'd had a little tequila. The stars were brilliant. Nora located every constellation and pointed them out. He sung her Lyle Lovett songs. All before drifting into the endless, beautiful night, their bodies intertwined, grounded again, floating into endless, beautiful, night. Sleeping...

...when the rattlesnake found them.

The reptile didn't mean any harm. She had only ventured out of her lair to shed. Upon returning, she discovered another of her kind inside. The interloping serpent, facing out, had all the advantage. Her only recourse was to find a new home.

The rattler slithered into blackness, wondering just how it was that so many snakes had come to be. She would have settled for an outcropping of rock, an abandoned, even occupied, prairie dog hole. The snake only required a few hours rest before new skin hardened and she could begin the routine search for a morning meal.

She found a doublewide sleeping bag. The inviting fissure drew her in. Their body heat meant nothing. If anything, it was bothersome to the creature. They seemed like prey but their smell was different. This was not a rodent or reptile.

Nora was dreaming, of all things, about smoking cigarettes with her best friend in the girl's lavatory at Percy High School. Security was making the rounds and she had to duck into a stall to avoid detection. Unfortunately, the maneuver also caused her to shift in the bag and she landed on top of the rattlesnake.

The reptile retaliated, sinking its venom-filled fangs into the intruder's lower back.

Nora yelped upon waking. She screamed even louder when she heard the hissing and determined what was happening to her.

"What! What! What!" blurted Raphael.

The snake answered before his girlfriend could with another strike, three quick hits, into Raphael's arm and torso. Well beyond startled, the rattler thrashed inside the sleeping bag, fangs bared and spewing venom. She bit into nylon, into arms and legs, whatever was in her way.

Raphael's trachea swelled, rendering him unable to breathe.

Nora miscarried and died, convulsing, trapped under her lover's dead body, an angry rattlesnake tearing into her midsection.

And then it was over.

Dazed, the reptile slipped out of the bag. Missing one of its fang teeth, she bolted, unaware, really, of what just had transpired, only that she would have to go without food for a while.

Whatever forces brought them together, broke them apart, and brought them back, was done.

A poisonous snake had taken them out of Eden.

Save for vultures, no one would ever discover their bodies, much less the irony of their bittersweet, cut-short lives.

Their vehicles went unclaimed as well, leaving two more rusted hulks in the desert, atop the mounting fossil record of the 21st century and the Last Generation.

During periods of regret, individuals can become obsessed with positive qualities perceived in others.

Sympathetic participation in the experience(s) of another person is the coping stage known as...

Idealization

After 120 days, it was called an "Event Pregnancy." If at all possible, the expectant mother was admitted into a special government facility for the event's duration, all expenses covered for all cases. That was the policy and it was a popular one. Four months, in. Period. The eyes of the world watched.

Being in her fifth month, Shawano Rollins was an exemplary candidate for such admission, and Mrs. Harris knew it. The problem was Shawano did not want to be admitted into a special government facility. She'd been incarcerated before. She loathed it and saw no difference here. Of course, Mrs. Harris said her fears were "nonsensical." Mrs. Harris had proxy over her on account of Shawano's volatile legal and medical history. Lots of mess there, Shawano supposed. But she still didn't want to go to any facility, hospital, or whatever it was. She envisioned the long, strange-smelling hallways patrolled by uniformed, unfriendly men pushing horrible machines that took blood and other bodily fluids. No, Shawano wanted no part of any more hospitals.

"No! No! No! No!" Cornrows swaying as she rocked, Shawano resembled a bobbing dashboard figurine.

"Listen to me, Shawano," Mrs. Harris said, trying to pacify the disturbed woman. "You are–"

"No! No!"

"You're five months pregnant, girl!" she yelled, cutting her off. "That's a goddamn miracle!"

Stunned, Shawano quieted. Mrs. Harris got mad, but she had never raised her voice. Not to her. Not to anyone.

"Mrs. Rollins," continued Mrs. Harris, making an effort to compose herself, "you should be excited. You're one of the lucky ones. You could be the one. You hear me? The one." Harris would have loved being pregnant. "Five months." She kept repeating.

Having made her point, Shawano kept mum. She liked Mrs. Harris well enough, but not always her words. If only the social worker would let up. The visit would be a lot more fun.

Exasperated, Mrs. Harris sat, regarding her client. Sometimes it was hard to tell if she even understood the English language. Shawano was slow but not clinically slow. Which was unfortunate, because if she were, Harris could and would have mandated hospitalization a month ago. It only took a phone call. The law was explicit. In the second trimester, a woman of unsound mind didn't have a choice. She was put in the hospital. Too many others depended on her. Society's need far outweighed her rights as an individual. Still, it all came down to mental competency. Was Shawano Rollins competent?

"I just don't want to be put away, Mrs. Harris," Shawano said, after sharing a long piece of quiet. "I'm sorry if it don't agree with you."

"Agree with me?" Incredulous, the social worker took off her glasses and looked hard into the other woman's eyes. "Since when do you care what agrees with me?"

"I don't know," answered Shawano. "I reckon when you started caring about me." She played with her fake pearls around her neck, sliding them up and down on the strand.

"Girlfriend," Mrs. Harris sighed, "you'd be treated like a queen."

"I'm not the brightest light on the Christmas tree, Mrs. Harris. But then you already knew that." Shawano tittered. She tapped the slight protrusion in her belly. "Hell, I don't even know who the daddy is." She thought harder. "But the fact of the matter is, locking me up won't change neither of those things."

No, it won't.

Mrs. Harris closed her eyes, and this time she saw Shawano Rollins as well as the truth. Here was not an opportunity to save the world, or even a shot at personal redemption. Here was a messed-up simpleton who'd no business getting pregnant, let alone having a child. And here was a social worker trying to save herself instead of a client.

Even tearful, she kept her eyes closed. Did she not want to be seen weeping, or just seen? "Forgive me, Shawano... can you?"

Shawano rocked back and forth, giggling, then whispered, "Big girls don't cry. Big girls don't cry. Big girls—"

"Okay, then," Mrs. Harris said. "Enough." She got up, straightened her suit, and headed for the door. "See you next week?"

"If you say so," mumbled Shawano, no longer paying attention to the social worker. She began picking at a cuticle on her thumb. "Look, Mrs. Harris. Blood."

"I see," she said, easing back the metal door so as not to slam it. "But at least you're not in any pain."

Jack in a Box

Everybody had the same idea—leave—and thus they exited their rooms early… and simultaneously. They convened in the parking lot, not making eye contact, mumbling "Hey" and "What's up?" Hung over more from weirdness than beer, all four were still sorting out what to make of this tiny town whose populace coalesced over home movies. It had gone from a delightful evening in Small Town, USA, to something more akin to an acid trip at Small World in Disneyland. Creepy and surreal, it had been like Muriel's haunted carnival or a Patricia Highsmith story. "The Twilight Zone."

Not pleasant.

Opening the trunk to load his bags, Jack saw the empty cans of film and realized he was out. How much had he shot last night at the theater? Reaching for an unopened cartridge, he paused. The whole movie thing seemed unnecessary.

Irrelevant.

Jack heaved his duffel bag into the trunk. It wasn't the futility of making his film that bothered him. Hell, every human endeavor had become futile. Writing books. Achieving world peace. Losing weight.

It was something else.

He put his sister's bag in the car next to his, and then it hit him. Jack understood why he felt so profoundly disinterested. He'd been trumped, plain and simple. Jack's concept was never about making a documentary. He was making art, a statement. The thing was, everything he hoped to accomplish had already been done. The Last Generation had its film for the ages. He saw it last night.

Fucking home movies.

Cinema verité had become just that–truthful film. Conceptually, Jack's movie was at best *B-roll Futurescape.*

He slammed the trunk. His anger was palpable, yet unfocused. For now, he just wanted to hit the road.

M & M

Muriel caught her reflection in the motel's flimsy bathroom mirror, thought she looked, well, wrong. Not bad, mind you. Not ugly. Just not right. Massaging the flesh around her nose and eyes, feeling the wrinkles she now saw, anxiety beset her. The person she looked at seemed, in some ways, unfamiliar to Muriel, like a cousin or a woman wearing the same outfit.

She sat on the toilet, head in hands. Sighed.

One of the home movies last night featured a trio of teen-aged girls dressing up for a Halloween party. They all wore the same outfit. Black tights. Cute little ears. Tail.

Cats.

Naughty and cute.

Cat women.

Muriel didn't have a real boyfriend. She hadn't ever really. Since Father died, her brother was the only man in her life. Jack never brought the subject up. But then, she never questioned his social life either. They had each other, but what kind of relationship was that?

And what if he did ask questions, certain questions? Would she have answered them honestly anyway? Did she even know how?

Honestly?

The fact was the girls in last night's film had aroused her. There.

And so did Maura. That small scar over her left eye, the pine-colored hair uncut by professionals and that nasty leather jacket smelling dangerously of gasoline and cigarettes. "Hmmm," Muriel sighed, eyes closed, her imagination riding where it feared to go.

It was a terrain she'd only glimpsed on websites and in magazines, peeked at during private moments.

At those times she'd touched herself.

And knew.

"Whoa!" exclaimed Maura, about as politely as one can say a thing like that, not sure if Muriel was sick or what. "Jack asked me to see how you were doing... um, how are you doing?" Maura couldn't help but notice she was sitting on the toilet, not using the toilet, and moaning. This was the second time she'd walked in on her. "We've got to stop meeting like this, kid."

Speechless, Muriel crossed her legs, moved the hair out of her face. She looked up at the intruder.

More vulnerable than ever, thought Maura. She felt the need to protect her from—from what?

"I'm gay," Muriel said, looking right at her. "Nobody knows."

"How about that?" Maura replied. If anything, she was more surprised by the time and place of the confession rather than the confession itself.

"Do I look... gay?" Muriel fought the urge to check in the mirror. The bathroom seemed warm, like if someone were taking a shower. She felt beads of sweat forming on her upper lip.

"Well, you hang out so much with your brother," answered Maura, though she did not want the comment to come across as mean-spirited. "I figured one of you was."

Muriel laughed, her funk already lifting. She wondered how many other people she'd encountered over the years felt the same way. But then again, Muriel thought, it's not like she met a ton of people.

Maura resumed. "But Jack ain't the type. Too sloppy, know what I mean? Gay men like to cut their hair once in a while, tuck in their shirts." Having this conversation, Maura began feeling a bit warm herself.

"What makes you the expert?" Muriel was genuinely curious. She'd wanted to have this kind of talk for the longest time. Even if it was in a motel bathroom with some biker chick. Thinking of it, especially if it was. She smiled, feeling sexy and empowered, which came first she had no way of knowing. *Both.*

"I go two ways," Maura admitted, sensing the other woman's flirtatious tone and responding accordingly.

Muriel's eyes widened. She said nothing.

"It's not uncommon," continued Maura. "There was this guy in our club who went gay overnight. Know what? Nobody gave a shit." She reached in her jacket for a smoke but didn't light it on account of the room being so small.

"Cool." Muriel intoned, engrossed in the conversation. In Maura. Something about the way her dirty blond hair spilled over that black leather shoulder. The way she talked. The way she walked.

"Well," said Maura, reflecting. "I guess being queer just isn't something you'd associate with a biker gang. For a guy, anyway. Wink-wink." She leaned on the sink. "Once upon a time a member of The Last would've gotten his ass kicked good for coming out. Especially choosing to, going pseudo."

"How would you know he wasn't gay all along?" Muriel played with a long tendril of her hair, wrapping it around her pinky finger.

"You mean like you?" Maura said. It was barely a question.

"How do you know I'm not, um, just…"

"Just what, curious? Looking for a little excitement to keep your mind off the road or the end of the world? Look sweetie," she said, "people that go pseudo, they want to be gay. They like the idea of it. I catch you crying in the bathroom, I get the impression you don't."

"I wasn't crying," said Muriel, looking at her feet. The tiniest little red ant she ever saw scurried along a dirty groove between the beige floor tiles. It was hopelessly lost, or, at least, so it seemed.

"I wasn't kidding," said Maura, touching the side of Muriel's face. The move caused her to jump, then blush.

"About what?"

"I like women. I like you, Muriel."

Maura had never used her name before in conversation. Or more likely, Muriel had just never heard it said before in that context.

She got up and—and Maura kissed her hard, pushing into Muriel's mouth, fishing for her tongue and catching it. When they pulled apart, a glistening strand of saliva bridged between their open mouths.

"Okay," drawled Maura, "the world can just go away because I'm done!"

"But I'm not," said Muriel breathlessly, leaning in for another kiss.

Reluctantly, the two women separated. It was getting hot. They were supposed to be making tracks, not making out.

"Ever ride on a bike, kid?"

"Nope."

"First time for everything, right?"

"Apparently," Muriel answered.

Maura licked her lips, turned, and walked out of the bathroom.

Muriel followed, a cat having tasted cream.

Indian Head Rub

Seth assumed that Muriel was having female trouble and Maura had merely been helping her out. He asked Jack if he "minded minding the fort" and detoured to a bar. Even though early, he fancied a beer and perhaps a shot of something stronger. Surely Husker Heaven could provide, its neon sign beckoning from across the street, promising refreshment. Last night's movie odyssey agitated Seth even more than it had the others. It reminded him of why he needed the road so much and a good belt from time to time. People freaked him out. Once again, he acknowledged an up side to the world's diminishing population.

Husker Heaven was as much a shrine to the University of Nebraska's storied football team as it was a saloon. If one didn't know the Big Red Machine upon entering Husker Heaven, it wouldn't take long getting acquainted. Its walls were painted a violent shade of crimson and covered by an endless array of Cornhusker memorabilia. Faded photographs of corn-fed, massive athletes adorned each nook, while game schedules and programs occupied every cranny. Nebraska never had a professional sports team. Subsequently, the Cornhuskers were the only game in town or had been. EFS shut them down like no competitor ever could and in doing so, wiped out spectator sports in this state forever. And, as it happened, years earlier than it had in other states where folks clung to their pro teams for as long as they could.

Which explained why Husker Heaven felt more like a museum than a bar. Maybe mausoleum was the better word, or shrine. It being early, the place was nearly empty, adding to its maudlin feel. An old craggy-faced man with long black and gray hair sat on the farthest stool nursing a beer. Seth looked behind him and everywhere for the bartender.

"He ain't here," the old man said, without looking up or turning around.

"Can I get a beer then?" asked Seth, seeing his.

"You're part Sioux. You should be able to manage."

Seth approached the elder to stand before him. "How did you know that?"

"I am too," the old Indian replied, turning around and facing Seth.

They stared at each other not unlike two dogs of the same breed would upon meeting. Sizing each other up, seeing themselves in the other.

"I know it's early for a drink," said Seth. "But–"

"But your spirit is acting up and you need something to calm it down," he nodded. "I know how that goes." He lifted the short beer glass to his lips and took a sip. "I know."

And so Seth made his way around the bar and helped himself. He poured Budweiser, knowing somehow that that was what the old man was drinking as well. He took a long pull from his glass and then topped it off again. He returned and sat on a stool next to the man.

"My name is Seth Little. What's yours?"

"Marvin White. Um, sorry, it's not more Indian."

"No problem." Seth laughed. Then, shifting gears, he said, "I guess it's sort of a bummer. Two Indians drinking this time of the day." He pulled out his cigarettes, offering one to the old man.

He declined. "What is it with you and the time?" the man asked. "Something is troubling you. You don't know what it is. Beer feels good. These things are true at any time."

"Yeah, I suppose, but still... you know the stereotype." He took a big swallow, emphasizing his point.

"I know that you are too young to keep your spirit down. You should release it, brother. Let it take over and show you."

"Show me what?" asked Seth.

"You went to the movie theater last night, didn't you?"

"Again I ask, how did you know?"

"Maybe it's magic," the Indian chuckled. "Maybe the stereotypes are true."

"Seriously." Seth was confused and taken aback. "Do you mind telling me what is going on here?"

"We are having a chat, Seth... among friends. Among Sioux."

Seth shook his head. He had no idea what they were having, but he was having another drink. "Can I get you one?" he asked, wagging his empty beer glass.

"I told you. Stop pushing your spirit down. Let it out, brother." Marvin put his fist down hard, making the point. "Those movies are unsettling. I know. I have seen them. They make you see the world through the white man's eyes. A world that begins and ends with people. It is... disconcerting."

Halfway around the bar Seth stopped. "Okay, old man. So what are you trying to say? I mean, you know stuff about me, other shit, I'll give you that. But hey, you're sitting here drinking too." At the tap he drew another beer. *Fuck it.*

"I am not you, Seth Little," he said. "My spirit is not trying to get out. I am not screaming inside. I am not blind. You need to see better, Mr. Little."

"Okay then, how?" He wasn't sure what he was supposed to 'see better,' but there was something about the old Indian's tone that Seth couldn't ignore. Something about the whole situation.

"You need to unburden the spirit, Mr. Little. Find your bloodline and what connects you with the Sioux."

Seth blew a series of smoke rings over his head. "Heap big smoke rings, eh chief?"

You're funny but not so happy," said Marvin. "Ever wonder why?" Without waiting for Seth to answer: "Perhaps the old movies, all those laughing, smiling children, were bitter reminders of your own deep sadness."

Seth stared at the Indian, almost trying to see inside him. The guy knew things, he'd give him that. "This ... inner spirit?"

The Indian smiled. Sipped his beer.

"How do I—"

"Find it?"

"Yes, find it," repeated Seth quietly.

"First," Marvin said, "you must eliminate all the distractions from your life and from inside. This can take time. It is like pulling bark off a live tree. Eventually you come to what is pure and unfettered. Piece by piece, you return yourself to yourself and achieve the basic architecture of your ancestry and soul, the one of your father's father's father and the creator of him too. Go back, Seth Little. Go back to the first ring on the tree. Become ancient. Become new." With a shaking hand, the old Indian lifted his beer glass to his mouth.

"Or," he said. "You can take a few of these." He placed what appeared to be three small pieces of cat dung onto the worn wooden surface of the bar.

Seth picked up one of the clove-like objects. At first, he did not recognize it, but being a member of one of the largest motorcycle clubs in the world, he also knew that it wasn't a clove or a cat dropping either.

Marvin explained. "They are peyote buds, Seth Little. They will make you sick. But they will make you better. Much better," he said.

Peyote was a natural hallucinogen like mushrooms and mescaline. Derived from the pre-flowering tips of a small desert cactus, it was also very potent and quite rare, at least where Seth came from. But he'd heard the stories. He'd even seen a show on *Cooler Heads* about it. Certain Western Indian tribes used the stuff as part of their most sacred, bizarre rituals. And since peyote was considered part of their religion, the authorities couldn't bust any of the Indians for using it. Come to think of it, Seth knew plenty about peyote. He'd just never seen any before. *Or taken any.* The idea of doing so turned him on.

"Right now?"

Marvin laughed. "Somehow, I doubt you want to find your inner spirit in a crappy sports bar."

"No argument there." Seth laughed.

"I know you are not from around here," Marvin guessed. "And I can tell you're not staying. So, which way are you going?"

"West. Utah… maybe."

The Indian pondered. "There's a place in Colorado, near Durango. Go there instead. Look up a woman goes by the name of Elke Morningstar. She's Cheyenne and knows the spirit world well. Call upon her, Seth Little."

"Well, what if–"

"The others don't follow you?" he stated, finishing Seth's question. "I don't expect they will. These buds are for you only, Seth Little. It is your journey. Not theirs… Now if you'll excuse me I have to take a leak." And with that the old man rose, shook Seth's hand by the wrist, and headed for the men's room. "Elke Morningstar," he said again, walking away.

"Mr. White!" shouted Seth, causing the man to turn around. Hardly one for long good-byes, he still thought he should say something, if for nothing else, the free goodies. But what?

"I really do have to piss," Marvin prompted.

"Thank you… I guess," Seth mumbled, sheepishly but sincerely. "I really hope you're right, you know?"

"Well, I have been so far," replied Marvin.

Fate, Et Cetera

They get stuck in a closet or what?" whined Jack in Seth's general direction. He didn't really care. He was still sulking over the derailed movie, the fact that they were in a motel parking lot, and so on. He sat on the bumper of his car, smoking a cigarette. A couple of dead butts lay on the cement between his feet.

"Some shit. Who knows?" Seth answered, sidling up to Jack on the fender. He sensed the man was in a funk, but he was preoccupied too. Seth could use the moment and a smoke to collect his thoughts. He still had to tell the group he was leaving, in particular, Maura. They hadn't been intimate in a while, but she was still his partner, if not paramour, with a lot of highway behind them.

Might as well start with Jack. "I'm gonna split."

"Say what?"

"Go. I'm leaving the group. I have to."

"I see," Jack said, not seeing at all. Part of him didn't give two shits. Still, he asked why and where he was going.

Seth considered his run-in with the old Indian and the business last night at the theater. He thought about all of it before answering.

"Believe it or not, Jack, I'm going to find my inner spirit."

"I see," Jack said, still not seeing at all.

"Well, I'm not sure I do," said Maura, towering over them, Muriel by her side. "Mind filling me in?"

"Are you all right?" Jack asked his sister, ignoring Maura. Muriel had been in the can a long time. He worried she had the flu or something.

"Never better," she smiled.

"Last night was weird," offered Seth, gearing up for his big exposition. "But something happened to me just now that was, well, weirder."

"Bit of that going around," Muriel said, amused.

"Bottom line," he continued, "and this is going to sound funny... I have to–"

"He's going to find his true *inner spirit*," blurted Jack, not trying for sarcasm but achieving it nevertheless. Of course, he had no clue as to Seth's actual intentions. He didn't believe he was leaving them. He assumed the man was venting, maybe having relationship problems, that sort of thing.

"Care to elaborate?" Maura demanded. She was hardly furious, especially given her recent behavior, but she was intent on getting an explanation.

"I'm afraid I just can't go to Utah," he said, picking at a worn corner of his leather jacket. "A new wrinkle," he added, inspired by the frayed garment.

"You're not afraid?" asked Maura, though she doubted it. Seth was a lot of things but coward wasn't one of them. If not for her, they would never have second thoughts at all. Still, he had been acting different as of late. Not *bad* different, just not the slovenly drug addict she knew and loved. "Because, you know, we don't have to go to Congress. It's not like–"

"You know damn well that's not it, Maura," Seth said, cutting her off. "I don't know if inner spirit is the right phrase," he said, shooting Jack a nasty look, "but I do need to find something, and I need to look for it alone."

Even though she was curious, Maura elected not to ask Seth what the mysterious 'it' was. He'd had a change of heart, simple as that. About her. About him. About the journey. All of the above. When it was all said and done, he was entitled. She looked at Muriel. Had not it been the same with her? And while she was at it what about yours truly?

"We can always hook up later, back in Madison. Anywhere, really," bargained Seth, holding up a map to illustrate his point. He wasn't so sure though, wondering if their history together would mean anything in his future.

The group shared a long silence. The mission was at an impasse. They all sensed it.

"Oh, hell," said Maura, forcing a grin. "I'm taking a detour as well." She smiled at Muriel. "We both are."

"What the hell is going on?" exhorted Jack. Okay, so he misjudged Seth. He could deal with that. *But his sister?* This was a curve ball. He stood up, sat back down. What about his fucking news?

"Can you finish the trip by yourself?" asked Muriel. "Find Dan's wife and daughters, keep filming? After all," she paused, "the show must go on."

The show must go on. "Easy for you to say," sighed Jack. "For one thing, there's only the one car. For another–"

"The car's not an issue. I'm riding with Maura," stated Muriel with noticeable enthusiasm. She strode over to Maura's motorcycle and stroked its leather saddle. "You can have the car."

"Huh?" questioned Jack, still in the dark.

Muriel found Maura's hand and squeezed it. She had no interest in hurting her brother, loving him profoundly. But her coming out had been long overdue. No way she was going to cop out, settling for business as usual. Life was too short. Especially now.

As for Seth, he had ears and eyes. He knew a few things about Maura, kinky things. He'd picked up on the subtext. Maura had herself a girlfriend. It wasn't the strangest thing that had happened. Par for the course, actually.

"So, everybody's doing their own thing?" Jack asked the whole group. "Is that the plan?"

"Oh, Jack," Muriel barked, feeling like one of those home-wrecking antagonists from a soap opera. "It's not like that. It's not part of any sort of... *plan*. It's just something that happened." She looked at Maura, Seth, then back at her brother. The others all seemed to be in agreement with her little summation. None of them presented tangible resistance to it anyway.

Thus, Jack accepted his sister's meager explanation. Why not? He'd just abandoned his beloved camera. Seth's departure was imminent. So what if his sister was barreling out of the closet on a motorbike?

Another tricky day, right? Sand through the hourglass.

"Fate, fuck it, et cetera," Jack said, employing an old saying belonging to his father. Or was it Dan's? "I'll just do this myself then. We're all going to be alone some day. I might as well get used to it." Resigned in stature, his words came out calmly and without prejudice. "It's all about accepting our fate, isn't it?"

No one answered. No one felt like they had to. Muriel gave Jack a hug. Maura followed suit, giving Seth a kiss as well.

"I guess," Jack said, after they all let go of one another, "that this is what 'making the best of it' means."

"And we will," replied Muriel, kicking the gravel beneath her feet. She was happy and sad at the same time, like they all were, only her skew was better.

"Well, here's to making the best of it, then," chimed Maura, injecting a note of frivolity, or at least trying to. She brought a shiny, silver flask to her mouth, drank, then offered the bourbon to whomever.

"Fate, fuck it, et cetera!" said Jack again, taking the flask, "and everything else."

After loss, a period of fearfulness may exist. There is a tendency to remain aloof, particularly from those who serve as reminders.

This anxiety-born symptom is known as...

Avoidance

G iven his position, given the history of his position, at fifty-two, one might say the pope was spry. Yet Michael felt ancient. Weary. Inept. He could not reconcile his faith with what was taking place. Embryo Fatality Syndrome was not the Apocalypse, nor was it Armageddon. The scriptures did not foretell it. In all that was known, even the devil had never been so thorough.

Michael was bereft of options. Yet his constituency, nay, his flock, awaited a message from him, their pope. One he did not have.

He paced over carpeting a thousand years old. The axioms were not cutting it anymore. The clichés of his faith were not cutting it. Ridding the world of all its children had no precedent. Even the first-born sons of Egypt had been taken for a reason. For the many who were eliminated, countless more had been spared. Once again, God had shown his people the way. God had been merciful.

Where was God's mercy during this epic blasphemy? Despite all mutterings to the contrary, EFS could only be construed as heinous, a scourge without moral or rationale. Abortion was a crime against God. What was this?

Had we truly sinned to that point where even the Lord no longer forgave us? Or worse yet, were we being punished? And if so, for what, for which sin? What did or didn't we do? Pope Michael needed an explanation. A sign. Something.

None was forthcoming. The pope treaded back and forth, not knowing what to do. For once, Michael wished he were a boy again, back home in Tuscany chasing jack rabbits in the vineyards or catching butterflies. He rifled through his notes, rereading the words he wrote, searching for just the right ones among the uninspired combinations. Mostly, he prayed.

"Your Excellency?" the vicar beckoned, intimidated beyond measure. He'd been ordered to check on His Excellency by Bishop Paulson, leaving him no choice but to venture into the pope's chambers. In the Vatican, as in a game of chess, bishop always takes pawn. With utmost trepidation, he did what he was told. "Your Excellency?" he beseeched again. "I beg your pardon, but are you all right?"

"No, my son, I am not," answered the pope. He gazed upon the prelate, seeing a man who was maybe ten years younger than he was, if that. Michael put his papers down. "I am afraid that... I am afraid."

Not the answer the priest was looking for. He assumed the pope was fearless. Nor did he think they were supposed to confide in lowly servants. Don't be silly, he wanted to say. For obvious reasons he did not. His befuddled expression spoke volumes.

"Afraid," continued the pope. "As in frightened. Scared. In America, I believe they call it chicken." Pope Michael considered the vicar, recognizing him from this or that function. He was a good man among good men. "Alfredo, isn't it?"

"Yes, sir." Alfredo swooned, delighted the Pope knew his name. Still, he had to show restraint. Something was wrong with the Pontiff. "What can I do?" he asked, eyes averted. "Just tell me and it will be done."

Bittersweet, Michael smiled. As always, he appreciated the gratitude, but it also saddened him. Unconditional servitude never set well, but now it almost seemed blasphemous, like pagan worship, idolatry.

"Please," Michael said. "I am not worthy of this admiration."

"But Your Excellency–" Alfredo put his hands to his ears. He could not listen to such things. The pope was beatific, incapable of failings of any kind.

"I'm of course flattered, Alfredo." Michael approached his sovereign, placed a hand upon his shoulder. "But do stop. I must insist."

"No. As our revered conduit to the Lord Jesus Christ, you are most dignified and holy." Alfredo knelt before his pope, crossing himself.

Michael parted the huge hanging tapestry in front of the huge window. Sunlight streamed in from the crack. He stepped back, motioning the prelate to come forward. "Alfredo, would you mind opening these doors?"

Alfredo stepped into the light, reaching for the curtains with a shaking hand. He knew what was behind them, outside, below and waiting.

"Do it," the pope said, sensing the other's trepidation. "Godspeed."

Alfredo gripped the glass door's ornate lever, then froze.

"Is there a problem, Alfredo?" questioned the pope.

"I can't do it your Excellency." Alfredo was having trouble maintaining his composure. "I'm afraid."

"Hmmm," replied the pope. "Now you know how I feel." Michael sat down on an elaborately rendered 17th-century chaise. "Come sit by me." He patted the spot next to him. On it wolves were tearing open the stomach of a writhing hog.

"But–" Though he wanted to, Alfredo was not about to argue with the Pope. He sat down beside the great man.

Relative silence, save for the clamoring outside.

"I do not know what to tell the people anymore," the pope said wearily.

And yet, a half-million of them waited in the courtyard below.

Hors d'oeuvres

Well, well, well, if it isn't my best girl!" exclaimed Matthew upon receiving her at his door. "Don't we look divine?"

"Good evening, Matthew." Kathleen gave him ample time to appreciate her still-comely features. She wore a lavender gown, cinched at the waist. Her hair was pulled back into a tight bun, which Matthew took pleasure untying, and on her face, she had a fair amount of make-up, certainly more than usual. With her get-up, Kathleen looked like female crew on the U.S.S. Enterprise, one of Captain Kirk's dolled-up lieutenants. And in a way she was. "How are you?" she said, catching a chill on the step.

"Better now," Matthew replied, moistening his lips. "Won't you come in?" He stepped aside, allowing her to enter.

Nothing had changed in the yellow room except the flowers. Textured by numerous brushings of oil-based, glossy paint, the walls shone brilliantly in the romantic light of myriad candles, reminding Kathleen of sunflowers. Warm in tone, blissfully muted, the room was designed for lovemaking.

"Would you like some champagne?" Matthew delighted in Kathleen's appearance and the obvious attention she'd put into it.

As of late, some of the girls had been slacking in that department. This was more like it.

She nodded.

Humming, he uncorked the bottle. "Tonight we are having wall-eyed pike with new potatoes and French beans. Something you adore if I remember correctly."

"You do," she said. Indeed, pan-fried walleye was among her favorite things, a holdover from years of summering in Northern Wisconsin. Dad caught 'em. Mom cooked 'em. She ate 'em. If only they could see their little girl now.

"Splendid," Matthew said, smiling. "It is so good to see you again. So good. As your mother aptly pointed out to me earlier, the garden has done wonders for your complexion and disposition." He touched her cheek, letting his manicured nails play across it. "Lovely. Just lovely."

She sighed, hoping it came out as wanting. "Hmmm," she added.

Matthew poured the champagne. The White Star came right to the lip of each Tiffany tulip, breaking into bubbles, just like a TV commercial. He handed her a flute.

"To a lovely evening," he toasted, raising his glass to hers.

"And to the next child," she retorted, feigning pleasure and selling sincerity. The charade was difficult but not impossible. She remembered all too well when it had been sincere. Alas, it wasn't that long ago.

They drank, tapped their glasses, and drank some more.

Matthew put down his flute and reached across the table, placing his hand over hers. "What say we forgo dinner?" He narrowed his well-practiced bedroom eyes, replicating the look from his own television commercial.

Okay, now what? He was usually a stickler for romantic protocol, first dinner then sex, and Kathleen was somewhat surprised by his sudden breach. And taken aback. For the plan to work, they needed to eat before the clothes came off. Hopefully, instead.

"But I'm hungry," she pleaded. And then, to avoid coming across as disinterested, she added, "I promise to leave plenty of room for dessert." She flashed her own bedroom eyes.

Matthew laughed. And why shouldn't he? This was a game worth playing, like it should be. Like it used to be before some of the girls started questioning things, losing their zeal.

"We are having tart for dessert," whispered Matthew, playfully responding to the come-on.

"Two of them," Kathleen replied, not skipping a beat. She chuckled throatily, but not too deeply. Matthew could get angry if he lost control. The sex was a given, therefore it was, in a sense, less critical than the foreplay. This was still a mission they were both on. Before Casanova, Matthew embraced the role of Messiah. One had better play along. Besides, she needed him hungry not horny. She was on a mission too.

Thankfully for Kathleen, a bell sounded from the other room indicating that dinner was being served.

"Saved by the bell," she joked.

Tripping

As per Elke Morningstar's instruction, Seth ingested a second peyote bud only after throwing up from the first. His insides purged, he was an empty vessel ready for replenishment. Unimpeded by foodstuffs, the hallucinogen was capable of opening the most steadfast door, toppling the thickest wall. Under its influence, psychological borders became porous, spiritual traffic flowed in and out. Binge and purge. Body and soul. Elke said it could go both ways and it often did.

"Rid yourself of all distractions. Peel away the bark." Morningstar had seconded the Indian's words. Unlike conventional therapies where the source of pain was key, here one went further back.

To that place... to that place... before one went wrong. That, that, that... Like the tapping of a drum. He was thinking out loud now. That place he was at before he went wrong.

The name of the place is *I like it like that.*

Seth watched smoke rising from the fire, curling and wispy, silver tendrils tickling the night. A piece of bark ignited, sizzling as it peeled from the mother log. Bubbling and lunar-like. Macro-apparent. And so it was that Seth's trip began with a mesmerizing bonfire and a Cheyenne woman named Morningstar.

Who, *good lord*, was now gone.

Which meant he was alone in these dark woods. What fierce creatures lurked in the pitch, just beyond the glowing, waning fire? Mountain lions, tigers, and bears? Oh my! Oh, shit.

"Where are you, Elke?" He either said it or thought it. Sounds confounded him. The fire crackled obscenely. Shooting stars seemed to explode over his head like fireworks at a carnival.

A carnival of lost souls.

Where had he heard that before and why was he thinking it now? Sight and sound had become one. All five senses blended. He could touch sound and feel smell. Seth tasted fire and remembered a barbecue. His lips stung from sauce his daddy made. Dad flipped meat over fire. Get Mother, get plates, and get the lemonade out of the fridge because that sauce was hot, hot, HOT!

The stars fell like snow. It was snowing stars. Seth hugged himself, touching fingertips around his back. How could he accomplish such a feat? But he could! He was!

A bear licked Seth across the face. The slurp was tremendous. Bear tremendous! Then the great beast disappeared into the surrounding tall pine trees bending in the wind. Temperature ceased to matter. Wind was just space moving. His clothes moved upon him like molting snakeskin.

"What do you see, Seth? What do you see?"

Morningstar. But where was she? He looked up. *Up?*

"Looking for something?"

"I... I don't want to be alone." Again, he wasn't sure if he was speaking the words or thinking them. Grabbing his ankles, he pulled his legs inward as hard as he could. The strain on his body alarmed, yet also comforted him. He must have been really doing something. Muscles strained that Seth only imagined possessing, like the kind one saw in comic books, cavorting beneath his loose skin like rodents trapped under a tarp. Electric eels pulsated through his arms and legs.

More than living and breathing, Seth felt inhabited by his alive-ness. His body was truly electric, a matrix of conduits, plugged in, and receiving.

The flames crackled and roared. Were they being fed?

From beyond, he heard a rustle and sensed a presence. Footfalls in the darkness. Movement. Seth felt someone's soles crunching upon the gravel and sand. He discerned every pebble being pushed into the ground, back from whence they must have come millions of years ago.

But he wasn't frightened anymore. Not Seth Little, the mighty Sioux.

"Come out, come out, wherever you are," he did or didn't say.

Elke emerged from the fire, or so it appeared, unscathed. The flames were caressing, pliant, and lukewarm. Her long black hair spilled back, framing an angular face darkened from sun, illuminated by the fire. Elke's white blouse coolly shimmered like the moon. It was as if she were surrounded by clouds, a collar of mist.

"One little, two little, three little Indians…" the woman sang, laughing at the baby-like O's Seth made with his mouth. "Four little, five little…"

"El… ke," Seth spoke in slow motion, transfixed, stoned. His smile was a broad fissure, saliva dribbling from its corners like lava.

"Six little In-di-ans," sang Elke, grinning as well.

She took Seth's chin in hand, stroked it, rubbing the growth of beard.

". . . Eight little Indians…"

Seth felt, even heard, each follicle moving under her touch, so pronounced. He flashed on an image from his youth, a television commercial for a shaving razor. The man's beard bent and broke one hair at a time. Bink, bink, bink.

"Hi, Seth," whispered Elke, the song over. "How are we feeling? I imagine pretty well." She continued to hold a hand to his face.

Her fingers felt like feathers. "Yeah," Seth drawled in response. "I'm very fine. And you?" The talk felt big, like dialogue from an important movie. Scripture. "How are you?" he said again and again, meaning it profoundly. "I really wanna know," he slurred, pointing a finger at and then touching, Elke's forehead, "How... are... you?"

"I'm wonderful, Mr. Little," she cooed. "And thank you for asking." She shuffled closer to him on the bench.

"Are you going to help me find me, I mean, my–" Seth couldn't complete the thought. A rush overtook him from all sides, and he was unable to finish his sentence, let alone remember it. A piece of wood on the fire exploded, the pop echoing through him like a brick of firecrackers.

"No more talking," Elke said, touching his lips with her index finger. She kissed him, putting her tongue inside his mouth, flapping it between his jaws like a moth trapped inside a lantern. Then she found his tongue, sucked on it like a baby would her mother's nipple.

Moans filled the campsite, the fire layering its own hysterical vocal to the chorus, and it all became hot, smoky, and loud, a tumultuous mix of heavy breathing and sighs, the snapping and pulling of straps and belts, crackling embers, sizzle.

Hands grappled goose-pimpled flesh. Bodies intertwined.

The velvety feel of him inside her was like a warm bath below the waist, like a hallucination.

Then she was on top, riding him like a horse. Making whoopee. Elke fell upon his torso, found his penis, and engulfed it.

Feeling wetness and teeth, Seth feared he was being devoured, and so he pushed her away.

The Indian only laughed, climbing back on top.

A long time ago he visited the state fair with his niece. The rides were cheap, colorful, rusted, busted things with names like The Mad Hatter, Screaming Meanie, and Mad Max. Relentless, the Mad Hatter spun and threw him, first into his squealing niece and then the other way into a stringy-haired teenager. Thinking something was going on between them, she put her hand down his pants. The ride just kept going and going and even though his niece was right beside him, he came in the other girl's hand…

…And into Elke Morningstar.

Last Supper

K athleen was surprised at how not nervous she was. She even
had an appetite, enjoying the walleyed pike. Pan-fried as opposed to deep, it had a subtle, greaseless crunch. Only salt,
lemon, and butter accentuated the freshwater fish's robust flavor.
Her mother had prepared it the same way.

Matthew was serving the fish with an Oregon Chardonnay, although Kathleen opted to stick with champagne, which he topped
off for her. There were no servants in the room, only the two of them.
Again, under normal circumstances, lovely.

Kathleen made the best of it, getting by on pretenses and veneer.
She *appeared* to be enjoying herself, hardly the precursor of murder.
If the ploy failed... well, she had done all this before. If not, he died.
Kathleen was prepared for either eventuality. Matthew had manipu-
lated countless lives, ending some, in pursuit of his dubious agenda.

Hopefully, now it was his turn.

Funny how an obsession with creating life could get in the way of
living one, Kathleen thought, pushing bones to the side of her plate.
She recalled times at her family's church, listening to the reverend
sermonize on abortion, how wrong it was, how evil. And yet, when a
group of youngsters from nearby Racine required a venue for their

basketball tournament, that same priest turned his back, keeping the empty gym doors locked, claiming the children a threat of some kind. They were miscreants fraught with trouble, bringing only regret. No, let them go elsewhere. More talk about the unborn, for they are the ones who matter.

Kathleen picked up the charred tail fin–God's potato chips her father called them–and popped the thing into her mouth.

"I'm not a tail man myself," Matthew chuckled, aware of the double entendre.

The couple dined slowly, silent for long periods, then stepping on each other's words, like a date, almost.

And finally the pie came, along with coffee service and choice of cordials. "Time for dessert," Kathleen said, ready. She didn't even wait for him to ask, slicing off a piece. God forbid he wasn't hungry.

Matthew accepted the prodigious slice. He continued to marvel at how well the evening was going, nary a glitch or awkward moment. Just like old times. As it should be, he mused, licking berries off his fork.

"Delicious," said Kathleen, savoring her portion as well. And it was. The inclusion of gooseberries gave the pie an unusual but delightful tartness. Plain strawberry was generally sweeter. Kathleen wondered if Matthew could tell the difference. She eyed him, measuring for odd reactions, but as berries varied in their flavor, so did homemade pies, something hopefully he knew.

"Tarter than usual," said Matthew. Furrowing his eyes, he took a sip of coffee.

Shit.

"But excellent," he added.

Not only did he clean his plate, they even split a third piece.

"You know," Matthew said, pouring them each a glass of port wine. "I have a special feeling about tonight. I really do."

"How so?" *Stall. Draw this thing out.* Berries, do your thing, she prayed.

"Well," he said, easing up from his spot at the table and making his way around to her. "I'm not ignorant. I realize the goals of Congress have not been met. I know there is an ebbing of confidence. I know–" Matthew stopped short. Placing both hands on her shoulder, he began massaging her from behind.

"Don't be silly, Matthew," said Kathleen, trying to avoid a show of alarm. "You're hardly ignorant." *He's making his move.*

"I know this may sound odd," he said, going lower, squeezing biceps, then slowly trailing his fingernails down her forearms. "But," he continued, "if past efforts with another would have been fruitful, then we might not be having this opportunity now." Faster now, up and down her arms, raising goose bumps. "I want it to be you," he said, voice deepening. Leaning over Kathleen, he kissed below her ear, down along the nape, his tongue making ever so slight contact.

"Hmmm," Kathleen murmured, allowing him to continue, faking arousal.

He found her breasts, gently squeezing the nipples, making circles there.

The pie was having no effect beyond that of an aphrodisiac.

Kathleen tilted her head back, receiving his kiss. Was she still faking? Prior to dinner, she'd told herself not to freak out if the plan didn't work. If rape was inevitable you might as well enjoy it. God help me, she thought, if either part of that statement were true. God help me.

Matthew began undoing her dress.

With horror, Kathleen realized she was wet. That's how strange, no, fucked-up, her life had become. "Shall we then?" she asked with anger, shame, and, sadly, desire.

"We shall," he purred, grinning like a cat.

Hung Over and Over

For lack of a better word, Seth awakened. Or better said, he regained consciousness. His hangover was as untraditional as the high had been, the common denominator being misery. Head whirring like an old refrigerator, thoughts rattling like bottles and cans. The pain was audible, for Christ's sake.

Sitting up created a mutiny within his body. The rush of blood to his cranium knocked him back down. He assumed the hallucinogens had devastated his bloodstream, polluting him for years. For a few days he'd been clean. Had been. Last night constituted the mother of all relapses.

Examining himself, Seth discovered he had on a pair of long johns, and, regretfully, not the blue jeans he felt certain he'd been wearing last night. His shirt was still on, thank God, though oddly buttoned, one side hanging lower than the other. Shoes? Gone. And where the hell was his watch? A piece of shit, yes, but he'd never taken it off before. With palpable dread, he tallied other missing items–wallet, keys, watch, pager, money. And–oh, fuck–his motorcycle.

Not that.

But yeah, *that.*

Okay, okay, mustn't panic. First things first. Find your pants. They had to be around here somewhere.

Then he remembered the sex. Given that, his pants could be anywhere.

Seth rose carefully, making sure he had full control of his legs, but he didn't and down he went. As he hit ground, it hit him. He'd been had.

Ripped off.

Seth looked around. He located the remains of the fire, a huge pile of ash and blackened shards. He spotted a rumpled blanket here, a sock there, and one of his shoes. Seth saw his pants draped over some brush. Heaving a sigh, he crawled over to them.

Pinned to one of the pant legs, Seth found a note. He held the piece of paper before his eyes, waiting for clarity. Like ants, the words crawled, and at first only the larger letterhead was readable.

MORNINGSTAR, GUIDE AND CLAIRVOYANT. Centered above were a tee-pee and an unblinking eye not unlike the one used on back of every dollar bill in America. The note read–

Seth,

Help yourself to whatever's in the trailer.
Clothes, food, beer. Mi casa su casa!
I'll take good care of the bike.
Don't take it personal. You were looking for
something and so was I.

PS: I left a twenty in the pocket of your jeans.

- X, Em

Dropping the letter, Seth watched it blow into a cactus and shred. Oh, well. It wasn't like he'd need it for evidence. Doubtful the law had much patience for a strung-out biker missing his wheels.

"Like hell," Seth bitched, struggling to put on his pants. Not out here. The West was wild again, a lawless frontier with every man for himself. And guess what? He was the Indian, literally and in fate. Seth ventured into the spirit world looking for answers and got burned just like his ancestors, robbed of all earthly possessions, to say nothing of his spirit. Welcome to Marlboro Country, Seth Little. Yee-Fucking-Ha!

Uninvited and noisily, last night's drug-induced debacle played out once again in his mind with a final hallucination, an epilogue, and an end. He thought of the film Jack and Muriel were making and of the strange home movies they'd seen in Maxwell. Weird how much everything seemed like part of a movie now. People were merely characters. Places visited were just locations and sets. Maybe it had something to do with the incontrovertible fact that you knew, just knew, how it was all going to end.

Seth had an epiphany of sorts and suddenly getting ripped off didn't piss him off. It was only a scene. His beloved motorcycle was just a prop. He'd survived and he'd gotten the girl. He was still a member of the Last Generation. Still a player.

Gathering what belongings he could find, Seth headed for Elke's beat up Winnebago to hunt down some chow. There wasn't a phone, a working one, anyway, or any viable means of transportation. And the nearest town wasn't anywhere close. Nope, chasing the diabolical Morningstar was out of the question, as was getting help, at least in the interim. But Seth didn't worry about that or her. What he wanted more than anything right now was an omelet, glass of milk, hot shower, and clean shirt. Some real sleep would be nice.

Funny then, he mused, approaching the vehicle. In the end what man really needed was food, clothing, and shelter. Seth opened the screened door, a cobalt blue offsetting the trailer's hot pink.

Hopefully, some other paint was lying about. He might be there for a while. The hermit crab had found a new shell.

Feelings of helplessness, hopelessness, withdrawal, and the loss of pleasure are typically seen in the most common stage in the grief cycle known as...

Depression

The former general was bored, not because there weren't myriad issues and problems but rather because of the one remaining problem. EFS superceded everything. Matters got ugly or remained ugly, such as the Middle East, but outside of a few beleaguered nations, who really gave a damn? Certainly no one on Capital Hill or the Pentagon. Maintaining a ready militia seemed just as ridiculous as an antiquated feud. Why fight, and for what? With plenty of it, land disputes were easily settled. Species going extinct rarely fought, the Middle East, being the one mind-numbing exception.

The national scene offered no new challenges either. Even a blown-up high school wasn't all that horrifying without blown-up high school students. These days, crises were moot points. People didn't get mad, only sadder. Pointing fingers, punishment, retribution, it just didn't make sense in a world without progeny or benefactors.

The unusual foe was indifference. Previous administrations had gravity, dammit. Situations. The president craved relevancy. But to achieve that he needed a cure. Alas, the chief executive knew better. He gazed down upon the White House lawn, wishing he were looking at a little league tournament, an eighth grade class, tourists on Pennsylvania Avenue. As usual, the grounds were empty.

Even the Secret Service lacked presence. Enemies of the State? Boredom and malaise.

President Connor sighed, plodding back to his desk. His big, dumb presidential desk. The same desk Kennedy lingered over during the Bay of Pigs. The same one he, himself, had signed a bill, which eliminated the income tax forever, not that people had been paying it.

He plucked a shiny, silver pen from its brass mount. A blue eagle perched at the crest. It was half as old as the country. God, he envied that pen and the riveting and controversial things it had written. Policy to a dignitary. Orders to a spy. Mash notes to an intern. That pen, the president thought, had had a more interesting career in this office than he ever would.

"Ah, nuts!" He almost hurled it across the room. Instead, ever the good Republican, he placed the instrument back into its holder. There, there, there. Be a good president. Mort's making ribs tonight. And wasn't that a bottle of very rare Kentucky bourbon in the cabinet, a gift from the speaker of the house?

The bottle showed off its amber color nicely. At least, the commander in chief thought, he wasn't a despised leader. Nobody wanted him out of office or was burning his effigy.

He cracked the waxen seal and pulled forth the cork. A pungent sweetness filled the room. The president selected an engraved crystal tumbler from the top of the cart. Had Truman ever enjoyed a nip from this heavy glass? He hoped so. Tru was his favorite president. President Connor aspired to be just like him and had admitted to as much often during his lengthy career in politics.

The president poured himself a large dollop. He twirled it, let it breathe, then held it up to the light like a thing of beauty.

In two swallows it was gone.

Closing his eyes, the president sat down. When he'd first taken office he vowed to find a cure. Indeed, it had been one of his campaign promises and one that he believed. To this day, he still couldn't comprehend how the world's greatest super power, with all its resources marshaled and focused, still couldn't find a cure.

Reaching for the bourbon again, he topped off his glass. Simply put, he wanted to be the president who solved EFS. In public he feigned optimism but he knew the fight, without an identifiable enemy, was over. Like some weepy kid, President Connor could only watch befuddled as the circus began folding up its tents.

This time he took a hit right from the bottle. Hardly presidential, and a safe bet Tru never did that. He took another sip. And another. The stuff was good. A cigar would only make it better.

"Up we go," the president said aloud, righting himself.

The antique humidor had been a gift from the Dominican ambassador. Made of rare and costly tropical wood, it shattered when the commander in chief toppled into it.

Woozy but unhurt, the president sat amidst the cigars and broken wood. "Ah, nuts," he said when he saw the broken bottle. "Now what the hell am I gonna do?"

Consummation

The great leader of Congress, the messiah, the savior of human kind, the presumed father of the next child was atop Kathleen when his windpipe began closing. Or so that's what the struggle for air felt like, for the harder he tried to breathe the less oxygen he received.

Below him, his face at her neck, Kathleen first mistook Matthew's belabored breathing as a sign of increased ardor. It was unlike him to approach orgasm this quick, but given the circumstances she wasn't complaining. On the contrary, she encouraged Matthew. Modulating her breaths to replicate his, she tightened her legs around him. However mixed her feelings, it seemed irrelevant now. Her body language said let's get this thing done.

Now.

She'd never made love to a man before. She'd done *this*. But, then as now, the act had been a means to an end or at best a diversion. When Kathleen first slept with Matthew, it had been some of both. At the time, she'd thought otherwise. Regardless, love had nothing to do with it.

Not like the love that she'd read about or seen in movies, between hero and heroine, husband and wife, lovers.

"Come on, go," urged Kathleen, angrily and passionately. Strange, she thought, how similar the two emotions were.

Fuck.

"Please... just go!"

There was nothing joyous in her beckoning. The plan hadn't worked. The sooner he finished the better.

"I'm... I'm..." Matthew was gasping, still inside her. He couldn't speak. Pushing himself up on his arms, he was now above her. Maybe air would come easier.

It didn't, and he continued straining for every breath, each one harder than the last. His chest heaved, his lungs gripped up like a tightening fist. Death's frenzied motions perpetuated the act of intercourse, his penis remained hard, and rapture and rupture were one.

In other words, he was unable to stop fucking. The pistons continued to fire. He was like a praying mantis that copulated even as its head was being eaten.

Kathleen held fast, now sensing something wrong.

Matthew's reaction to the pie came late, but it was now furious, manifesting itself in the form of a seizure. The heightened activity of his body had proved the catalyst, evoking black magic from the dark berries.

Intent on closing the deal, Kathleen pulled him back down, increasing her motion underneath. Grasping his head by both ears, she looked him dead in the eyes.

"Fuck me harder, you prick," she yelled into his reddening, shocked face. "Don't you dare stop now."

Matthew gasped, unable to form words, yet unable to stop.

And so for her sister and for her mother and for all the women whose lives he'd ruined, she said to him, "I'm going to send you to hell!"

Matthew began convulsing. No longer in control of his body, it vibrated hideously. Fluids emitted from his mouth.

Kathleen felt herself coming. Over and over, each wave a watershed of impossible wonderfulness. Erupting like a volcano, she let go everything, including the man holding her, especially the man holding her.

"Yes!" she screamed.

"No." It was the final statement from the self-proclaimed savior of the human race. Leaving her just as she came, Matthew slid to the floor in a clump and died.

Kathleen stayed put, skin quivering, eyes open but not seeing. I fucking killed him, she thought, amused, yes, amused, by the pun.

The feeling didn't last. Reality encroached. What the hell was she supposed to do now?

Ideally, he would have taken ill sooner, calling for help himself and thereby creating the illusion that an accident had occurred. This made it harder, less clean. Getting up, Kathleen gathered her things from around the room as well as her wits. She would need it all.

* * * * * *

Summoning help was still her only move. The man died having sex. That's what happened. That would be her story and waiting was not going to make it any easier. What she needed now was a decent poker face... again.

So far her demeanor had been remarkable, even she had to admit. Most women would have considered the evening an ordeal of the highest order. Adjusting her hair, Kathleen reasoned that perhaps the last two years had been the ordeal. Now was merely the beginning of its end.

She put on one of Matthew's robes. It would look odd if she were dressed. She walked around the other side of the bed and studied Matthew's body.

Damn, she would have to pull him back onto the bed. Kathleen wanted no questions. He died having sex. In bed. Case closed.

* * * * * *

Two goons showed up within seconds of her call. Rushing by her to him, they crudely began administering CPR and whatever else they could think of. One guy prayed while the other worked over the corpse. Having already told them what had happened on the phone, they did not ask Kathleen for any more details.

"He's dead. We better call a meeting."

The praying man was less composed. He blubbered, holding his head in his hands.

"Pronto!" ordered the other. Clearly more a man of action than compassion, he grabbed the phone punching in a number. "Matthew's in trouble. We need a stretcher in the yellow room. Call the doctor. Call everyone at level one... Well, wake them up. Big problem... *Huge.*"

He considered Kathleen. Then, after a slight pause, he added, "bring the other two Connely women to holding."

"The man died. I don't see why anyone should be taken into holding," said Kathleen, concerned. And just what the hell was 'holding'?

"Be quiet," replied the man, not even looking at her.

Once again, the emotional one began sobbing over his leader's body.

Saying nothing, Kathleen tightened the robe around her and sat in the corner. This was not over.

Slice of Life

D an parked within a block of the spectacular domed Capitol. Congress was not in session, as it never was anymore, and there were plenty of spaces. Was he depressed? Claustrophobic? Whichever it was, Dan fancied a walk. Maybe he'd go up State Street toward University and Bascom Hill. He wondered how the bars, cafes, and pizzerias were faring with the student population so vastly depleted.

Not so well, he realized, as he came upon a closed and boarded tavern. Bucks was its name. And, man alive, had it ever been the place. College kids, as well as Madison's working class, would come nightly for the generously poured wells and cheap bottles of Blue Ribbon. PBR ME ASAP! The slogan had been on everybody's lips. And there it was, in quotes, on a gigantic poster still hanging from inside of the door. A woman donning a Badger-red bikini and holding up a bottle, PBR ME ASAP, she said via callout, oblivious to the lack of ogling twenty-year-olds. Bucks had closed to regular traffic, opening only for reunions and other purposes of nostalgia.

Crossing the street, Dan headed for the hill and passed a pair of long-haired old men. He marveled to himself that guys like that even existed. Had they even gone to college? If so, why hadn't they left?

Fake bums used to piss him off even more than real ones. Now he just found them ironic. A small boy during the tumultuous sixties, Dan hardly even remembered it, them, or whatever one called such a silly period of history. Living fossils these two.

"How ya doin'?" said one.

"Getting old," replied Dan. "Just like you."

He walked.

He wondered, given the prevailing circumstances, if maybe there wasn't something legitimate to their dropout mentality? In a few more years the same thing was going to happen to everybody anyway. Did it honestly matter whether Dan had built a family and a business? While you never could take it with you, now you couldn't even leave it behind. What was the legacy now and who was it for?

He walked and he wondered.

Maybe a few pals and a bottle of wine were all a body really needed. The long-haired freak and his "End Is Near" sign wasn't so farfetched anymore, no longer that eccentric or freaky.

Was he?

Shit, now the son-of-a-bitch was right.

Perhaps half the businesses Dan walked by remained open.

A group of lawyers or politicians or maybe some of both were having coffees at Starbucks.

Pentium 20s were on sale at the computer store but there appeared, at least at present, to be no takers. A bored clerk thumbed through a magazine.

Impulsively, Dan entered a pizza joint called Rocky Rococo's. Even in its heyday, it was a low-end franchise. Still, his wife loved the place, often telling friends they'd met there even though they had not. Infinitely better pizzas could be had in a college town like Madison.

Dan ordered a slice of sausage.

It was served in a distinct triangular carton, same as always. "Salt, pepper, and Parmesan are on the table," said the counter man, taking Dan's money without looking at him.

To his right, a trio of women sat around a pepperoni and black olive, talking and laughing. Having a good time.

Taking his slice, Dan found a small table up front overlooking the boardwalk. He took a seat facing away from the ladies. He found it unusual and a bit unsettling that they were having such a good time. Were they really that happy? Could anyone be? Laughing sounded like a foreign language. Uncomfortable, he turned away.

Not surprisingly, his pizza sucked. Its crust was a dry sponge. Dan picked the sausages off the top and ate them, leaving the rest. He felt like an old ape picking beetles out of a piece of bark.

Nothing was how he remembered it, save for the bad pizza and triangular box.

"You're kidding," chirped one of the old birds behind him. "What else did she say?"

"Stop it. You know we promised not to gossip."

"Just this once," said a third, faking a whisper.

"Oh, please!"

Gabbing women. Crappy pizza. A silly triangular box. He didn't understand how such idiotic totems could be part and parcel to the end of the world.

Just that they were.

Dan wasn't aware of his tears until he saw them. Until that moment, he hadn't cried in years. Not since Connie had left him.

Maybe they could tell the old man was crying. Maybe it was just an awkward moment among friends. But the table of women fell silent.

Dan missed his girls.

About-face

It was Frederick's job to take Kathleen to holding with the rest of her family. He came in wearing aviator sunglasses and a New York Yankees fielder's cap, the consummate chopper pilot, all American, all business.

He examined Matthew's corpse a good five minutes. Saying nothing, arms limp at his side, he looked like a corpse himself. "Let's go, Ms. Connely," he said with appropriate graveness.

Breathing a heavy sigh, Kathleen got up. She didn't know Frederick very well, only having ridden in his helicopter once. He'd been quiet then as well, all business, like now. She knew he was one of Matthew's lieutenants. Associating him with the Good Walk, she was distressed to be leaving with him now. Doubtful the man was escorting her to dinner.

"We'll be in holding area two," said Frederick to the other men, talking right through her. "Doctor Wells is waiting for Matthew."

"Doc gonna do a full autopsy?" the tough guy asked.

"The sooner the better. Find out exactly what went on here." He looked at Kathleen when he spoke.

Talk of autopsy further upset the other man, and he continued blubbering.

"We'll do the meeting in an hour... maybe two," said Frederick, checking his watch, alternating glances between the room's occupants. "We don't want to alarm the general population. This has to be kept quiet."

"Only the principals know," said the tough guy, proud at being one of them.

"Let's keep it that way," snapped Frederick, sharpening his tone.

"Wha-wha-what about the leader?" asked the crybaby. "How do we transport him to the–"

"Here's what you do," replied Frederick, stepping on the question, though recognizing it as a good one. "Put Kathleen's robe on him. There's a set of wigs in the blue room. Don't ask. Get one that matches the girl's hair color." He pointed to Kathleen. "Wrap Matthew in a bed sheet and carry him out. If anyone asks, it's *her*." His finger remained pointed at Kathleen.

"And what about her?" the main goon asked.

"Matthew has a set of fatigues in every closet. She'll be him." Fred tossed Kathleen his cap and aviators. They landed on the bed in front of her.

"That'll work," said the goon.

"All right then, we have a plan," announced Frederick. "Let's do it."

"Can I at least change in private?"

The men said nothing, but their leers spoke volumes.

"The closet," Frederick sighed. "You've got two minutes."

And that was that.

Being a late hour, chances were good neither group would run into anyone. Frederick and Kathleen left Matthew's boudoir, heading toward what she assumed was some sort of holding pen or jail. At least maybe Kathleen would get to see her kin. She'd heard them say as much back in the bedroom. Kathleen almost started a conversation with Frederick but refrained. Matthew's strange death had created some serious doubts. After all, she'd just had intercourse with the man, and he knew it. Speaking with Frederick was probably a bad idea. Silently, Kathleen walked by his side, listening to their feet upon the sandy gravel and to the crickets chirping in the brush nearby. Again, she was taken by her own calmness. For all she knew she was about to be severely punished, her family as well. But yet, her heart beat normally, her skin felt dry, and she was focused. What was that famous passage? "And though I walk through the valley of death, I shall fear no evil." There, but for the grace of God went Kathleen.

"You won't have time to pack," Frederick said, breaking the silence. "But your mother was able to put a few things together for you... some necessities."

So that was it. The Good Walk. Banishment. Kathleen sighed. If she was surprised, it was on account of the punishment's lack of severity. Still, she didn't know if she had another Good Walk in her. And this one was bound to be a doozy. Something else piqued her curiosity as well.

"Look," Kathleen said, choosing her words carefully. "I'm not trying to indemnify myself, but what happened to the leader certainly isn't my family's fault. I don't see why any of them have to be subjected to the same –

"Stop calling him that." Frederick cut her off.

"Excuse me?" Kathleen halted. Some lights went on in the building in front of them. She envisioned her family being roused from their beds. *Stop calling him what?*

"You don't have to call him the leader anymore. Not on my account," Frederick replied, managing a bit of a chuckle.

"What's so funny?" asked Kathleen. "Begging your pardon, but am I missing something?"

"Well, Kathleen, you're right about one thing. Your family is going with you... But I'm pretty sure you've all had about enough of this place." Frederick smiled. "We all have."

"I'm sorry," said Kathleen, confused. "But given current events, you don't seem very upset."

"I am upset. Big time. I'm upset that I let myself get sucked into that man's bullshit. Upset that I let him get away with what he did. Upset that I helped him. I'm especially upset about that... But you know what, Ms. Connely? This evening I'm starting to feel somewhat *less* upset."

"So you know?" asked Kathleen slowly. She was far from comfortable. She couldn't be sure this dialogue wasn't part of an elaborate trap.

"I know Wisconsin is pretty this time of the year. Daffodils and tulips. I bet the pike are getting hungry." Frederick took off yet another pair of sunglasses, putting them in his pocket. He seemed to be enjoying their exchange. Reveling in the cheerfulness of it.

To clarify, she said, "I'm referring to Matthew. The circumstances of his death."

Replied Frederick, "Let's just say I'm aware he got his just *desserts*." Another laugh, even bigger.

Kathleen shuddered at the illusion. She still did not know what to make of this man, to say nothing of their bizarre conversation.

"Can I be frank with you, Ms. Connely?" asked Frederick. He couldn't help being coy. Like intricate wrapping paper, belaboring his point only made the gift inside more appealing. For him anyway.

"Please do," responded Kathleen, unaware of imminent gifts, although she did have the distinct impression the danger had diminished and that she was being herded away from the wolves as opposed to towards them.

"I'm well acquainted with your sister..." Frederick blushed. "It's a long story but, well, we're going to be an item."

An item? Kathleen shook her head in disbelief, gaping. When was the last time she'd heard that phrase? And coming from of all people this helicopter pilot? It was just too much.

Somewhere a door slammed, disrupting them.

"There'll be plenty of time for this later." Frederick grabbed her on the elbow. "We really should get the hell out of here."

They resumed walking.

"Are we honestly going home then?" questioned Kathleen. "I mean, my whole family, all of us... *really?*"

"If we hurry."

"What about everybody else?" she said, motioning to the dorms.

"I'm afraid they won't fit in the chopper." It only sounded like a joke.

"Look, I'm going with you, but I need to know what will happen to them?" Kathleen waved her arms over her head and around her. It was almost as if she were also referring to the universe as opposed to the rest of the women in Congress. Maybe she was.

"What's going to happen to all of us?" Frederick sucked air. "Matthew's dead. They can just leave."

Kathleen wasn't pleased with his answer. Either one.

Frederick stared at the ground. It wasn't like he was satisfied with it either. Leaving Congress wasn't that easy. For some, it might not even be an option. Ever. It was far from over for them either. Things could get dicey, and fast.

"Without Matthew there's no imperative to stay," continued Frederick. "Nobody is going to make them. Creeps like Frick and Frack," he said, referring to the two men in the yellow room "will no doubt take the money and run. Lord knows there's plenty of it to take."

"You know I don't give a shit about those morons. And who even cares about money?"

"They do. It's all goons like that ever cared about. Next to power."

More noises in the distance. Both felt a growing sense of urgency. Having passed the dorms and mess hall, they now approached the compound's lone aircraft hangar.

"The women here?" Frederick dug hard for an appropriate closing remark. "I'm sorry but they're just going to have to deal with it."

"Haven't they been doing that anyway?"

Pause.

"I'm sorry," he said, meaning it.

"We're really going home then?" asked Kathleen again, a tear forming in her eye. She thought of her father and her mother and her sister all at once, something she hadn't done in ages. "Home?"

"Like I said," replied Frederick, appreciating the change in subject. "Only if we hurry."

Eventually, one learns to live his or her life regardless of circumstance.

This final phase is...

Acceptance

W e're getting something, Neil. This is real!" Wallace was beside himself. This was, as the cliché goes, the moment they'd all been waiting for. After years of sending, they were finally receiving. The audio was going nuts. "We're getting a communication from outer fucking space!"

Neil looked up from his book. He heard the signal, and noted it was an unusual pattern. Still, he was skeptical. Hackers had fooled them before. He had to assume that that was the case.

"No question about it," Wallace pronounced. "This sequencing is not random." Nor was it a fluke. The message they were getting was patterned within the perimeters of their unique code architecture.

"Come on, another chip-head figured us out." That's what Neil called them, chip-heads. He picked up his novel, already losing interest. The last 'alien' they'd corresponded with turned out to be a brother and sister in Boston. He had Wallace run the countering software and check the code architecture for level 3 aberrations. Even the most wired chip-head often missed the 3rd level.

"The message is legit, Neil. If it's a chipper, he's through level 3."

"So run the tran–"

"Transmitter scanner is on. Looking for earthbound transmissions as we speak." Wallace looked up, beaming. "North America is clear. Including Canada."

Neil put down his book. Most chip-heads good enough to break level 3 were American. This wasn't meant as a knock on another country's technological abilities. If anything, it was an indictment of certain pernicious individuals, generally of Western origin. Yes, the Japanese had the same core competencies, but using them to pose as intelligent life from another planet? Not possible. The Japanese just didn't do that, especially given the dire nature of the circumstances. Neil and Wallace were searching the cosmos for a solution to EFS. Only a fanatical monster would interfere. Only in America.

"Well, then, what does the message say?" asked Neil, allowing the door of plausibility to open ever so slightly.

"Not there yet," replied Wallace. He was creating multiple prints off the auditory cryptogram. He began each new version when the message repeated itself, which, the computer identified, was every 1.7 seconds. "But whatever it is, there's not much to it."

"Does it resemble our code?" asked Neil. He found it odd that the message was short, especially considering how long theirs had been. But all skepticism aside, any response from space was exciting, likewise even the remotest chance for a cure. "Maybe it's a form of cosmic shorthand," he half-joked.

"I don't think so," said Wallace, studying the computer's preliminary translation. "The crypts match too well. I don't see any anomalies or variations. It looks like three words. A small sentence..."

"May I?" Neil couldn't wait for the final translation. He took the first proof from Wallace.

$$(A-E-) \quad (-OU-) \quad (-A-E)$$
$$(A-E-) \quad (-OU-) \quad (-A-E)$$
$$(A-E-) \quad (-OU-) \quad (-A-E)$$
$$(A-E-) \quad (-OU-) \quad (-A-E)$$
$$(A-E-) \quad (-OU-) \quad (-A-E)$$

"It's only vowels, Neil. Give me a few minutes, and I'll have the rest." Wallace observed his partner pouring over the page. He had the message on screen as well. Whatever it was it sure didn't seem like the answer to all their problems.

The door to the room flew open. Being operations commander, Mariane Brooks did not have to knock.

"You see what we're seeing, eh, Mare?" When the transmission cleared Level 3, Neil figured it was only a matter of moments until she showed up. He didn't mind. He liked her. She was beyond smart and well deserving of her position. Plus, she had the wildest long, blond hair. It followed her like the tail of a comet.

"Boys, whatever you got, it's legit. A level 5."

"That's unprecedented," interjected Wallace. He was typically shy around his boss, but this was special.

"Damn right it is," Mariane replied. She was excited, too. "Do we have the final print out?"

"Coming." Wallace peered at the computer screen, waiting.

"As you know," said Mariane, "I never thought asking the skies for help was much of an idea. I almost pulled the plug on this project. More than once, I'm afraid."

He knew. "But you didn't," he said.

"I thought we were better off pooling our efforts with the Generation group." Marianne referred to the ongoing Space Fertilization Program. It had yet to be successful, but the majority of people in their field, and the scientific community in general, still believed it held the most promise. They'd just sent another couple into space yesterday. Hope and some other such name.

Mariane put a hand on Neil's shoulder. "It appears you have a valid transmission here. It checks. Even under normal conditions that would be colossal. But now... I can't find the words." She took a deep breath. "What if this is the answer? What if we just saved the human race?"

"I'm getting another translation," Wallace broke in. "Still not the final–"

Nobody cared. They huddled around the screen staring at the second translation. Wallace printed it out handing the paper to Neil who handed it to Mariane.

```
(A—E—)   (YOUR)   (—A—E)

(A—E—)   (YOUR)   (—A—E)

(A—E—)   (YOUR)   (—A—E)

(A—E—)   (YOUR)   (—A—E)

(A—E—)   (YOUR)   (—A—E)
```

Everyone remained silent, puzzling over the code.

"Oh my God," said Wallace, his voice wavered. "I know what it says."

The computer transmitted the third and final translation. For the record, Wallace had gotten it right.

A small piece of advice from beyond the solar system:

```
ACCEPT   YOUR   FATE

ACCEPT   YOUR   FATE

ACCEPT   YOUR   FATE

ACCEPT   YOUR   FATE

ACCEPT   YOUR   FATE
```

Hills Like
White Elephants

It was even darker inside the hangar than out. Frederick entered from the side door, beckoning Kathleen to follow.

She took his hand, stepping into blackness. For a second, nothing. No light. No sound. Kathleen barely made out the hulking shape of a helicopter.

"Excuse me," whispered Kathleen. "But where's my family?"

Before Frederick could reply, the lights came on, blinding.

"Going somewhere, Freddy?"

The crybaby goon from earlier was now standing by the hangar's other entrance. He wasn't crying. Only the helicopter was between him and them.

Now what? The question on everybody's lips.

Now what?

"Mike said he saw someone sneaking across the grounds," stammered the man. He hadn't really expected finding anyone, particularly not these two. "Aren't you supposed to be taking her to a cell?"

Frederick had no choice. "The lady lied," he said pointing to Kathleen. "She killed our beloved leader with poison. She confessed after we left. She even tried offering herself to me." He smirked. "A trial is a waste of time. This one's going on the Walk. And I mean right... fucking... now." Frederick didn't wait for a response. He grabbed Kathleen by the arm and moved toward the helicopter. He outranked the other and, as of yet, still gave no reason to be doubted.

"But..." the little man uttered.

"But what?" retorted Fred. "You want some damn tribunal to let her off?" Opening the helicopter door, he all but pushed her in. "This is right by Matthew. This is justice. Now make yourself useful." He gestured to the hangar's main switch and, for effect, slammed the door behind Kathleen, catching her on the ass. "Hurry, before it's too late."

The man did as he was told, opening the door.

Kathleen fell into the first seat, hitting the floor. Nevertheless, it appeared Frederick's fib had worked. They were proceeding. The only problem was, where the hell was her family?

Squealing on its rollers, the huge door clambered open.

Frederick got in beside her. "We're out of here."

"But what about my—"

"Hi, Kat," a familiar's voice came from behind.

"Your hair... it's so long." Yet another voice, equally familiar.

Kathleen whipped around.

And there they were, occupying the rear bench, her mother and sister grinned as if participating in some kind of hayride.

"I missed you so much," said Kathleen. Up until now she'd held her emotions in check, but she could no longer contain herself. Bawling, Kathleen leaned over into the hands and faces of her immediate family.

Meanwhile, Frederick fired up the bird's engines wasting no time getting out. The helicopter's specially inset wheels enabled it to move ahead like a car.

"Lay low," he cautioned the group. "This could get funky." The machine lurched forward carrying them out. In plain view were the compound's many familiar buildings and structures, some lit up, some not. The little man had proved benign and so far there were no additional obstacles. Overhead blades began turning, and the jets roared signaling take-off. By the time anyone in Congress could get to a window, the chopper was airborne. By the time anyone ran outside they were but a disappearing dot in the starlit sky.

Silently, they bid good riddance to Congress. Matthew was dead, but his taint was omnipresent. More criminal than the mental and physical abuse, he'd robbed them all of time. Almost two years. If the Last Generation were counting minutes, the occupants of this helicopter now coveted them. Fraught with meaning-time. The Connely women could not wait to make up for the amount they had lost.

Mary leaned over, giving Frederick a kiss on the head.

"It's about time," he chuckled.

And indeed it was.

After a while, a long while, Connie looked away from her daughters and out the window. Heading east, the black shapes of more and bigger mountains began to appear. Many of them had snow on their tops, the whiteness popping in the pitch-dark sky. It reminded her of a short story she'd read a long time ago, before having babies, before the world had changed forever. Ernest Hemingway's *Hills Like White Elephants* was about a woman who'd recently lost a baby, who was traveling with her husband in Africa. To forget? Connie could not recall. Indeed, many of the story details were as distant as Africa. But the mountains, she was certain, had reminded the woman of her pregnancy. The snow-capped hills looked just like white elephants, she'd said to her husband.

Connie closed her eyes, shuddering.

Loss.

The hills were like white elephants, which in turn were like the rounded bellies of women.

Full of loss.

Connie gazed at her own children. They would never know what it meant to be a mother. They would also never know what it meant not to be.

"You know what I really want?" Frederick's voice rose above the din of the chopper.

"What's that?" asked Kathleen, leaning forward.

"A beer."

The sisters laughed.

"Last I checked we owned a bar," said Mary. "I'm sure Daddy will be happy to buy you one."

More laughter.

Not wanting to cut into their levity, Connie turned away. She thought about Dan, about his loss. After all, she'd taken away his children. Thank God she could at least give them back.

"Unfortunately, we got a ways to go," said Frederick. "But what's another few hours, you know, when you think about it?"

Which they did.

Jack Be Nimble

So much for teamwork, thought Jack. It was early, but he'd gotten up early, the sun just now rising. Granted, he was headed west but was it to finish the mission? Or just because? And had it ever really been a mission? Certainly it started out as one. But then again, he'd put away his movie camera and hadn't that been a mission of sorts? A mission statement? Funny… all the questions.

Jack hit the scan button on the radio. Between mountains and desert and the ever-growing lack of civilization, it was hard finding an operating station. He picked up an old country song and just as promptly lost it. Then some talk show: In lieu of a guest or topic, the program's announcer merely read from the newspaper. In a spaced-out, southern drawl, he reported that earlier today California abandoned local government. Legislators weren't attending to their duties and the public didn't care. And so, he said blandly, the state just shut down, deciding not to bother.

Deciding not to bother, Jack shook his head, bewildered. How do you report a piece of information like that without injecting some form of commentary? Hello! Insert California jokes here. Maybe, and most likely, the host wasn't very good. Or, like California's government, he just didn't care. Probably both.

Jack wondered how Muriel was faring in la-la land. He had a hunch they'd see each other again. And that, upon further review, she'd be mostly contrite regarding her distraction with Bikress Maura.

As for his own proclivities? At this stage, Jack felt secure admitting that he wasn't motivated one way or other by sex. He knew he wasn't gay, not if last night's fling with the motel porno channel was any indicator. He'd get by fine. Fantasy was enough, if not better, than the real thing.

Maybe if he had a sweet deal like this Matthew fellow...

Jack tried to get serious. Soon he'd have to. Could he honestly just pull into the driveway of Congress and ask to see the girls? Would he?

He thought about Dan. He should press on because of Dan. At least see if his girls were all right. If he didn't get in, maybe he could find some information. He owed Dan *that.*

"Matthew," said the voice on the radio, "the leader of the so-called Congress is dead. Apparently he was killed in his sleep–"

Jack didn't slam the brake. Rather, he took his foot off the gas, letting the car roll to a stop along the empty highway.

The announcer continued, reporting that a mother and her two daughters had fled the compound late last night in a helicopter with a high-ranking official. All four were considered suspects. He also added that Utah officials were not taking the matter seriously because they did not have a body.

Jack listened while staring out the window at a group of prairie dogs. The animals ran about, diving in and out of their holes. Did they have a leader? He didn't know. They all looked the same.

The law didn't respond to problems occurring within Congress' boundaries on account of it being "a lawless place in a lawless time," or so said the reporter. Matthew and his flock had divorced from civilization a long time ago. "Good riddance," said the DJ, deciding now to inject an opinion.

What law? Jack counted prairie dogs. Two, four, seven... Inside his car the still air felt charged, like right before a storm.

A majority of the women were going to stay on and run the farm and the Congress' various other enterprises. The reporter quoted one woman as saying she didn't care if she ever saw another man again in her life.

Okay, Jack laughed. He punched the gas pedal inciting the car into a wheel-screaming 360 and began driving the other way, back to Wisconsin.

At this point, all he could think about was Dan. He couldn't wait to see the look on his face. Not only was his wife coming back home, but so were his children. And this in a time when no one was having children, well that, that was as good as it got.

Something worth seeing.

This would make a great piece of film and a great ending as well. Jack opened the glove compartment fishing around for a CD. He had intended to use one of the tracks for his film. He popped it into the player, turning up the volume. At the chorus, he sang along with REM: *It's the end of the world, as we know it... It's the end of the world as we know it, and I feel fine.*

The sun rose in front of Jack. He looked right at it without wincing, feeling no pain.

An epilogue...

Curious George

No longer terrified, the simian approaches the compound. It has been a long time since she's heard the ripping and felt the tremors. Maybe the badness is gone now and she can relax. She's seen more of her kind lately and, in fact, has several prospects for a mate. Still, the animal proceeds with extreme caution along the periphery of the abandoned dwelling. These creatures are strong and vicious, and the tiny monkey knows not to take them for granted. Just because it is peaceful now doesn't mean they aren't here, just beyond sight lines, ready to pounce.

Yet she sees evidence to the contrary. Other creatures are nesting in the building, on the roof, in the eaves. She can hear baby birds, and lizards scuttling along the walls. And, most remarkably, for the first time in recollection, the great noisy machines remain hush, standing still.

No trees fall. Pale green new creepers and vines pop up along the various footpaths, winding their way around downspouts and gutters, overtaking fence posts.

Unfurling a tendril from one of the many rusted, yellowing hulks, she eats the tip. Feeling braver still, the creature ventures closer.

Their smell has disappeared, leaving her profoundly curious. These animals, which had brought so much misery, could they finally have disappeared like the four-legged beasts that once grazed in the clearings?

The monkey pauses in front of the building's opening. She peers in but is reluctant to enter. She remembers their long, sharp sticks that pierced the treetops, felling her kin. She would always be scared of those.

Yet, her acute nose detects only stale air, a faint odor of food and the pungency of rodents. Nothing of any threat, whatsoever.

Entering the vestibule, she discovers a large wooden object pushed up against the far wall. Rotting fruit is scattered across the surface. In one leap she is atop it.

Mango in hand, the monkey swivels from her lofty position and surveys the unfamiliar empty territory. She cannot help but be concerned. The inhabitants of this place were hardly nomadic. Quite the opposite. The hairless, tall ones always grew in numbers, not decreased. Their sudden absence, though appreciated, had to have some diabolical explanation. *Had to.* Even foul weather and disease failed to keep them away. They always came back and often nastier than before. Following the last rains, she remembers how they tore apart the jungle.

Settling into a crouch, she keeps one eye on the door, the other on the room's lone window. Had some new predator emerged from the earth or from the sky? The monkey looks up at the mottled ceiling, stained from cigarette smoke and cooking fires. Perhaps the great river, tired of being fouled, had unleashed a creature even more powerful than they. Massive fanged things like the one she saw pull down an entire grass eater, so gruesome a sight she no longer takes refreshment in the spot because of it.

The monkey scampers from corner to corner, peers over each side, then returns to the center. Nothing of any interest present except the nothing itself. Her long tail flicks back and forth, high and low. The tip catches on something below the desk's front, a protru-

sion. She whips around, moves to the edge, looks down and discovers a handle. She pulls on it and the drawer flies out of its sleeve,
falling to the floor.

Inside are various items the animal cannot place–matches, pen-
cils, a few crumpled papers, and a bigger object, the color of bark, yet
softer and smoother. She can just lift it with both hands. She pulls
off the cover revealing countless thin white leaves. They are fragile
and tear easily. The monkey ponders the object, not sure what to
make of its fluttering contents. She only knows it belongs to them.
She can smell them on it. Their oils and sweat.

A small crack of thunder erupts and, startled, the monkey throws
the tattered Bible across the room. It hits a wall and falls harmlessly
to the ground.

Before the weather changes, she is out the window and gone.
Her clan is waiting in the nearby canopy, pleased to see her back
safely, excited by the coming rains and all the swelled fruit it pro-
duces.

Scavenging will be easy now.

Without them.

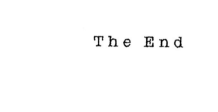

The End

About the Author

Steffan Postaer is Chief Creative Officer at LBWorks, a Leo Burnett company. A copywriter by trade, he is perhaps best known for his provocative work on behalf of Altoids, The Curiously Strong Mints. While he has accumulated numerous industry awards for this campaign, the author recognizes it is merely advertising and hopes you will read his book anyway.

This is Steffan's first novel, yet others are lurking on his hard drive. To find out more about the author go to LBWorks.com or search for him on Google.

Ironically, given the story, he has three children.

Printed in the United States
22829LVS00002B/43-111